D1565249

# Demon at My Door
## (The Collectors Series)
# By Michelle A. Valentine

Books by Michelle A. Valentine

# THE COLLECTORS SERIES

Demon at My Door
Coming Soon:
Demon in My Bed

# THE HARD KNOCKS SERIES

## Phenomenal X

# THE BLACK FALCON SERIES

# Chapter One

Someone in this room is about to die. The hum, deep in my bones, is undeniable. Shockwaves roll through me whenever I'm near a person who is about to bite the big one. I feel it now and I hope like hell it's not me. But it's definitely going to happen right here in the Grove City Country Club.

Soon.

I scoot back further in my seat and slouch down, trying to block out the incessant buzz in my skull. I hate when shit goes down where I work. This has been the best job for me while I attend college classes. The flexibility cannot be beat. Not many places would hold your spot every summer.

It's bad enough I got arrested at my last job for possession of a deadly weapon. Thank God I was underage at the time and that whole ordeal was expunged from my permanent record. I don't need a repeat of that here. I mean, it wasn't like I was going to hurt anybody or anything last time.

Well, I guess that's not exactly true. I had every intention of shooting the boy demon with the silver bullet I had loaded in the chamber of the revolver I scored from a local gun dealer, but he's pretty damn quick.

The vibration in my bones increases in intensity, breaking me out of my thoughts and my teeth rattle a little. My eyes scan the area for the cause.

It's happening. Right now.

My heart thunders as my eyes lock on a rather plump man with salt and pepper hair with a spray tan from hell. He kind of reminds me of an over-sized Oompa-Loompa dressed in tennis whites. The heavy man curses at our newly hired receptionist that sits behind her desk to my immediate right and treats her like she's not fit to lick the mud from his boots. Every fiber in my body is drawn to him and I know without a doubt he's *the one*. My bones are like tuning forks for the damned and they are never wrong.

Sweat beads on his forehead and the vein in his neck distends while he growls at the girl. His protruding belly bumps against the marble counter in front of him with each labored breath he takes. "What the hell do you mean you can't find my tennis reservation in the computer?"

He says he has one, but the petite blonde girl wearing a 'required' smile isn't able to locate his name in the computer.

"Where is the manager? Do you even know who I am?" the fat man yells at the girl before he blots his forehead with a perfectly pressed handkerchief.

My heart bleeds for the receptionist. I hate it when people are rude, but when the ones who are about to die are jerks, it helps lessen the guilt I feel for them when the sadistic creature from hell comes.

The girl chews her bottom lip. Her pale skin shows a hint of red in her cheeks, no doubt caused by sheer mortification. "I'm sorry, Mr. Wellington, but my manager is out sick. Let me—"

He holds up a chubby hand, and his face turns the shade of a beet. "I don't want your damn excuses. I want a court, and I want it now!"

"I'm sorry," she apologizes again. Her bottom lip trembles like she's about to cry, but he's doesn't care. He points his finger under her nose and continues to berate her during his little tantrum.

"I said—" He grabs at his chest in mid rant and grunts in pain. That's when it happens. Time stands still. There's no movement or sound in the crowded lobby. The silence in the room allows the faint sound of my breath to echo around me. The receptionist is frozen in a look of fear, hair stuck in mid-swing, her eyes still glued in Mr. Wellington's direction. Two little boys in front of the entry door across from me are stuck in a game of catch and a cleaning lady, wearing a blue uniform, is in mid-sweep—all of them unaware that time has stopped and true evil is about to enter the room. None of them will have a clue they were even put on pause, like a DVD. The only people still able to move at all are Mr. Wellington and me.

My eyes search the immaculate room. He's here somewhere—the little demon who stole my soul. Now, I just have to wait on him to make his grand appearance.

The fat man falls to his knees in front of me with a heavy thud, and a combination wave of sweat and fear blows in my direction. His eyes widen as he gasps for air and clutches his chest. They always look at me, probably because I'm the only thing moving around them. They all have the same look in their eyes, too.

*Fear.*

I should be used to this. But no matter how many times I see it, soul bargains still creep me out.

"Help me," Mr. Wellington rasps.

My mouth pulls into a frown, and I bite my bottom lip. I shake my head. There's nothing I can do to help him, even though I want to. He's going to die, and the demon has already come to offer him a deal. There's no stopping it now. I've tried before, countless times, but each time my attempt is overcome by the sheer strength and power of the demon boy.

Mr. Wellington collapses on the floor, riddled in pain, and stretches his hand toward me. I press my back into the chair. The fancy buttons in the fabric press against my skin through my thin, black t-shirt. I bring my legs up to my chest to get out of his reach. I hate it when they ask me for help. It makes me feel like crap when I can't.

A vortex of air blasts into the room and whips my black hair in my face. My eyes water as loose strands snap into them, so I close them tight and begin to hum. Thank God no one can see me. I know I must look insane rocking back and forth like this, but I don't care. It's not anyone can see me. A distraction of any kind is better than bearing witness to another death.

When the room grows still, I know he's here and my pulse quickens. I can sense his presence and, after all, this is his trademark tornado entry. One of the daggers I had blessed by a priest off the internet a few days before presses hard into my back. The steel handle warm against my skin as the blade remains covered in the waistband of my pants. It's the next method I'll use to try and kill the little demon bastard.

"Hello, Natalie." I open my eyes to the sound of the dark-haired demon boy's voice. He looks innocent as he stands in the doorway of the lobby in his black slacks and white button down shirt and vest, definitely not what first comes to mind when you think of an evil creature from hell.

My eyes roll. Here we go again. I wish he wouldn't address me like we're friends, because we are so not. Sure, I'm grateful he didn't kill me when he had the chance, but still, he's ruined my life with his little visits. The whole town thinks I'm a crazy nut-ball thanks to him. Hopefully this dagger will take him out once and for all, and I can finally get my life back.

My right hand inches behind my back. The hilt of the blade is firm in my palm. This is it. It's now or never. My muscles tense in my shoulder as I start the motion to jerk the weapon from my waistband.

Wind whips in my face, and I suddenly find myself pinned against the chair. Damn. He's quick.

The demon grips my arm with his tiny fingers. "I wouldn't do that if I were you. You know your plans to kill me never work. Why even try anymore?"

He grabs the dagger from my hand and examines it, flipping it over and over in his hand. He smiles at me, takes a couple steps backwards then throws it straight up into the ceiling. It sinks into the fancy marble clear up to the handle, like it's cutting through butter.

My mouth goes dry. Damn it. There goes that idea. I really thought that dagger would finally do the trick. Now, I'm forced to sit here and watch. Powerless, yet again.

His dark gray eyes stare into me, and my insides churn. Why does he look at me like that, like there's more he wants to say? It scares the hell out of me, but I can't let him see my fear. Fear is a weakness to him, and I can't let him know he has that much power over me.

I clamp my eyes shut again. Taking a breath in through my nose to stop the quivering I feel prickle in my throat as I say, "Just do what you came here for and leave me alone. I'm not in the mood to chat today."

His footsteps echo off the marble floor, each one sounding closer than the last. When he stops, I can sense he's about an arms length away. "Have it your way, but you did promise to be mine. You'll have to get used to talking with me eventually. We made a deal, remember?"

How could I ever forget what I had done when I was just five years old to save my mom? If only she hadn't chosen to make us hot dogs for lunch that day, she wouldn't have choked. And he would've never came to my door and been able to trick me into promising him my soul.

When I don't answer, he takes a slow breath and then sighs. My eyes snap open in time to watch him squat next to the dying man. Mr. Wellington's humongous frame dwarfs him, but the boy exudes power and is in total control of the situation at hand. Mr. Wellington's skin is a faint shade of blue, signs of no circulation—heart attack victim this time.

The demon bends down and slips a faint whisper in Mr. Wellington's ear. He closes his eyes and slowly nods.

I've never figured out what the demon says to the people he steals souls from, but whatever it is he promises them, they always say yes. He knows what gets to a person. He knows what it takes for someone to give their soul to him, just like he knew how to get to me when I was a kid.

Mr. Wellington attempts to extend his shaky hand to the demonic boy. The boy's eyes light up, and his little pink lips curve into an angelic smile. The demon shakes Mr. Wellington's hand. When their hands meet, my palm screams with the same electrical shock I felt the first time I shook the boy's hand. I can feel the energy that flows between them as they seal the deal. A low grunt escapes my lips, and I grimace from the pain. Every time he makes a deal—more times than I can count—in my presence and shakes a hand, I'm tortured.

Without warning, the little boy whips his head toward me, his gray eyes flash a blinding, white light. "Natalie, close your eyes."

The vibration in my bones heightens as the demon exerts more power. On command, my eyes snap shut once more, and I bury my face into my knees. He always tells me not to watch. My index fingers jam into my ears, but I can still hear Mr. Wellington's screams while the demon finishes off what the heart attack started.

Curiosity wins out and I peek over my knees. It's like a car wreck. I can't help but to look.

My body trembles as the soul of the man darts through his open mouth. It hovers like a see-through angel above him. Pulling a black-glass vial from his pants, the demon chants something in a foreign language that kind of sounds Arabic, and his eyes glow a brilliant white as he says the last word. His fingers twist off the lid. Mr. Wellington's soul morphs into a ball of white light and bounces in a current of air. It's ready to be collected.

The demon extends the black vial away from his body. His white eyes stare at the hovering ball of energy, like if he blinks it will disappear. The soul shrinks to the size of a dust particle and plummets into the tiny, glass container. After the demon double checks the lid, he stuffs it back into his pocket like it's a pack of gum. Mr. Wellington's lifeless body is all that's left behind.

The demon always kills them. Not once has he ever left a person who made a deal alive. Not one, except me.

# Chapter Two

Tears stream down my face as the demon's words reverberate in my brain, haunting me every night since I made the deal with him. *"You belong to me now, and I'll be back to get you after your twenty-first birthday, when the time is right. No one else can touch you until then and I'll always be around to make sure."*

I dry my face with the sleeve of my pajama top and check the clock. It's 3:33 in the morning. Why am I not surprised? I've been waking up at this time for sixteen years now. At first, the same dream every night kind of freaked me out, and telling Mom about it is one of the reasons I ended up in therapy when I was a kid.

After my body calms down, I glide my legs across the cotton sheets, feeling their smoothness against my skin. I stretch my arms over my head and yawn. Slowly, I sit up and the memory of the dream floats into a foggy haze. My hand slides into my night stand drawer and opens it. I pull out a picture of Stew from between the worn pages of my favorite book. A smile tickles my cheeks.

For the past couple of months, I've had a nightly sneak-out date in the old, backyard tree house with my neighbor, Stewart Masterson. We've had to slink around all summer since we've both been home from Capital University because his dad doesn't approve of me. Stew says it's not *me*, per say, just what my reputation says I am.

Crazy.

Sure, if I saw Stew walking with me hand–in–hand down the street, I'd do a double take, too. We couldn't be more opposite if we tried. He's like perky golden sunshine while I'm an overpowering eclipse.

I shimmy on a black tank top, pull up my dark-green pants, and slide my feet into my black Converse. After I run my fingers through my long hair, dab a little lip gloss on, and pop a piece of gum in my mouth, I'm ready to meet Stew.

My bedroom window opens with ease and I make sure the backyard is clear. I straddle the windowsill and then start down the trellis. Thank God, I'm light enough not to break it or this would be a hell of a lot harder to do every night. That's one good thing about being petite.

Butterflies fill my stomach when the tree house comes into view. A rush of adrenaline flows through me as I creep in the backyard like a spy on a covert operation. I wish our relationship didn't have to be a secret. Falling in love with Stew was so easy. Did I ever imagine Stewart Masterson, our college's golden boy, would be my friend? No way, at least, not until we discovered each other in the backyard at four in the morning this summer. Not only do we both not sleep, we also have parental issues. It's a match made in crazy heaven.

Stew is the only person, other than my sister, Alicia, that I'm close to. I tell him everything. Well, almost everything. I didn't tell him I see a shrink—no sense in scaring off the one person I want around before the junior demon comes to drag me to hell—but I did tell him demon stuff freaks me out. He thinks I have Demon Phobia. A term he discovered on the internet after Googling "fear of demons".

Stew thinks all my issues stem from my dad always working late and my mom's frustrations falling on me. He believes he has me completely figured out. I don't have the heart to tell him that he's not even close—that my problems are way bigger than bickering parents.

Most of the time we just hold each other, make-out and talk until the sun comes up, but last night we came close to having sex.. He told me I was perfect, and I turned into putty in his hands. It was almost the best night of my entire life, but I decided at the last minute it'd be best to wait. I don't think I'm ready just yet. I know I'm a little old to still be the big 'V', but sex hasn't exactly been the top priority on my brain.

Fall semester starts back in a couple of days and we'll finally spend some daylight hours together...in public—away from all the parental authority. Stew's dad, Mr. Masterson, would split us up in a second if he knew, which I think is pathetic he still lets his father boss him around like that. He's a grown adult, not a little kid.

His father made it quite clear he wants him to stay away from me. One evening when he spotted us talking across the fence in the back yard, Mr. Masterson grabbed Stew by the arm and practically dragged him to the back door.

My heart crumbled when his dad referred to me as a 'crazy demon lover' before shoving Stew into the house.

I climb up the ladder. Stew already has the little shack aglow with a teacup candle. The tiny flame flickers and the light dances around on the old, wooden walls. After our first two extremely dark visits, we decided to cover the windows with black trash bags to keep our nighttime adventures a sealed secret. We don't want people to discover our secret spot or interrupt our private moments. How embarrassing would that be?

"Hey," Stew says, as he sits up on his knees on our makeshift bed of old comforters. He runs his hand through his brown hair. "I've missed you."

He reaches for my hand and pulls me down so I'm on my knees, mirroring his stance. He's almost a foot taller than my five-foot-two frame, but sitting like this, our faces are much closer. I breathe in the scent of cinnamon and earth as he rests his forehead against mine. His chiseled features look even better than I remembered from last night as he brushes a stray hair away from my cheek. The touch of his fingertips on my skin makes my whole body tingle.

"I've thought about you all day. Did you miss me?" he asks. A smile flirts across his face.

Since elementary school, I've had a major crush on him. When he sat behind me and pulled my ponytail, I knew he was special. We spent almost every day together in this tree house when were little kids. Before Stew's mom died, his dad was okay with us hanging out—back when I still owned my own soul. But after that, his dad was hell bent on us not being friends.

It was like he knew I had been touched by evil and was no longer good enough to be Stew's friend. He separated us when Stew needed me the most, and he went through the grief process of losing his mom alone.

I wish we hadn't listened to his dad back then and been friends anyway. We lost so much time we could've spent together. It took until our second year of college to actually speak again.

I think I fell in love the first time Stew smiled at me. It was like I was drawn to him, and the older I got, the more I liked him. I wasn't sure if he even remembered my name though, because he stopped talking to me just like everyone else back in high school. But I still harbored a secret crush.

Things changed this summer though. When I discovered the reason he pulled my ponytail back then was because he felt drawn to me, too.

I bite my bottom lip and nod.

His gray eyes sparkle against his tan complexion and hair, and a grin stretches across his face, putting his dimples on full display. "Good," he whispers, before his lips crush into mine. "God, you're beautiful," he murmurs between kisses.

Every inch of my skin aches, longing to be touched by Stew when he pulls me against his hard body. My hands run up and down the length of his back, tracing the outline of muscle underneath his blue t-shirt. Tonight is definitely not going to be a talking event. He's a little more aggressive, almost hungry. He kisses me deeply and intertwines his fingers in my black hair. There's no other guy that I'd rather spend what little bit of time I have left on this earth with. I've struggled with the thought that I shouldn't start a relationship with him because my twenty-first birthday is just a few days away, and I know that little demon bastard will be back to collect on my promise and ruin everything. But, I figured I should live a little before I die. The thought of dying a virgin is mortifying.

He leaves me breathless—my lips swollen—and pulls away. His hands, calloused from a summer of football practice with the college squad, cup my face and he stares into my green eyes. "Do you like me?"

*Oh my God!* My heart beats wildly in my chest and my stomach flips. All summer I've imagined this moment, the one where Stew says he wants more with me. This is what I wished for since the first night he pulled me into his chest and wrapped his arms around me.

"Yes," I whisper, unable to hide my huge grin.

His smile reaches his eyes. I knew he has feelings for me, too. "Do you want to keep meeting me?"

Of course I do. What kind of question is that?

Without a second of hesitation, I answer, "Yes."

His fingers trail along my cheek, leaving a line of fire on my skin from his touch. "Good. I was worried with fall classes starting...you might want to stop."

He leans in for another kiss, but I shove him back a little. The smile now erased from my face. "What?" Now, he's got my full attention and my guard, which is usually down around him, springs into action. Why would we stop meeting if we finally admit we have feelings for each other? That's insane.

He sighs and shrugs. "I figured you wouldn't be cool with all the secrecy."

That makes no sense. "What does keeping our relationship secret from your dad have anything to do with school? We can be together at school without him finding out."

He lets go of my face and sits down on the blanket, not looking at me.

Nausea rolls through my belly. "Stew?"

"Natalie, I'm being unbelievably selfish. I'd be pissed and never want to see me again, if I were you."

My lip twitches as I fight back the emotion that threatens to expose how uneasy I feel. "You aren't making any sense, Stew."

His gray eyes appear deep in thought. "Not secret *just* from my dad," his whisper barely audible.

I gasp. "What?" My pulse pounds in my ears. I can't believe what I'm hearing. Do I mean nothing to him? He's the one person I thought I could trust and spent most of the summer opening up to.

He reaches for me, but I shy away. "I do have feelings for you, Nat. I want to keep seeing you—" My arms cross instinctively and uber-bitch mode goes into effect. Alarms continue to sound in my head.

How could I be so stupid? He's only with me because I'm next door and convenient for the summer while we were both home from college. Practicing with the team for a school as big as Capital doesn't exactly leave a ton a free time to find girls. I was just accessible and seemed overly eager. What a jerk. "But you don't want anyone *else* to know." I lift my hand to cut him off, finally understanding he never wants to be seen with me.

He faces away from me, like he can't bear to see me as I call him out. "I've told you—people expect things from me. My dad doesn't want me to see you."

Expect things? That's the crap answer I get after a whole summer together? I should've listened to my sister, Alicia. She's the men expert, not me. Guys really do only care about one thing. "I only had one expectation of you, and that's not to be an asshole. Guess what? Epic fail, Stewart."

He picks at a loose string at the seam of the blanket and doesn't attempt to look at me. I wait for a couple seconds, hoping he'll redeem himself. When he doesn't answer, I shake my head in disgust. "Don't worry. You don't have to keep your dirty little secret anymore."

I fling my leg over the opening in the tree house and place my foot on the ladder.

"Please, Nat," he whispers and grabs my arm. "Don't go. We can work this out. I need you."

My hand balls into a fist and it takes all my willpower not to punch him in his stupid face. "Stew," —I jerk free of his hold— "when you decide you can talk to me in public, let me know. Until then, stay away from me," I huff, and then climb down the ladder without looking back. My feet pound the damp grass as I run away from the only man I've ever been close enough to develop feelings for. And now that I'm out of his sight, I allow the tears to roll down my cheeks.

"Who's the guy?" The voice stops me dead in my tracks in the darkness as I fly past a tree.

Quickly, I wipe my face before I turn around and attempt to slap all emotion from my face. "What guy?"

I might be ticked at Stew right now, but there's no way I'll serve up info to evil boy about him.

The boy demon steps from behind the shadows of the trees and nods toward the tree house behind me. "The one in there. You're not dating him, are you?"

I'm so not in the mood to deal with this little, demonic twerp. "Look, you may own my soul, but you don't own *me*. Not yet, at least. So I can do what I want with my life." My voice sounds a little hoarse.

He shakes his head and looks down at the ground. "I knew I should've checked in more as you got older." It's almost like he's talking to himself for a second before his eyes snap up to meet mine. "You know you can't date. You know the rules. You're taken."

"Taken?" I let out an exasperated sigh. "My soul may be taken, but I'm not." This isn't a good time for another argument over my eternal soul. My mission has always been to try and stay on his good side. If I piss him off now, I may never get my soul back. "If you aren't taking me to hell anytime soon, please leave me alone." I try to step around him, but he blocks my path.

He moves closer and glares up at me. "You are going to be with me, just like you promised. Like it or not, so you might as well forget about Romeo up there."

I step back. "There's no way I'm going to let you tell me what to do. Besides, I never agreed to being tied to you forever. You get my soul, as promised. That's it. You can stuff it in your vial or whatever, but you don't get to keep me as your side-kick for eternity. That wasn't part of the deal."

"You don't have a choice in this matter. Your soul is you, and I own it. You'll do whatever I say. This is how it is going to be." He reaches out and grabs my hand so quickly I'm not even ready to try and jerk away.

An electric shock jolts me. I drop down to my knees and groan as mind-numbing pain tears through my flesh. I open my mouth to scream out, but hold back when I think about Stew hearing me and getting involved in this situation. The intense jolt is gone within seconds, but my legs weigh a million pounds and are close to giving out on me. Winded, I plop down on my butt, unable to run away, and cradle my burning hands to my chest.

My eyes sting as fear overwhelms me. A single tear drips onto my palm. The solitary drop evaporates on contact, like my hand is a recently put out fire. I stare up at the boy demon, ready to scream at him for being so evil. His eyes narrow, like he dares me to say more.

Anger flows through me and I wish I had some demonic strength of my own to kick his little five-year-old butt. "You're an asshole!" Is all I can manage to mumble under my breath.

His lips draw down into a pout that would be cute on a normal five year old, so I know he heard me. "You hate me now, I know, but you didn't always. There's something you need to know."

Before I have a chance to come up with a snarky comment about not needing to know anything else about him, he touches my forehead with his index finger, and my breath catches.

At first, everything is pitch black, but I can hear a voice—my voice—in the distance. As I try to make out what I am yelling, a picture pops up in the darkness. It's far away, so I can't make it out. The blackness surrounds the image and it appears to be at the end of a long tunnel.

Colors swirl in a mixed up pattern. The greens and browns blur together, so I strain harder without much success to figure out what I'm seeing. Then I hear it—my voice clear as day screaming, "Run, Sarah! Hide!"

A gasp of air fills my lungs, and I am no longer in the dark vision. I clutch my chest trying to get my bearings as I try to recover from the sheer panic that I just heard in my voice and try to figure out who in the hell Sarah is.

As my eyes focus, I note that I'm still in my backyard with the demon standing over me.

He's dropped his finger away from my forehead and now stares up at the tree house where I left Stew. I hear the tree house creak.

Stew coming down the ladder has distracted him.

The boy turns to me and in a rush says, "Your human life is nearly over. Tie up your loose ends. You'll want a clean break."

"But, I—" Before I can ask what the vision he just showed me meant, he's gone just as quickly as he appeared. I stare blankly out into the dark yard. He's never done anything like that before, and it scares me. What did it mean, and why did he show me that? Whatever it was, I get the distinct feeling he isn't quite done with me yet.

My hands shake as I rub my face. I need to kill him so my promise won't matter anymore, and I can be free. Everything I've tried so far has lead to a marathon of failures. I need to get my soul back.

I don't realize I've clenched my hands until I open them up and see the imprints of nails in my palms. My brow furrows as I notice something strange. The life line on my hands glows like hot coals straight from a fire, and I know this isn't a good thing. I've got to find a way to get out of this deal and fast. Something tells me shit's about to get real.

# Chapter Three

Life lines. Most people don't think much about them. Me? I'm obsessed with them. Mine started fading last night. And there's only one thing, or person rather, I blame it on.

That sadistic, five-year-old soul-stealing bastard.

This is the fourth therapist I've been to this year—I wouldn't even do it if Mom and Dad make it a stipulation in paying for college. Each doctor causes me to question my sanity a little more, so there's no way I'll spill my guts about my newly discovered countdown clock of death. My chart's filled with enough crazy.

This particular doctor approached Mom at the country club yesterday when she brought me lunch and offered to treat me after she spotted me in the lobby. My daily look of dark clothes and hair must scream mental patient, along with I bet a shell shocked appearance of seeing a man just murdered before my eyes earlier in the day. The last doctor I saw kicked me out of his practice for not "trying" enough, so Mom was grateful when Dr. Fletcher eagerly offered to squeeze me in today.

I gaze around the office. The space feels tight since there are no windows and only one way in or out. The fluorescent light buzzes overhead and feels very institutional. I notice Dr. Fletcher's family photos positioned for display on the coffee table in front of me. It looks like she's married. One picture is of who I assume is her daughter and right next to it is one of a guy—looks like she has a son about my age, too.

He's tall with dark hair and gray or blue eyes. It's kind of hard to tell because it's not a close up of his face, but still, he looks pretty cute. And oddly familiar.

Her family is all smiling, and it occurs to me that people always seem to smile in photos. It's like they're always perpetually happy. Like they're in some fairy tale waving good-bye and ready to live happily ever after. Yeah, right. No family is that happy. *Ever.* Well, at least mine never is. But I'm sure Dr. Fletcher will cure me and make me the perfect, preppy robot Mom wants me to be. Whatever.

After eleven years of therapy, they decided to label me as a paranoid Schizophrenic. If I were actually crazy, like they say, that'd explain why I'm on constant look out for the boy demon. But I know I'm not mental, even if no one else does.

The door creaks open. A petite, brunette doctor in a white lab coat, wearing black stilettos, sashays into the room. Dr. Lilim Fletcher sits stiffly in her high-back leather chair across from me and crosses her panty-hosed legs. Her hair is in the tightest bun known to mankind and she's got a weird look on her face. Determination, maybe?

Great.

Instantly, my body stiffens and the defense mechanisms go up, as my brain morphs into uber-bitch mode. This one has to be kept at a distance. She seems dangerous, because of the mission mode vibe she's giving off. I hate shrinks that make it their goal in life to fix you, like they'll be the ones who will finally cure you with their overly huge brain and skills.

When I shrug without a word, she cuts the small talk. Guilt fills me for being such a pain. Really, who wouldn't feel a little snippy if they had to spend all their free time stuck in therapy? It sucks. Big time. Just one whole happy hour of *major* suckatude.

"Okay, since your mother gave me an introduction on your history, are you ready to talk a little more about why you are seeing me?" she asks and then places her glasses on her perfect heart-shaped face.

It's then, I realize, she's just like the rest of them, already diagnosed me as crazy before I've opened my mouth to speak. Is that something they teach in shrink school? I mean, I know it's possible for a soul to be stolen, so why doesn't anyone else? Have they never seen *The Exorcist* or *The Omen*? Sheesh. Since no one ever seems to believe me, I've learned to keep things bottled up.

"Um, you have my previous records." I point to the thick chart in her hand. "I'm sure you've read it by now. We can save the small talk. I've been through all this before. Why do *you* think I'm here?"

I wrap my arms tightly around my body. My gaze shifts toward her when she readjusts in her chair and she lifts her eyebrows.

"Hmmm." She clicks her pen and writes some notes in my file. "Well, according to your last physician's notes, you're having issues dealing with what you perceive as threats against your life from a" —she clears her throat but continues to look at her notes— "five-year-old boy no one else has ever seen. It says here that you often carry weapons for what you claim is personal protection."

Here we go again. I roll my eyes. After a moment, I force myself to unclench my teeth. I really, really hate it when people size me up for a strait jacket.

"I'm not crazy," I say with a sigh. "He *is* real."

She looks me in the eye. "Can you tell me where he lives?"

I shrug. "He's the spawn of Satan, okay? It's not like he lives down the street. He just sort of appears."

Again with the notes? Just once I'd like to see what they write about me.

"Natalie, if this boy first appeared at your door when you were five-years-old and he's never aged through the years, could it be possible that maybe the whole *incident* regarding this boy could be a bad dream? Have you ever thought about how this relates to your diagnosis?"

"Right. I made it all up. So never mind that I'm disturbed enough by it to dream about him every single night when I close my eyes." I shudder. The thought of his touch on my hand to seal the pact for my soul is enough to make my skin feel like a million fire ant stings simultaneously.

She flips through my file. "Do you ever dream of anything other than the day the boy came to your house to save your mother?"

I shake my head. "Nope. Same dream, every night."

It's amazing how the questions are always the same. I bet if I try really hard, I could give them all the answers they need before they even ask.

"Then it's possible it could be a dream, albeit a recurring one, but *just* a dream nonetheless?"

I shrug again because I don't want to get into this with her. How many times do I have to say I don't believe the stupid dream theory?

"According to Dr. Prior's notes, your mother says she doesn't recall seeing a boy matching your description in your neighborhood."

"If you read my file a little closer, you would've noticed that per my recount of the *incident* my mother took her last breath when the boy came into my house and stopped time to make the stupid deal for my soul." I still remember my mother choking – on a hot dog no less – and then everything stopped with the knock on the door, changing my life forever.

Lilim gets her pen out and makes extra notes. I've never figured out if standing my ground and telling the truth helps clear my mental diagnosis or not, but they've already documented my story. There's not much I can do to avoid the subject anymore. I just wish I'd found out earlier to keep my mouth shut. My life would've been a lot less complicated if I could've avoided therapy and meds altogether.

"Hmm," Dr. Fletcher mumbles. "Okay, let's say what you're saying is true"—whoa, wait a minute. Does she actually believe me? Wow, this is a first—"when do you *suppose* he's coming back to collect?"

I stare blankly at her. The world screeches to a halt, and for once, and I do mean once, I'm totally and completely speechless. No one has *ever* asked me that before, and it throws me off a little. Oh, she's good. Acting like she's on my side so she can poke around in my head, but I'm not telling her anymore than what she already knows from that file.

Collection day is always on my mind, especially now that my freaking life line started fading. I drop my head into my right hand and sigh.

"So you've never thought of it before?" she questions, after a moment of silence passes between us.

I shake my head slowly. Numbness fills my body. I swallow down the large lump in my throat and fight back the tears that threaten to expose my fear. Am I ready to die? There are so many people I'd miss: my sister, Mom, Dad, and even Stew. I'd hoped we can get past the fight we had last night and he'd come to his senses, but maybe he shouldn't. Maybe it's best to end things now. Demon boy did order me to tell everyone goodbye.

She removes her glasses and carefully folds them. "Well, Natalie, I can say, personally, death isn't something I like to think about too much. And I know you believe you're damned because you made this deal sixteen years ago, but I don't think you are. We are the masters of our own destinies. You have to live for today and not dwell so much on death. You're twenty-years-old. Worry about clothes and finding the right guy, not the Grim Reaper. You still have time to make choices about who collects your eternal soul." Her eyes narrow, and she stares at me with hardness in her eyes. There's a quick flash of sliver in her brown eyes, like a wave of mercury shimmering in the sun. The only other time I've seen anything like that is when the little, evil freak is about to turn on his demonic powers.

My mouth goes dry, and my pulse pounds like I'm running for my life. Her eyes won't let me go. It feels like she's peering into me, taking inventory of my insides. My breath catches, and before I completely pass out, she looks away. The rhythm of my heart slows the moment her eyes leave me, and I grip the arms of the chair to steady myself.

A moment later she glances back at me, one eyebrow raised in question. There's no trace of anything odd in her eyes.

I shake my head. What the hell was that? Maybe I am going crazy.

She slides her glasses back on, wearing a satisfied smile. "I think if you take a step back, you'll see there's more to life than *just* death. Maybe start small, like wear something other than black for a change."

Not wear black? The whole campus knows me as Natalie Sugarman, the Crazy Goth Girl. Why would I ever want to mess up that stunning reputation? Before I can stop myself, I snap, "Sure, I look great in pink."

Lilim ignores my reply. "Good. You see, progress already. We are going to be great friends, Natalie." She smiles and glances down at her watch. "Well, it appears that our time is about up. We'll talk again next week." She holds out her hand and waits for me to shake it.

I start to reach for her, but instead I bolt from the couch. I don't do handshakes anymore. They can cause your life to be hell. Literally.

# Chapter Four

Today is the first day of the fall semester, and I haven't talked to Stew since the night in the tree house a week ago. I've wanted to call, but my pride won't let me. Besides, he owes me an apology, not the other way around.

The steering wheel glides with ease under my hands as I turn onto the street campus is on. I've been extra careful with my driving – I don't want to wreck the car a week after getting it - so I look both ways at the stop sign. I don't see anything coming, so I cautiously accelerate. Out of nowhere a black, sports coupe zooms into the intersection. I slam on the brakes. My hair flies in my face, the sound of screeching tires echoing in my ears. When my car grinds to a stop, my neck whips back a little.

I watch the black car streak past me, missing me by inches. I punch the horn and curse under my breath. The driver is concealed behind black-tinted glass, and for a second, I entertain the idea of chasing down the driver and beating the crap out of them.

I run my fingers through my hair, an attempt to calm my nerves. Reality sets in and my anger turns to rationality. It's probably not wise to track down a stranger and scream at them for nearly killing you. It could be a three hundred pound raging crack-head with a gun. God knows I don't want to start my eternity any sooner than I have to.

I whip my custom, bright green Focus into the empty parking lot and put the near crash out of my mind. A tingle trickles down my spine as I eye the practice field for our school's football team. Passing Stew and pretending I don't still have feelings for him will be hell. My insides quiver, and if I'd let myself, I could cry all day over him. Instead, I decided it's better to just ignore him.

My teeth grind together. Next time I get involved with a guy I'll make sure he likes me for me. If there is a next time, that is.

With a sigh, I throw my satchel over my shoulder and trudge through the parking lot. Not much has changed over the summer. Capital University's campus still looks exactly the same as it did the last time I was here, this past spring.

"Wonder if I should waste what little bit of time I have left in this place?" I question myself quietly. I check my vanishing life lines to see how much they've changed. They fade a little more each day. Last night I did some research on the internet about life lines and demonic soul possession. There wasn't one site that was even remotely helpful—probably because most people don't live through demonic encounters. But I did order some holy water and a bag of salt from a demon hunter website. One can never be too prepared when their soul's at stake.

A couple of sites mentioned winning your soul back after a demonic deal, but basically they said I'd have to make another deal with the demon that currently owns it. No way do I want to make anymore deals with that little shit. Shivers erupt through me. He could be anywhere, just waiting to pounce on me like a lion does its prey.

"Hey! Wait up!" I hear someone call, but I don't stop. No one ever talks to me. Well, at least not in public. My reputation as a certifiable nutcase precedes me.

"Hey!" the male voice calls again. It's closer this time, and there's a light touch on my elbow.

I glare down at the hand on my elbow and then allow my eyes travel up the tattooed arm of the brown-haired guy holding it. He's cute in that bad boy, biker kind of way.

My eyes narrow.

He immediately releases me and holds his hands up, palms out. "Sorry," he says.

He's hot and all, but I doubt he's here to ask me out. Most people at school never actually talk to me – unless you call making fun of me "talking." I stare up at him and demand, "Are you talking to me?"

"Yeah." He raises an eyebrow and smiles. His teeth are perfect—probably cost his parents a mint. "Who else would I be talking to?" He chuckles as we both look around the empty parking lot.

"Okay...soooo... what?" I ask a little more brusquely than I meant to and then take off in the direction of the school before he can answer. I am so not in the mood to be messed with.

"Whoa, hold on there." He catches up to me and matches my pace. "I was just wondering if you could show me where Administration is. This is my first day on campus. By the way, I'm Rick." He holds out his hand as a standard greeting, but I just keep walking. "Rick Steele." He tries again. I glare at his hand for a second before he shrugs and drops it down to his side.

He's new. That explains the tinge of southern accent I hear in his voice and why he's not afraid to be seen with me. He's got a great smile and a deep throaty voice that makes me think of hot caramel over smooth, cool ice cream. He'll do well in the girl department here. Especially with those intriguing gray eyes—the kind that can peer into your soul – and thick, dark hair that nearly touches his shoulders. Girls eat that crap up.

Even though I'm not really feeling hospitable, especially to a guy that's going to eventually ignore me like all the others, I decide I can show him. He hasn't done anything to me. Yet. "Sure. Follow me."

I pick up the pace, wanting to get into the building before anyone tries to use me as target practice with their half-empty, fancy iced-coffee cups. For some reason the prep crowd around here think that kind of shit is hilarious.

We arrive at the main office. I smile faintly at Rick. "Here you go. See you around."

"Wait," Rick says, as I turn away from him. I whip around to meet his gaze. "What's your name?"

I roll my eyes. Why does he care? "Most people call me Sugarman."

He tilts his head to the side. "That's your last name, I take it."

I nod and walk backwards, trying to get away as quick as I can without looking like a total bitch.

"What's your first name?" Yep, he's a smooth-talker.

"Natalie."

A slow grin spreads across his face and his smile leaves me feeling a little light headed. "Thanks for helping me out, *Natalie.*"

My name rolls off his tongue with ease, like he's said it a million times. His accent gives it a special twist. Damn it. I can feel my cheeks grow warm with embarrassment. I duck my head, trying to hide my reaction.

He chuckles and then heads into the main office.

Ugh. What a flirt. I flee back across the courtyard, completely baffled in this guy's interest in me. He probably plays all the girls like this and causes them to swoon all over him. I'm sure Rick will fit in just fine.

After surviving my morning classes, I head to lunch. Usually, I sit alone outside under a big oak tree—trying to disappear—until it gets so cold we're forced inside.

Ah, the lonely life of an outcast. Was I always seen as social pariah? The answer is no, not always. As hard as it is to believe, I was once accepted, and - I might even dare to say - semi-popular.

At least until I went to Taylor Gee's freshman year sleepover seven years ago in high school. Thanks to Mom, she revealed my psycho status to practically every girl in my grade by storming over to Taylor's and making a huge scene. Talk about mortifying. Going on and on about how I'd forgotten my 'crazy pills' at home and how it would affect my 'condition' if I missed a dose. From then on people started avoiding me like I had leprosy and lucky me that status followed me on to college.

I saunter over to the lunch line and grab an apple and a bottle of water and head out to the tree.

Great, so much for being alone out here. The entire student population seems to be spread out across the quad and— wouldn't you know it?—there's someone in my spot.

"Hey, again." Rick grins as he looks up from his book to meet my stare. His long legs stretch out in front of him, and his black tee shirt clings to his chest as he moves his books out of the way. "You want to sit down?"

Ugh. What's the deal with this guy? I might as well set him straight about my social status around here and hope he goes away. Now's not the time for new friends, especially a guy friend. Demon boy made that quite clear.

"You do realize that's not the smartest move. I'm probably not the best person to be seen with," I say as I take my satchel off my shoulder and toss it down. "This is usually where I sit." He looks at me, like he doesn't get it, so I state the obvious. "Alone."

He laughs and crosses his legs at his black, booted ankles, like he doesn't plan on moving anytime soon. "Everyone needs a friend. And well, lucky for me, I'm not the kind of guy who cares what other people think. Come on. Sit." He pats the ground next to him.

I raise my eyebrows and give a quick shrug. If he wants to take on the wrath of the jock crowd to hog my spot under the tree, so be it. Doesn't mean we're friends, though. Finally, I take a seat in the cool grass next to him and bite into my apple, ignoring him the best I can.

It's epically silent, except for my thunderous chewing and the mindless chatter surrounding us. Rick seems oblivious of me as he reads his book. Even though I shouldn't, I glance around, hoping to spot Stew. It doesn't take me long to find him. He's at the picnic table in the center of the quad, not more than twenty feet away, surrounded by the entire puketastic cheerleading squad. Taylor Gee—the most vomit-inducing of all the cheerleaders and my previous best friend—is perched at his side.

I hate that half of my high school class got accepted into Capital University along with me.

Taylor giggles at Stew's every word and flaunts her A cups at him. Her brown hair twirls around her perfectly manicured index finger as she makes goo-goo eyes at Stew. Are they hooking up now? The whole scene makes me want to hurl. I don't know how I could have ever been her friend.

Blood burns in my veins, and I'm ready to explode. Frustrated, I squeeze the crap out of my apple and grind my teeth. From the outside, it looks like they're perfect for each other. But Stew told me he hates superficial people like Taylor as much as I do. The only reason he puts up with it, and pretends to be friends with those posers, is to appease his domineering father. He wants him to surround himself with only good people, and obviously, according to Mr. Masterson, that excludes me.

But God, Stew doesn't have to pretend he likes it so much.

My stomach churns for believing what we had together was real.

Rick pulls me back to reality. "Friend of yours?"

My head snaps in his direction. "Pssssh. Hardly."

"Hmmm." He lifts an eyebrow and then goes back to his book.

This guy thinks he knows me. Whatever. He's known me all of four hours. "What's that supposed to mean?"

He snaps the book shut and looks me in the eye. "It just means I've noticed you two staring at each other when you think the other one's not looking. It makes me wonder what's going on there because you two don't exactly look like you travel in the same circles. No offense."

I shrug. "Not much to tell. He's my neighbor. That's all."

He cocks his head, almost like he's suspicious of something. "Right." He smirks. "You know, I want us to be friends, so you should be honest with me."

For a second, I think about how amazing it'd be to have a friend like Rick, someone who isn't afraid to be seen in public with me. But I haven't had a real friend –not counting Stew, for obvious reasons - since the Taylor incident, and the one thing I've learned since then is to protect myself.

I roll my eyes. "Whatever. Think what you want. I gotta go."

I stand, throw my satchel on my shoulder and turn back to address him. "What makes you think we're friends?"

I hear Rick call my name as I walk away, but I don't look back. No way do I need the new guy knowing any of my secrets. I'll have to make sure I'm more careful with the Stew situation so the demon doesn't suspect there's something still going on between me and Stew.

Because if the new guy can see through me, so will everyone else.

# Chapter Five

Abstract Art is the only course I'm really excited about on my schedule. I wish I could major in it, but my parents would flip their shit if I did. Here I can express my darker side—my inner most demon fears. Dr. Woods, one of the main art professors, just refers to it as soulful and slaps an A on my work, yet never questions where I draw my dark inspiration from. This is also one of the only courses where people willingly talk to me. Even if it's only questions on how to make their project better so they can score a good grade from the hard-to-please Woods.

I find myself back at my old faithful corner desk and peer out the window, while I wait for the other students to come in. I try not to make eye contact as they pour into the class room because I don't want to scare anyone off. Believe it or not, I like to have people around.

The chair next to mine scrapes across the floor as it slides back and the table rumbles slightly under the weight of a big pile of books. I breathe a sigh of relief. Having a partner this semester will be awesome.

I'm shocked to see so many empty desks around when I scope out the class. This person intended to sit next to me, since there are so many other places to pick from. My most friendly smile goes on display as I turn to greet my tablemate.

My jaw drops when I look at my partner. It's Stew. His legs stretch out under the desk as he scoots his chair closer to me. Has he changed his mind? My stomach tenses and my palms grow clammy. Holy crap! This is it. He's going to let everyone know we're together. Guilt fills every inch of me for believing he was a worthless user.

I can't tear my eyes off him. If we weren't in class right now, I'd leap into his arms and kiss him with all my might, but since Woods doesn't tolerate any funny business, it probably won't fly. The smell of cinnamon and soap wafts off of him and my fingers ache to touch his skin. It's been too long and I've missed the feel of him.

"Hey." He wears a sheepish grin as he cradles my hand in his under the desk. Fire courses through me, and suddenly it's hard to breathe. I can't look him in the eye so I focus on the little black bruises Stew has on his right bicep. It looks like a finger marks, like someone grabbed him really hard. I wonder which one of his football buddies did that during practice. "I picked up this class as my elective since I knew you'd be here. I thought this would be the best way for us to talk."

*The best* way? I give him a lukewarm smile while my heart thumps against my ribs. It's a good start, but I'm not giving in so easily. "I've missed you, Nat. I've been to the tree house every night, hoping you'd come. Meet me tonight? I can't take not seeing you. It's been hell."

His thumb rubs the skin on the back of my hand. Every nerve in my body wants to meet him in that tree house, but my head is screaming for me to stand my ground. "I told you what I want."

"Come on, Nat. Please, be reasonable," he says in a hushed whisper while he looks around the room.

"Reasonable?" I say through clenched teeth and try to pull away from his grip, but he tightens his long fingers around my hand. "You think I should be okay that you're too embarrassed to be seen with me?"

He furrows his brow. "I'm not embarrassed of you."

Maybe I should give him a chance? "Great, then meet me at Drakes tomorrow for lunch."

He shakes his head. "Nat—"

"Stew," I growl, "if you say no, I suggest you get up and find another place to sit."

His gray eyes soften, and his voice shakes a little. "Nat, please. I think I love you. I can't stop thinking about you."

I don't answer. Instead, I jerk my hand free and turn my attention to my backpack, pretending to search for something so I won't have to look at him. My eyes sting as he rejects me yet again, and I blurt, "You don't love me."

"Yes. Yes, I do," he whispers. "My Dad won't let me see you. You know that. If word got around campus that we're together, it's only a matter of time before he finds out."

"So that's it then. Your dad says no, and you won't fight for us. Stew, if you loved me, you'd stand up to him."

"Do you know how hellish my life would be if I defy him? I'd loose everything."

"You're being dramatic. He wouldn't kick you out on the street because you're with me. He isn't that evil." My eyes meet his. "If you love me, you'll prove it."

He bites his lip. "You don't know my dad. He would send me off somewhere...away from you."

"No he wouldn't." I shake my head and then turn away from him. "Besides, you're an adult. He can't control your life or force you to go anywhere."

He sighs heavily and starts to gather his things. "You don't get it."

He's really going to move. Do I mean nothing to him at all? My body trembles and I debate on running from the room before I burst into tears.

Just as he rises and his tall frame towers over me, Woods turns her attention to him. "Have a seat young man." Stew slumps back in his seat with a thud while the professor explains we need to work together with our tablemate on our project.

Great. Forty more minutes to go and the last thing I want to do is talk to Stew. I need to toughen up. If he's going to write me off, then I have every right to give him the cold shoulder and treat him like every other snob on this campus.

I take out my black notebook and turn to a crispy new sheet. "Ideas?" I ask dryly, not making eye contact with him.

"Nat?" he whispers.

No way am I going to forgive him for this. "Look Stew, I'm done talking. Let's just get through this project, so we can go our separate ways."

He raises his eyebrows, blows a rush of air out of his nostrils and looks away from me. "Fine."

# Chapter Six

I have to come up with an idea for my art project A.S.A.P. because my list of possibilities is due at the next class, and I don't think Woods will find a blank sheet of paper very amusing.

I park my car in front of the local bookstore and go into mission mode. I head through the front door and make my way to the books on famous paintings. Something in here has to spark my masterpiece. It's nice in the store and I can totally get lost in the sea of books. This may be just what I need to clear my head and get my mind off Stew.

I search through all the titles and pull a few books from the shelf. There's not much to choose from in this little Mom and Pop shop, but still, I'm able to find a few to thumb through. The smell of paper and coffee fill the room, relaxing me. I sit Indian style in the middle of the aisle and get to work.

"Are you my secret stalker?" My zone is broken. Rick, the hot new guy I saw earlier today, cradles a bundle of books in his hands. When I meet his gaze, he winks at me. I roll my eyes.

What's this guy's deal?

"Maybe I should ask you the same question," I retort and direct my attention back to my book.

He smiles as he sits beside me. After tilting my book so he can read the title, he raises an eyebrow. "Art books, huh?"

"It's for a project. What do you have?" He runs his hand through his thick, dark hair, almost like he's nervous. I sort through the stack he set on the floor. There are several creepy titles and my breath catches as I read through them. *Soulless: Real Accounts of Deals with the Devil, Demons in the Western*

*World*, and *Lucifer: Friend or Foe*. "Wow. Obsessed with the Devil much?"

He chuckles as he piles the books back into a neat stack. "No, not really. I just find this stuff...interesting."

I raise my brow. "I guess I don't have to ask why you're trying to be my friend."

He cocks his head to the side, and I notice how gorgeous he is. Definitively not someone I picture as a demon fan-boy. "What do you mean?"

"Look, I'm not into worshipping the Devil or anything. Dressing in black has nothing to do with liking evil. It's a personal choice, and believe me, befriending demons is the last thing on my mind." I shudder, getting a tiny flash of the five-year-old soul stealer.

"So, no Devil worship, huh?" He smirks.

I flip to a new page in my book. "Nope."

"Well good thing that's not why I'm trying to be friends with you."

I set my eyes sternly on him. "Why *are* you trying to be friends with me? Most people try their best to avoid me."

Rick draws a ragged breath. "Let's just say I know what it's like to be an outcast. Not accepted by the rest of society." His face is deadly serious, and his gray eyes thrash like there's a million lighting bolts trapped inside ready to burst free. Maybe he's not like the rest of the assholes around here. He doesn't seem like them at all.

I nod, curious about why *he* would ever be an outcast, but knowing it's too soon to push for details if I want to make a new friend.

"Come on. Let me buy you dinner?" he asks. His crooked smile invites me in and fills my belly with tingles. "Please?"

I can't believe I just swooned a little. Even though Stew's being an ass right now, I still have some sort of feelings for him. Why does Rick have an effect on me?

My bottom lip slides back and fourth between my teeth. Rick's offer is tempting, especially since I am hungry. An apple for lunch doesn't last long, and I want to find out more about this guy. His interest in me has me curious, but this is strictly as friends. "Sure."

He smiles wider and hoists himself up from the floor. He's taller than I remember, at least six foot, and his thin, black tee shirt outlines his muscular frame, leaving little to the imagination.

I trail behind him to the check-out counter and wait while he pays for his evil reads. He grabs his sack, and I turn toward the exit. He rushes in front of me to open the door.

"M'lady," he says, with a hint of southern twang, and bends at the waist as I pass by.

Is he for real?

We head to the parking lot and suddenly I wonder if this is a date. I'm *so* not ready to date anyone else, but a friend I can definitely handle.

"So what sounds good to you?" he asks.

I shrug. "Doesn't matter. Whatever you want is fine."

"Get in." He unlocks the doors to his sleek black sports car with his keyless entry remote. "We'll figure it out on the way."

His car looks like the one that nearly crashed into me this morning. "You ever speed in this thing?"

He grins. "Sometimes I do like to take things a little fast."

I roll my eyes and shake my head. Should I even ride with such a maniac driver? I look over my shoulder at my little green Focus and bite my lip. Riding with him makes this a date, doesn't it? Maybe I should just follow him.

I stop in my tracks.

"I'll bring you back to get your car." It's almost like he read my mind. Can he sense how hesitant I am? "Now, get in." I meet his stare as he opens the passenger door. "Promise I won't bite...unless you want me to."

He smirks as I walk toward him. If I wasn't desperate for a friend, I doubt I'd get into some random guy's car, but my life is what it is. Lonely. So, I nod and get in.

I slide into his passenger seat and inhale the scent of leather and spice that fills the interior of the vehicle. He hops in the car with the agility of a fine tuned athlete. It's funny how things work out. I hoped to have friends this year, and my relationship with Stew led me to believe that I was actually going to have a social life. Instead, the cute new guy has stepped into the friend role. Maybe this will show Stew there are guys out there who want to be seen with me.

Rick pulls into the parking lot of Drakes', a local sports bar, and cuts the engine. My muscles tense at the thought of going in that place. "Um, I know you're new, and as your friend I should tell you this isn't the best idea," I say.

He furrows his brow. "Why?"

I run my fingers through my hair and stare at the neon "OPEN" sign. "Because this is, like, jock and sorority central. A place I don't belong."

He chuckles. "You worry too much. You belong anywhere you choose to be, Natalie. Besides, it's just a restaurant, and the asshat crowd doesn't own this place. Come on. I'm starving."

Before I can say another word, Rick is out of the car. He opens my door and my body stills like the stone statues from the art books I studied earlier.

He leans in the car and his face is just inches from mine. "Come on. What are you afraid of?"

I tear my eyes away from his stare almost immediately. "I'm not afraid of those assholes. I just don't want to hang out with them."

He touches my arm. His fingertips are hot on my bare skin. "Then come on. I'm starving."

With a little huff, I fumble my way out of the seat belt and follow him into the restaurant. I feel like there are cinder blocks strapped to my legs, and it's twice as hard to make myself move. The strategically placed cowbell on the door announces our entrance to the rest of the patrons. I lock my eyes on the ground and run my fingers though my hair, wishing it could become a black veil and shield me from prying eyes.

Rick leads me to a corner booth. I slide onto the red vinyl seat across from him and slouch down, praying for the power of invisibility.

"Relax, Natalie. No one's going to kick us out. Trust me," he says as he hands me a sticky-worn menu.

"What'll it be kids?" The red headed waitress appears out of nowhere with her pen and paper ready.

Rick directs her attention to me. "Natalie?"

"Um, a Coke and the hamburger platter," I say.

"Make that two," he adds.

The sweaty red-faced waitress nods and scurries off to get our order.

The front door bell rings and then I hear cackles and chatter coming from somewhere behind me. Rick stares behind me—his eyes set on taking inventory of the people who walked in. Even with my back toward the door, I can tell it's the crowd I'm trying to avoid. I don't dare turn around because I can lay money it's probably me they're laughing at. And if it is, honestly, I don't want to know.

Rick doesn't take his gaze off the people behind me. He has this intense stare like he could melt them if they crossed him.

Just as I was going to tell him to stop staring at them before he starts a fight or something he starts to speak. "So what's your story, Natalie?"

With more confidence then I even knew I posses, I lean in close and give my most mischievous grin, hoping to throw his cocky ass off a bit. "You mean you haven't heard?" I'm little surprised when he rests his elbows on the table, like he's into the secret I'm about to drop. "I'm crazy."

He smirks and leans back in the booth. His tattooed bicep bulges a little as he rests his arm on the back of the booth. He's totally relaxed in this place, like he could care less that we are in unwanted territory. I study every inch of him that's on display before me. He has a model face—well defined, strong jaw line, hair any girl would love to tousle around and not to mention that bad boy sleeve of tattoos that cover his right arm. It's then I notice he has the most mysterious, yet familiar, stormy gray eyes. They kind of remind me of Stew's color a little. Have I seen Rick before?

"I hoped those rumors were true," he says.

After a split second of uneasiness about the odd color eyes, I shake my head. "And why's that?"

His smirk becomes a genuine smile, and he makes a swirling motion around his temple with his index finger. "Because I'm a little nuts myself. Demon obsession, remember?"

He lets out a deep belly laugh, and after a few seconds of me trying not to be amused, I let a smile slip. He has no clue he's not the only demon obsessed person here.

His laugh invites me in and I crave to know more about him. "So what's your deal? What brings you to the big town of Columbus, Ohio?"

He leans back against the booth seat and stretches his toned arm along the back of the seat again. His boot touches my foot under the table. "You."

My mouth drops as I'm stunned by his answer, but then I feel foolish as he starts to laugh. "Jerk."

He smiles as me and then sighs. "Well, if you must know I needed a fresh start."

My eyebrows crunch in. "Why?" That sounded a little invasive, so I try to recover. "I mean, that's cool."

He rolls his eyes. "I had a bit of a mess and I needed to get my shit straightened out."

At that moment the waitress brings our food—completely interrupting the juicy details he was ready to spill. Rick tears into his burger, taking huge bite after bite. It's like he's a wild animal that hasn't eaten for days.

I grimace and wonder if he was raised by wolves. "Jeez, breathe, Rick."

He swallows and wipes a huge glob of ketchup from the corner of his mouth with his finger, then licks it clean. "Sorry, it's just really good."

"I see that." Totally grossed out, I try to get back on track and try to push the image of Rick eating out my brain. "So, anyway, what kind of mess?"

He swallows down his drink. "A mess with a girl." He states without hesitation.

I go into a coughing fit as I choke on my Coke. My eyes water from the sting in my throat, but I still ask, "You got a girl pregnant?" This is drama I don't need to get tangled up with.

He laughs and shakes his head. "No. Nothing like that. It's nothing really."

Talk in circles much?

I wrinkle my brow. "What is it then?"

He shrugs. "It's nothing, honestly. Forget I even said anything."

After pondering what that could mean, I decide it's best to let it go at that and not push him about it. God knows I don't need my only almost-friend frustrated with me. I suppose he'll tell me when he's ready.

Rick polishes off everything on his plate in record time and pushes it to the side of the table. The waitress clears out the plates and lays the bill face down in the center of the table. I reach into my satchel, dig for my wallet, and hope I have enough money. Mom is so crazy. Even though I know she can't legally control my money as an adult, I allow her just to keep her off my back. Sometimes she can be so damn overbearing.

She only gives me enough money for lunch for that day because she thinks if I have an excessive amount I might try to buy more weapons.

There have been a couple times that the demon unfroze time at the most inopportune moments for me right in public view. I've been arrested three times for menacing and possession of a deadly weapon. Mom always makes sure my doctors know that I am constantly arming myself to battle a demon, which makes me sound completely fucking insane.

"Stop looking for your money. You're my date, so my treat," Rick says.

My hand goes still and I meet his stare. "This is *not* a date."

He lifts an eyebrow. "No?"

I shake my head. "No." I can't have him thinking this is more than a friendship thing. The last thing I want to do is give the boy demon another target.

His lips twitch. "Well damn, just when I thought I was getting somewhere with you."

Since this isn't a date, I pull out my wallet. Before I can get the money to pay my half, Rick slips the waitress some cash and tells her to keep the change. Her eyes enlarge, nearly to the size of golf balls, as she examines how much money he slipped into her hand.

This so doesn't feel right. He's going to get the wrong impression, but I'm not ready to spill my guts about my problems with Stew. I need to explain I just want to be friends. "Rick—"

"You can pay next time, since we're friends now."

Relief floods me as he slides out of the booth, and I follow his lead while grabbing my bag off the seat. As I sling it over my shoulder, my eyes land on the prep crowd. Stew's at the table amongst them with Taylor at his side. His gray eyes glare—like they're about to wage war—when Rick and I pass by. The nerves in my back twitch as I feel Stew's stare on me.

"There's definitely something going on between you two that you're not telling me," Rick whispers in my ear as he opens the door to let me outside.

"I don't know what you're talking about," I say and avoid direct eye contact with him and zip past.

I attempt to rub the tension from my neck as I step out to the parking lot. Damn. Am I that easy to read?

Rick follows me toward his car. "I'm not the only one who's noticed, you know."

I swallow hard. "What?"

He opens the car door for me and continues. "Yeah, that Taylor girl made it a point to come talk to me after she noticed us together."

I stand before him and fold my arms. "What did she say?" I growl.

His mouth tweaks to the side in amusement. "Wow. Not a fan, I see."

My eyes roll. "Not really, no."

"Obviously." He chuckles. "Well you'll be happy to know, your nemesis felt compelled to warn me to stay away from 'The Psycho, Natalie Sugarman' and wanted to know if you'd said anything about Stewart Masterson. Apparently, she's afraid you're obsessed with him because of all the staring."

The blood drains from my face. This is a good reminder on why I hate Taylor Gee. She needs to mind her own damn business. Did he expose my secret about Stew to her? "Is that so? What did you tell her?"

He holds up his hands defensively. "I didn't say anything. I didn't even tell her that the staring is, well, a mutual thing."

I laugh nervously. "There's nothing going on between Stew and me."

I'll be damned if I get roped into spilling my guts, only to be laughed at later if this whole friendship thing doesn't work out.

I hop into Rick's car, and he props his arm on the roof and leans in. "I'm glad to hear that because I think it's lame when a guy pursues another guy's girl, plus Stewart Masterson doesn't seem too trustworthy. There's just something about him I don't like." He shuts the door and I can't figure out how to respond as he saunters around the car to his side. Of course he doesn't like Stew. It's only logical to talk crap about your competition.

I wish Stew would let everyone know there's something between us because then I wouldn't have to sit here and figure out a way to tell Rick I am taken. I wouldn't have to lie because everyone would know. Rick definitely likes me, and I'm not ready to jump into something new yet. A big part of me still holds a candle for Stew and maybe using Rick as arm candy will bring Stew to admit to everyone we're together.

I may just end up with a social life before I die, and I don't care what the junior demon thinks about it.

# Chapter Seven

It's my turn to clean up the supplies today since Stew and I figured out a schedule so we wouldn't have to talk as much. Stew bolts from his seat. I stare after him and waves of anger rolls through me. He still hasn't called me, and I get that we're over, but it wouldn't kill him to at least be civil to me.

I glance down at my phone after packing up my stuff. Great. I'm late for my next class. Figures.

The hallway is deserted like a ghost town. I debate on just skipping my Statistics class. Monkey Man Miller, as most of the campus calls him, hates when people come in late to his class. He loves to make a big embarrassing show of it.

Just as I round the corner, the janitors' closet door flies open, and a hand reaches out and places a firm grip on my arm.

"What the hell?" I screech when I see the hand belongs to Stewart.

He pulls me into the claustrophobic closet and closes the door. It's pitch black in here and smells faintly of mildew and ammonia. I run my hand along the wall and search for a light switch, but no surprise, the closet's too small to have a light. Stewart's fingers still cling to my arm and he's close enough that I feel his breath on my lips.

What is he thinking? "This isn't exactly public, Stew."

He doesn't say a word, only pulls me tight against his body. His chest heaves against mine. "Kiss me," he whispers.

My knees buckle below me, and I sway a little. My stomach flips, doing its own little happy dance. After a few days of the silent treatment, I wasn't sure how he felt about me, but I can hear the desperation in his plea for a kiss and I know he still needs me.

God, he makes me crazy. Why can't we just be together?

"Please, Nat." His lips practically touch mine. "I love you."

My arms turn to Jell-O at the sound of those three little words. My bag falls from my hand and onto the floor. Instinctively, my arms wrap around his neck. We fall back into our summer lovin' pattern, and the last few hellish days without him melt away. He hugs me tightly as his lips meet mine, gentle at first, then a little deeper. It feels like ages since he's held me, and it's been torture. I've missed everything about him. The hungry way his rough hands caresses my skin tells me he's missed me, too.

He pulls back slightly and nestles his forehead against mine. "I don't want you seeing that guy."

My mind is blank. "What guy?"

"The guy I've seen you hanging out with lately. Seriously, Nat, he's weird, and I don't trust him."

Ah. Warm, gooey feelings flow through me. He's jealous. "Funny. He said the same thing about you." I knew hanging out with Rick would bring Stew to admit he cares, but he's going to have to work to get back my trust. I can't let him pull me into a closet and still keep me his secret. I sigh. "Rick's just a friend."

"Doesn't look that way. You're *my girl*, remember?"

"Well, at least Rick talks to me in public," I snap, and hope he sees my side of things. "You want me to stop seeing other guys, make us official."

His shoulders tense under my hands. "Please, Nat. Don't start."

"*Don't start?*" I drop my arms from around his neck, and start to fold them, but he grabs my hands. I try to pull them free from his grasp, which only causes him to hang on tighter.

"Are you saying you still expect m e to be your secret girlfriend?"

He wraps my arms back around his neck again and squeezes me tight his body. "Come on. We can work this out. Meet me at the tree house tonight. I can't stand fighting with you anymore."

"You want to see me, ask me out—on a real date."

After a couple seconds of silence, I shove him away. Great. How big of a loser am I to think for one millisecond things are different. The only thing that's changed around here is my budding new friendship with Rick.

I snatch my bag from the floor. "I'm out of here."

He grabs my hand. "Alright. Friday night, meet me at My Frat's party. We'll make it a point to be seen *very* publicly together."

Finally, he's come to his senses. Thank God we're in the dark, because I know I'm wearing the silliest smile known to mankind. "Okay, then...Friday. I'll meet you there. What about your dad?"

"I'll tell him Friday. He'll just have to deal with the fact that you're my girlfriend."

"Good. It'll be fine, Stew. You'll see. Everything will be perfect."

"Great. I can't wait to show you off." I can hear the smile in his voice.

He kisses me one more time, and I wish I can stay in this dark heaven with him forever, but I can't. "I've got to go."

"Okay," he says, but still has holds me tight against him. "Don't bring your friend with you either or else I just might have to kick his ass. I want you all to myself on Friday."

I pull myself away and open the door. The light streams in and reveals Stew's beautiful profile and mussed brown hair. He runs his hand through it and smiles at me. How can one guy be so perfect? I give him a crooked smile. Does he know how happy he just made me?

"See you Friday," I whisper, give him another quick peck, and then step into the bright hallway.

I practically dance all the way to Mr. Miller's Statistics class—my entire body weightless and carefree. Stew loves me and we will make this happen.

Hopefully, everyone will fall in line behind Stew in their acceptance of me. If not, we'll be fine together, creating our own little world filled with the blissfulness of our love.

Damn, I sound like a fucking hippie. I guess that's the way people in love think.

Rick will totally understand if I ask him not to hang around so much and stop sharing my place under the tree when I'm there. I mean, it was my spot first, right? Plus, I'm pretty sure Rick has a thing for me and Stew obviously can sense it, too.

Why am I even worrying? I probably won't even have to ask Rick to move. He'll more than likely avoid me anyway once it's blasted across the entire campus that Stewart Masterson, Capital University's new quarterback, is dating a gothic freak like me after the party. I feel bad because I did kind of lead Rick on a little.

My gut clenches at that last thought. That makes me a terrible person, and I'll owe him a fat apology soon.

But, I can't worry about that now. I just hope Rick understands.

One more day, that's all I'll have to wait. Stew's Frat always has the biggest post-football game parties off campus, and everyone is there, like practically everyone from campus that's into the whole party/Greek scene.

Soon, Stew will officially—and very publicly—be mine.

Even though I'm ridiculously late, I saunter into Mr. Miller's class that's already in progress.

Monkey Man's pinstriped tie swings as he turns from the math problem he just wrote on the over head monitor board. His dark eyes bore into me as he adjusts his black, plastic glasses. He checks his watch and I slide into my seat, praying he'll let me slide. "Care to enlighten the class with why you are late?"

Hear we go. No doubt he'll kick me out of his class. "Nope."

He scowls while his boney fingers rest on his hips. After shaking his head, he pushes a loose strand from his comb-over hair style back into place. "I insist you explain why you're late to your fellow classmates and have wasted their valuable educational time. So, let's try this again, care to tell us why you're late?"

A grin spreads across my face as I think about the real answer to that question. I bite my lip and try to hide my smile. "Not really."

Monkey Man thinks I'm being a smartass. His face twists with anger. "Leave my class. Now."

I grab my stuff and start toward the exit.

In the hallway, I feel a nudge against my shoulder.

"Hey," Ricks says as he walks beside me.

I give him a faint smile a little weirded out by his sudden appearance. I didn't expect to see him so soon.

My hands tremble a little at the thought of hurting his feelings. "Hey."

"You feel like hanging out again later?"

Stew's request to not hang around Rick flashes in my mind. "Um, I don't think that's a very good idea."

He frowns. "Why not?"

I sigh. There's no easy way to say this, so I'm just going to throw it out there. "I don't think we should hang out anymore."

Rick places his hand on my arm, and it causes me to stop dead in my tracks. "Did I do something wrong?"

I shake my head. "No, no." I place my hand on his arm and look him in the eye. "You didn't do anything. It's me."

"Stewart got to you, didn't he? Told you to stay away from me?" I flinch at the mention of Stew's name. When I don't answer, he shrugs away from my touch. "Spare me the 'it's not you, it's me' speech. I'm smarter than that."

Is it that obvious I'm doing this because Stew told me to? My eyes shift from his face, the hurt in his eyes stings my core. "Rick, come on. Don't be like that. You're great."

"But, not great enough." he says as he backs away. "No problem. I get it. I'm not Stewart Masterson."

"Rick." I call as he turns his back to me. "Rick?" I try again.

Damn it. There goes my only friend. I thought he'd understand. For a second I think about running after him. I don't want to hurt him, but I don't want to jeopardize my relationship with Stew, either. Thank God Stewart finally came around or else I'd be totally alone...again.

# Chapter Eight

I finish the last coat of my Midnight mascara and take a deep breath. This is it. Tonight, Stew and I go public, which is why I decided to glam up a bit and steal some of my older sister's preppy clothes.

"Is that my Gucci shirt?" my sister, Alicia, asks as she passes by our joint bathroom.

"Yeah." I grimace. Busted. "I'll take good care of it. I promise."

Alicia shrugs. "No biggie. I'm just glad you're wearing something other than that black emo crap."

I'll miss her so much when she moves to Texas to finish up her graduate degree in a few days. Texas A&M is lucky to have her. She could've went anywhere with her genius level G.R.E. scores, but she chose to go to a state school, where she got a full ride. I think more than anything, she wants to prove to Mom that she can do things on her own. Alicia is not Dad's number one fan. I hear her tell Mom all the time she should be independent and break away from Dad and his money if she's unhappy, but Mom likes to insist everything is fine. Like the whole town doesn't know what Dad's out doing when he's not home.

Alicia is the only one in my entire family that gets me and says I'm the reason she wants to be a psychologist, to learn to help people like me. She actually tries to understand.

I smile. "Thanks."

Alicia studies me as she leans her slender body against the doorframe. When I make eye contact with her, I notice her blue eyes twinkle because of her smirky smile. We have the same eyes people say, like our father, clear, piercing blue ones that appear to see into people's soul.

"What?" I ask.

She flips her long brown hair over her shoulder then studies her nails. "Oh, nothing."

It's impossible to hide things from her. She knows something is going on with me and I have to find out what she knows. "That look isn't *nothing*."

Her eyes meet mine and she grins, like she knows she's about to win. "Okay, so spill. Who *is* he?"

Quickly, I look away. Damn it. How did she figure out there is a he? Maybe she really doesn't know. "Who is what?"

She steps into the bathroom and stares at me in the mirror. "Don't play dumb with me, Nat. Who's the guy you're breaking out of your emo shell for?"

Dang it. I roll my eyes to throw her off the scent. "There has to be a guy involved for me to wear a blue shirt?"

She laughs. "Yes. Why else would you care about how you look all of the sudden? Not saying you don't always look cute in your 'I'm so sad I wear black' thing. But that blue top looks awesome with that black skirt and boots. I might have to take that outfit to school with me, actually." She studies my clothes. "I'd look fierce in a club wearing that."

My face heats up, and I know my blush is giving away my embarrassment at her gushing.

"I knew it!" she squeals. "Who is it? Tell me, tell me, *tell me*."

I sigh and figure she's going to find out anyway. We're going public tonight, after all. "Promise not to tell anyone? Including, Mom or Dad."

She crosses her heart with her finger.

A deep breath fills my lungs. "Stewart Masterson."

Her eyes grow a mile wide. "Dean's little brother? As in our neighbors?"

I nod.

"Oh. My. God. The Masterson boys are hot! I had the biggest crush on Dean until he moved out of state. Good job, sis." She walks in my room, mimics fainting, and falls on my bed, only to quickly prop herself up on her elbows. "Since when? And why didn't you tell me?"

I pick at my black nail polish. "Not long, just over the summer. And we've kind of been keeping it secret."

She cocks her head to the side. "From who?"

I shrug. "Everyone."

Alicia sits up on the bed and crosses her arms while she glares at me. "And you let him get away with that shit?"

"You know how his dad is. He thinks he's all high and mighty since he became a big time judge. Stew and I didn't want his dad to find out."

That did it. That totally pissed her off because she furrows her brow and twitches her lips. I know that look. The look that says someone is about to go down. "Who the hell cares about his crotchety dad? It's not like he's better than us. We're neighbors for God's sake, and our dad is a freaking doctor." She pauses for a minute, like things are sinking in. "Maybe it's just him. You know, Nat, if Stewart isn't willing to tell his dad about you, he doesn't deserve you."

My lips pull down into a frown. Deep down I knew this is how she would react and it's one of the reasons why I didn't tell her about sneaking around with Stew. We usually share everything, but this wasn't only my secret to tell. "I know, believe me, I've told him I'm tired of sneaking around and either he tells everyone we're together or we're done."

She smiles, pleased with my answer. "Good. So you guys are going out tonight?"

I nod. "Kind of."

Alicia rolls her eyes. "What the hell, Nat? Kind of? I thought you were a tough, kick-ass chick? Why the hell do you let him get away with that?"

"We're meeting at a fraternity party tonight." I try to redeem our relationship.

She shakes her head and gets up from my bed. "You know college parties get crazy." She steps toward me and puts her hands on my shoulders. "Do you want me to go with you?"

I know what she's thinking. I probably won't be too welcomed at the party since all the jock crowd hangs there and the connected sorority's queen bee, Taylor, and I have this unfriendly rivalry. Actually, now that I think about it, showing up with Alicia may not be a bad idea. She might be able to keep me safe from the prep crowd jerks until Stew finds me and shows everyone I'm with him.

I shrug, but hope she'll say yes. "If you want."

She claps her hands. "Great. Give me twenty minutes," she says, before she scurries out the door.


We pull up to the big white frat house in Alicia's college graduation present, a little red sports car. The place looks packed, and people have actually parked on the grass. Bodies are everywhere, and for a minute I hesitate as she puts the car in park.

"You ready for this?" she asks.

There's a lump in my throat that's about the size of a baseball and I struggle to swallow it down. "Yeah."

We step out of her car, and Alicia flashes me her pearly whites. No surprise a party would be fun for her. She was very popular on campus her entire four years here. I think that's why I got into the prep crowd so easily back in high school, before my psycho status was revealed. Everyone was envious of her and expected her little sister would follow in the most popular girl role. Goes to show how stereotyping and profiling people are totally bad ideas.

My beautiful sister is greeted with smiles and waves and is fully accepted back into the fold. People clear a path for her like she's royalty back to rule her kingdom. Suddenly, in her shadow, a tinge of self-consciousness creeps into my body. I fold my arms across my chest. Why did I have to pick tonight to step away from my comforting all black ensemble?

"I see nothing's changed," Alicia says to me. "I still feel like an undergrad student here."

I grin. "I'm sure you'll feel different once you're all settled into your apartment in Texas. You'll probably rule there, too."

She throws her arm around me and leads me into the house. "Oh, Nat. I'm *so* going to miss you."

Once inside, Alicia grabs a couple red plastic cups, fills them from the keg, and hands one to me. "Let's go be seen in the living room."

I follow her obediently toward the brick fireplace, which is the focal point of the room. She always tells me "you should always stand in the best location to get guys to notice you." I could learn a lot from her if I was interested in picking up any old loser from this party. She always gets noticed. Her strategy must work for her. But me? I only have one guy on my mind.

Stewart.

Bodies fill every inch of the house and they all seem to acknowledge my sister. Most of these people never speak to me and tonight is no exception.

I'm living proof popularity isn't genetic.

People clamor all around Alicia, practically pushing me out of the way to get to her. I was once told by a geeky, science nerd that when Alicia touched his shoulder and said "excuse me" was the best moment in his life. Pathetic, right?

I fight to stay involved in her social circle for a few minutes, but finally, I give up and sit on the hearth and sip my bitter beer. If I didn't know better, I'd say she sold her soul to a demon for popularity while I sold mine to save a mother who practically hates me.

I study my watch. It's nearly midnight. Where the hell is Stew? He's the one who wanted to meet here, and it's not like I'm early or anything. As I scan the room, the warmth of someone's arm next to mine sends a rush of excitement through me. I can't help but grin. Stew.

"Who ya lookin' for?" My grin immediately fades when I hear the voice. My stomach drops. This is not the voice I expected to hear. Sitting next to me is Stew's best friend, Trevor Humphreys. Trevor looks good as usual, with his dark hair and eyes. He's kind of a big man on campus around here, too. Kind of comes with being a college ball player.

Seeing Trevor is a good thing though, because it means Stew's somewhere close. But I'm not about to spill the beans to Trevor that I'm looking for him.

I bite my lip. "No one."

He raises his brow. "Well, if you're lookin' for Stew...he's not in the living room."

I shake my head. "I wasn't—"

He laughs. "Relax, Sugarman. I know...*everything*."

My eyes grow wide. "Everything?"

He nods and smiles. "Come on. I'll take you to him."

Trevor stands, and I follow suit. I risk a glance over at Alicia. She's laughing and having a great time. Not wanting to interrupt her fun, I don't bother telling her where I'm going. I follow behind Trevor through the crowd and then up the stairs. The stairway is crowed and a heavy smell of pot wafts around me. This is some party. Maybe the heavy partiers hang out upstairs, although Stew never said he was into the whole drug scene.

Trevor goes to a door once we're on the second floor and knocks. When no one answers, he opens it and motions me through. Trevor is creeping me out a little with the way he's grinning like a baboon, but if this is what it takes to see Stew, I'll trust him.

I step into the darkness of what I can only guess is a bedroom and turn toward Trevor as my eyes adjust a little to the darkness. "Well?" I ask, after looking around the empty room.

A deep, coarse laugh from Trevor reverberates around me. "Well, what?" My palms start to sweat as he closes the door and locks us both inside. Alone.

My heart pounds with a nervous flutter as I ask, "Where is he?"

"Where is who?" He steps close enough for me to smell the bitter-sweet odor of hard liquor on his breath.

I swallow the building bile in my throat down as Trevor fingers a loose strand of my black hair. "Where's Stew?"

He shrugs his shoulders indifferently. "He's not here." I take a step away but he moves in even closer. "But I'm here, and I know everything, Sugarman."

Taking another step back, I bump into what I imagine is the bed in the room. "Why did you tell me he was up here?"

He drinks down the last of his beer and tosses his cup on the floor before he wipes his chin. "I wanted to get you alone because I want to be *secret friends*, too."

That's it! I'm out of here. The way he's looking at me with lust filled eyes tells me he's not just talking friendship here. I try to make my way past him, but he blocks my path. His massive frame towers like a brick wall. "I'm not having sex with you."

He pushes his dark brows over his dark eyes, which makes him look evil and menacing. "Why? You think you're too good for me? You little Goth freak. You gave it up to Stew, now how about me? We share you know."

I *so* don't need this crap right now. What I need to do is find Stewart and ask him why the hell he told Trevor Humphrey's I'm an easy lay. "Fuck you, Trevor."

The next few seconds play in slow motion and my brain kind of detaches itself from my body. As I attempt to leave again, Trevor grabs my wrists and pulls my body against his. I struggle to break free from his steel grip, but the more I fight, the angrier he gets.

"Come on. Don't fight it," he slurs before he grinds his mouth against mine.

My teeth pulverize the meaty flesh of my bottom lip and a metallic taste covers my tongue. I need to get away from him, so I try to worm my hands away from his grasp. Finally, my right hand breaks free from his tentacle-like hold. Instinct takes over and my palm makes contact with his face. My body lunges forward as I smack with all my might.

"You bitch!" he shouts.

The back of his hand flies across my cheek, knocking me off guard. I stumble back and cover my face with my hands. Before I have a chance to fully recover, he shoves me onto the bed. The springs coil under my weight, and my head bounces back, rattling my teeth inside my skull. I push myself up with shaky arms. I need to get my bearings because I need to get the hell out of this room.

Trevor's face contorts in anger when I make eye contact with him. I open my mouth to tell him to calm down, but before I can get anything out, he tackles me with the full force of his body and knocks the wind from my lungs.

His two hundred pound frame crushes me into the mattress, and I gasp for breath. He pins my arms above my head with his massive grip, even though I'm fighting against him with all my strength, virtually rendering me helpless. His hands burn against my skin and I twist to get away from him.

Sheer panic stings my stomach as I struggle to free myself from his clutches. My legs pump wildly as I try to buck him off me. It's no use. He's just too damn big. A scream rips up from my throat out of sheer frustration and panic. A growl reverberates in Trevor's chest, and he uses his free hand to slap me again. The force of his blow knocks my face to the side. Pain shocks my core and my cheek throbs instantly. Blood drips into my mouth from a gash in my lip. The fight from inside of me starts to fade.

I squeeze my eyes shut. Trevor Humphreys is about to rape me. I always thought I would be tough enough to fight off an attacker if I was ever in this position, but I was dead wrong. My only option now is to beg. Maybe it will make him realize what he's doing.

Bile rises up in my throat as I think about what he has planned. "Please, Trevor," I whimper. "Please. No."

Warm tears flow into my hair, and I attempt to get Trevor's bloodshot brown eyes to focus on me, to realize he's doing something wrong. No such luck. His eyes burn with unfathomable rage—rage he's ready to take out on me.

His hand runs roughly up my thigh and reaches under my skirt. My breath catches. His fingers turn into claws as his nails scratch my skin in attempts to pull my panties down.

"See, Sugarman, I can be just as nice as Masterson," he says between ragged breaths. He leans in for a kiss, but I whip my face away from him, so instead he kisses my neck.

His cologne overpowers me, and I grow light headed from the strong stench of spicy musk that crams my nostrils. I breathe through my mouth and shut my eyes. I just want him to stop and go away.

"Please. I'm begging you. Please, stop."

He ignores my pleas, and his sloppy kisses continue to leave a trail of slobbery wetness on my neck. I try to force my brain to take me to another place, far away, so I won't have to endure the guaranteed torture he has in store for me. I begin to zone out.

There's a knock on the door. "Natalie?"

My body tenses at the sound of possible help, and once again I have enough energy to fight back. I open my mouth to scream for help, but Trevor's massive hand quickly muffles the sound.

"Natalie?" Rick calls again. "Are you alright?"

"Get lost, fucker! Sugarman's busy," Trevor shouts. His body stills like a statue, allowing a blanket of silence to cover the room. He stares daringly at the door with narrowed eyes.

"Natalie?" Rick calls, his voice agitated.

I whimper under Trevor's disgusting palm and try to squirm away from him. He locks his eyes on me. "Sugarman, I swear to God, you better not say a word."

At this point I figure I really only have two choices—lay here and take it, or make a scene and let Rick know I need help. I decide to go for door number two, and before I can think about it I sink my teeth into the fleshy part of Trevor's palm. Warm blood seeps into my mouth before he jerks his hand away. I know I got him good. Here's my chance.

"Rick!" I scream before Trevor raises his hand to smack me yet again. I cover my face to avoid any additional blows.

There's a loud crack, and the white six-paneled door nearly flies off the hinges as Rick kicks it in. The light shining from the hallway casts an angelic halo around him, like he's my own personal savior.

"What the hell, dude?" Trevor shouts, but the murderous look in Rick's face tells me he's not here to discuss the situation.

Rick storms over and grabs Trevor from behind with the strength of ten men and throws his sick ass to the floor.

Trevor attempts to stand, but he's quickly shoved back down and lands with a heavy thud. "Don't get up until I say you can," Rick orders.

Trevor doesn't listen and tries again. "I think you need to mind your own fucking business!"

Without warning, Rick springs on Trevor like a wild animal and lands a hard right-handed punch in his face. "She." Another punch. "Is." And another. "My business."

Rick releases Trevor's shirt and lets him fall to limply to the floor. My knight in shining armor splays his fingers, trying to shake the pain from his hand. Then, he turns to me. "Are you alright?"

I look down at myself and realize my skirt is still shoved around my waist. I quickly smooth it down. There's a smear of blood the back of my hand. My bottom lip still throbs, so I trace it with my fingers. Blood covers my fingertip and I wipe them on my skirt and then run my fingers through my hair. Slowly, I peer up and meet Rick's intense gray eyes, then quickly break away. Bodies pile into the room to check out the commotion. It seems the entire party has found its way into this enormous bedroom to witness my rescue. "I'm fine. Can we go?"

He nods, reaches over to take my hand, and then leads me through the gawking crowd. Every couple of seconds through the staircase gauntlet, I hear my name whispered.

"Can you believe someone would fight over Sugarman?"

"She's such a freak."

"Rick's too hot for her."

Tears threaten to spill from eyes at the sound of their words. I let go of Rick's hand and place my hands over my ears. I follow close behind him and try to block out the world around me. We reach the living room, and I feel the warmth of his hand on the small of my back. He guides me out the door into the cool night air. I drop my hands from my ears, feeling safe from the judgmental whispers in the house. I wipe the fallen tears from my cheek with the palms of my hands.

Rick grasps my hand in his large, warm fingers. "Are you sure you're okay? I can always go back in and finish the job on Trevor."

I sniff and shake my head. "No, that won't be necessary. Besides, I think you already did a pretty good job whipping his ass." I pause and take a shaky breath. "I'm just really glad you showed up when you did. Thank you."

He pulls me into a hug beside his car. "Me too," he whispers. The heat of his body pulsates from him and envelopes me in comfort for some strange reason. "I would've killed him if *anything* did happen."

There is an odd feeling in the pit of my stomach. I don't deserve his kindness, but I appreciate he's given me a second chance. The thought of disappointing my only friend earlier makes his words sting. "Why are you so nice to me? Especially after how I treated you?"

He pulls back, and I stare into his charcoal-gray eyes. "Because I care about you, Natalie. And even though you pick that asshole Stewart Masterson over me, I'm still glad you're my friend."

My head drops instantly at the sound of his name. "That's over."

It's harder than I thought to hear myself admit it out loud. Stewart was using me. Trevor made that quite clear. I know it's over now. Stewart doesn't even have the balls to tell me to my face. Instead, he leaves me stranded at this party and made me look like a complete moron.

Rick frowns, like he's concerned for me. "Really?"

I nod. "Yeah, really."

Rick's lips meet my forehead in a gentle kiss and I close my eyes. An electric tingle zings through my entire body. He cradles my face in his hands and his thumbs caress my cheeks, and before I'm ready, he slowly breaks away and I open my eyes.

"Good," he whispers. "Come on. I'll take you home."

# Chapter Nine

"Natalie?" the voice sounds like it's down deep in a five gallon bucket somewhere. "Natalie!" This time I roll over to find my sister, drunk and kneeling at my side whispering so loud she might as well announce to Mom and Dad she's just getting in. "Are you awake?"

"I am now," I grumble.

"Good, because I wanted to talk to you." She giggles. "So, what's up with you and that Rick guy? I thought you were dating Steeeeewart," she slurs his name, stretching it into three syllables instead of just two.

God, I so don't want to talk about this. "Yeah, well, he stood me up and apparently he told his douche friend I'm easy. That asshole Trevor tricked me into going upstairs with him and he tried some stuff."

She sways as she leans back and grimaces. "Stuff? What kind of *stuff*?"

I roll over and pull the comforter over my head. "I really don't want to talk about it. Nothing happened. Rick made sure of that." I need a subject change fast because I don't want her to go nuts over the situation. "How'd you get home anyway? You didn't drive like that did you?"

"Of course not!" She sounds appalled.

I yawn, causing my cheeks to stings and I'm glad it's really dark in here. I'm sure I look horrendous after taking those smacks from Trevor. Alicia, in her drunken state, would completely freak out and wake up the entire house if she saw me.

She pulls down my comforter. "I hear Rick kicked Trevor's ass over you, but no one's really sure why."

Nobody would believe the truth anyway. They think Rick is too good for me. No way would they ever believe I was with Stew. "Humph. Well now you know. If Stewart would've been there like he promised, none of this would've happened. I hate him so much."

We sit wrapped in dark silence for a couple of minutes, but it doesn't last long. Alicia is a talker and she babbles constantly when she's tipsy. "Well, tell me more about this Rick guy. He's really cute. Someone pointed him out to me before the whole fight thing went down. It was like he came straight to the party to find you or something, because he wasn't there long. Who knew you were such a hot guy magnet."

A smile spreads across my lips. The right side of my face aches with pain, and my grin quickly fades. Rick is cute, but I don't need to jump into another relationship so soon. It's going to take a while before I get over Stew and what he did to me.

What am I thinking? I don't need to focus on *anybody*. Only me. It's not fair to drag a guy into a relationship when I won't be around much longer. But I am glad Rick cares enough for me to beat the ever-living sit out of Trevor for me.

Alicia still waits on me to acknowledge my relationship status with Rick to her. I have to give her something. There's no way I can pretend I don't know him. "We eat lunch together sometimes. He's really...nice."

"Nice?" Alicia questions. "That's always what you say when you want to avoid something."

I sigh. She's digging. "Okay, he's interesting, but I'm not ready to, like, date him or anything."

"Natalie." She leans in close and rests her elbows on my bed. "To hell with Stewart. He's an ass. You should give Rick a chance. I mean, the guy beat up Trevor Humphreys over you. Besides, what better way to get back at Stewart than date a hottie like Rick?" She taps my arm. "Show old Stewy what he missed."

I shouldn't care about Stew, but I do. I turn my head toward her. "That could really hurt Stewart, though."

Alicia growls in frustration. "Yeah, so? That ass deserves it. Didn't he hurt you?" Her words feel like another slap in the face. More reminders of all the trouble Stew caused me tonight.

"Yes," I whisper. It's hard to admit it to her as well as to myself. Stew's betrayal sends waves of nausea through my belly. This was his second chance and he blew it. He never really cared for me after all.

"So what if you hurt him? What goes around comes around. Plus, you'd probably really like Rick if you gave him a chance." She stands, swaying back and forth a little. "Think about it, Nat. I love you, and you should be treated like a queen. Don't take shit from anyone." She kisses my forehead before she wobbles from my bedroom. "Good night."

Way to plant the seed, sis.

Now visions of Rick flash in my mind. He really is kind of beautiful with his cool gray eyes set above chiseled cheekbones and full lips. Long hair and tattoos on a guy have never been my thing, but on him they totally work. And even though I've never seen him without his shirt, I imagine from the tone of his arms that his body is quite solid. Another plus is he's definitely nice. Look at how he stood up for me tonight, like he'd take on the world if I asked him too. No one has ever done that before.

I can't think about this right now. I need a distraction.

I snag my Mp3 player from my nightstand, poke in my earbuds, and study my alarm clock while mentally calculating how much sleep I'm going to get before the dreadful three-thirty-three nightly wakeup call. If I can manage to slow my brain down, I'll get at least two hours of sound sleep. My breathing flows into a rhythmic pattern as I attempt to relax and search my playlist to choose a song.

"I didn't think she was ever going to leave." My eyes fly open at the sound of the demon's voice, and a gasp releases from my mouth.

I yank the earbuds out and stare at him. His tiny body rests against the side of my bed as he leans over me and inspects my face. My pulse pounds in my veins and I try sit up. He places a tentative hand on my forehead and forces me back against the pillow. "Wait! I'm not ready." I plead and try to get to my nightstand where I keep a jar of salt stashed.

He shakes his head and a dark lock of hair falls into his gray eyes as he stops my hand. "Relax. I'm not here to kill you."

My bottom lip trembles. "Why are you here then? You never used to check up on me so much, and you've *never* come into my room before."

His little palm traces the contours of my face. "I'm here to fix you."

My mouth feels like I have a wad of cotton balls in it. "Fix me?"

"Close your eyes," he whispers—the side of his face illuminated by the moonlight shining through the window.

My eyes narrow and I stare him down. He matches my intense gaze and sighs. "I'm not going to hurt you. I would've done it already if I was."

What choice do I really have? I don't have a weapon or another plan of attack yet, so I do as he asks. But when a bright amber glow flickers, I sneak a peek. His tiny hands are red, like hot coals. The same brilliant white eyes he gets when he's about to claim a soul are on full display. I knew I couldn't trust him.

"Wait!" I beg, but he presses his hands on either side of my face. My legs buck wildly beneath the blankets, and I claw at his hands. I'm not ready to die yet, and I'll fight my hardest against him.

At first, my skin burns, like a million tiny flames trying to melt my face from the bone, but then it changes. A cool sensation covers my skin. A combination of fire and ice fills every inch of me. My legs calm down and stop pumping all over the place. My fingers go limp and fall away from his. The pain is gone. The gash where my lip split is now smooth under the glide of my tongue, and I'm totally relaxed.

He removes his fingers from my head. "There. That should fix it."

Sleep tries to overtake me, but I fight to stay awake. It's almost like he gave me a sleeping pill.

"Wha'd you do?" I manage to choke out.

He smiles, and it seems genuine. "I told you. I fixed you."

I'm too tired to try to escape. My legs wouldn't move even if I attempted to budge them. "Why?" is all I can manage to ask.

"It'd be easier if I showed you." His index finger touches the middle of my forehead.

Suddenly I'm in the dark. There is complete nothingness around me for a few seconds until a light flickers before my eyes. The tunnel reappears just like before when he tried to show me something—blurry at first, but then it grows clear. There's an old, wooden cabin surrounded by trees. The path in front of the house is dusty and worn. To my right, I see a horse trough filled to the brim with water. The birds chirp while the smell of wild flowers and fresh air feels real. Why is he showing me this? I'm not scared at all. Matter of fact, I feel completely comfortable here in this vision. It's peaceful here, like this is home.

There's a little girl in a faded, blue dress sweeping the front porch. She looks like she's straight off of *Little House on the Prairie*—very plain. I glance down and notice my outfit nearly matches the little girl's. My fingers touch my hair. It's braided into two long plaits that rest on my shoulders and feels strange between my fingers.

While I wonder why I'm here and why demon boy is showing me this, I hear a man shout in the distance, followed by the sound of hooves pounding the ground. The haze of the hot summer sun causes the three cowboys riding over the hill to shimmer. They're strangers. Strangers I can't let get the little girl. For some reason, I just know this. Fear causes my entire body to tremble, and before I can stop myself, I yell, "Run, Sarah! Hide!"

The little girl drops the broom on the porch and takes off toward the barn. I watch her tiny eight-year-old legs carry her, but I feel like she's not moving quickly enough so I scream again for her to hide. I think about hiding too, but no one else is here to defend the farm, and I can't let them destroy what I feel is our home. The men bring their horses down to a trot as they approach me. They look rough—like they haven't had a bath or shaved in weeks. I swallow down a lump in my throat. Suddenly, I'm really afraid, more than I've been in my whole life. It doesn't look like they just want directions.

The largest of the three men stops his black horse in front of me. "You there, girl, yer daddy here?"

I shake my head. "No sir, but I 'spect he'll be along any minute." Those words don't sound like anything I'd ever say, but it's like I have no control over my actions or words. It's like I'm in the passenger seat of my body.

The three men laugh as they dismount. The big one smiles at me and I notice he's missing his right, front tooth. "The horses need tending to. You see that they get water and then get on in the house and fix us something to eat. We're mighty hungry."

Bossing me around doesn't sit well, and I'm sure as hell not their servant. "Papa doesn't like strangers 'round here. Y'all need to get back on your horses and be on yer way. There's a town a little ways up the trail."

Toothless marches over and grabs me by the arm. Hard. "You sassing me, girl? I don't take to kindly to being sassed by no woman." He spits, and it nearly lands on my shoe.

"Let go of me!" I shout as I smack his face. Nobody grabs me like that without asking for a fight.

He rubs his face and smiles evilly. "Looks like we've got a feisty one here boys. Maybe we should cool her off."

Bile fills my throat and I nearly throw up as I'm brought out of the vision. The room rocks back and forth as I focus on the demon boy. Then he presses his finger to his lips and then points toward the door with the other hand.

"Natalie?" It's Alicia. "Can I sleep with you tonight?"

I look at him, my eyes still wide from what'd I'd just seen. Alicia cracks the door open and my gaze dart in that direction.

"Why—" before I can say another word, he's gone. That vision felt so real and has left me with so many questions and absolutely no clues on why it's important. Now, I'm just further confused about him and what exactly he wants from me.

I clear my throat to regain my composure before I answer Alicia. "Sure." I pull back my covers and slide over.

She snuggles in beside me. "I really don't want to leave for school."

She's still drunk. I rub her arm and whisper, "It'll be okay."

I'm safe from a return visit from the demon as long as my sister is here with me. For some reason, I think he's only able to freeze time when he's collecting a soul, which is why I used to always climb in bed with Alicia when I was younger. There's safety in numbers. He did seem different tonight, though. Not as scary as usual.

This visit showed me a different side to him—a caring side. Maybe I can convince him to renegotiate my deal? The next time I see him, I have to try to bargain with him and ask him about the vision he showed me. I sigh and close my eyes knowing I won't get my answers tonight.

The next thing I know Alicia shakes me vigorously. Damn it! I wish I could be an evil sister and yell at her to leave me alone because I only have a couple hours of sleep time left. I love her too much to do anything mean to her, though.

"Nat, wake up."

My heavy comforter becomes a shield over my face. "What, Alicia?"

Footsteps come to a halt at my bedside. Why is she up already? "Come on. Get up. You don't want to sleep the day away. I've got big plans for us."

I groan. "You're still drunk. Can't it wait until morning?"

She laughs and yanks the blanket off my face, then opens up the drapes that keep my room pitch black. "God, Nat. It *is* morning."

What the hell? Startled, I sit up and rub my eyes as the streams of bright sunlight shoot across my bedroom.

She gasps. "What the hell happened to your face?"

My fingers trail along my right cheek. Crap! I bound up from my bed and dart over to the mirror. The bruises aren't nearly as bad as I thought. There's a faint yellow spot on my left cheek. They're almost healed. Impossible. The baby demon really fixed me just like he said.

Not wanting to drag the topic of me and Trevor back out, I quickly cover the faint bruise up with make-up. "It's nothing. I got drunk last night and kind of fell on my face."

Alicia crosses her arms and glares at me through the mirror. "Are you sure? That jerk-off Trevor didn't touch you, did he? Because you told me last night that Rick came in before anything happened. Don't lie to me, Natalie. You know I can always tell when you're lying."

Nervous laughter spills from my mouth. "I wouldn't lie to you. I fell. That's it. I promise. It's not even that bad. See." I turned toward her.

She inspects every inch of my face. After a thorough assessment, she nods, believing me. "If you say so. Cover that up good. Mom won't let us out of the house if she knows we were both hammered last night." She walks over beside me. "I've got a surprise for you. Get dressed." She pauses and looks me up and down. "And make sure it's cute. None of that all black shit."

I stare after her as she leaves my room. I've never slept through the nightmare. *Never.* The constant 3:33am wakeup call is what always reminds me my soul is promised to the miniature devil.

Another warning that things are about to change, maybe?

After dressing, I clink my way down the stairs in my boots and find my sister gossiping with my mother. My defenses shoot up as they always do around my overbearing-want-to-be-perfect mother. I raise an eyebrow as they both turn their focus on me. Mom's dressed in her work out gear with her dark hair smoothed back into a tight ponytail. Her eyes glisten when she looks at me, and my heart sinks. Has Dad finally asked for a divorce?

"Oh, Nat. This is going to be great," Mom says as she stuffs her platinum credit card in my hand and closes my fingers around it. "Buy *whatever* you need."

What? With my eyes glued on the shiny plastic card, I answer, "Uh, Thanks?"

"Oh, Mom. You're going to ruin the surprise," Alicia spouts off.

"All right." Mom wipes a solitary tear from her right eye. "Have fun girls," she says before she leaves the room with a goofy grin plastered on her face.

I shoot an inquiring glance at Alicia. "What was that about?" Mom never treats me like that—like she's happy with me. I'm the troubled kid—the one who gave her early gray hairs with all my demon antics. And giving me permission to use her credit card is huge. She's never let me near the thing, because she knows I'd buy more demon killing items with it.

My sister is definitely up to no good.

She shakes her head and then grabs my arm. "Nuh-huh. No questions. Let's go."

Knowing she always has my best interest at heart and means well, I let Alicia drag me along without objection, but I'm still on high alert, trying to figure out where she's taking me. She opens the driver's door on her little red car, and I mimic her movements on the opposite side. The black leather is already a little warm from the early September sun, and Alicia's signature floral perfume mixes with the strong leathery new car smell.

She slides on her sunglasses, and I do the same. "Are you going to tell me where we're going?"

"Nope." She laughs as she backs out of the driveway. "You'll see when we get there."

Once on the road, she cranks her stereo up and bops around in her seat. She never gives any hints on where she's kidnapped me too. "Come on, Nat. Sing with me."

I roll my eyes and laugh, but give in like I always do when it comes to Alicia. The lyrics to an old song roll off my tongue. Sure, we've had moments when we want to rip each other's hair out but usually we stay pretty tight. She's the only one who gets me, the only girl I actually consider my friend. Alicia was there. Even though she's only a couple years older than me, she seems so much wiser.

After a quick fifteen-minute drive, Alicia whips into a huge parking lot. "Um, why are we at *the mall*?"

Alicia grimaces for a split second. "Oh, don't be a party pooper." She pats my leg. "This is going to be fun." She sets her eyes on me, and her face totally reads with the 'duh-look'. She's lost her mind. No way is she dragging me around that place. I hate the mall and all the preptastic people that hang there. People like Stew. "I'm giving you a makeover."

My head flies into instant no-motion. "No, no, no. No way!"

Her eyes narrow. "Yes."

"No!" I fold my arms over my chest.

"Nat?" She puts on her best puppy dog eyes. "Please do this for me."

I sigh. "Alicia, I can't! Look at what happens when I just wear a blue shirt. All hell breaks loose."

She grins. "You've already shocked everyone. You might as well go all out. Please let me do this. My main goal here is to help you in the man department. With my help you can have any guy you want. You are super-hot, and it's time the rest of the world knows it." I could use some help there. Maybe if I looked a little more like Alicia, Stew's dad would have been cool with us dating, and last night could've been avoided completely.

Ugh. Instantly, I'm upset with myself for thinking about any relationship at all with Stew. He's a dick and it's time to forget him.

This could be helpful. Not that I want anything to do with most of the assholes I know, but a little acceptance would be nice.

After I stare into her pleading eyes, I let out an exasperated sigh. Her fashion intrusion is irritating. "Okay, but let's not go crazy."

She squeals and squeezes me against her. "This is going to be so fun. We're going to make Stew so jealous, and Rick won't be able to keep his hands off you. Where's Mom's card?" I hand the card over. "Okay, let's go do some damage."

After ten gazillion hours of shopping, my feet are on fire from these stupid heels Alicia put me in. I'm starting to regret the decision of throwing my old clothes—including my boots—in the trash can. It was such a liberating experience, freeing myself from the current bullshit of my old life, so I try not to complain about the bubbly white blisters forming on my heels. I do really kind of love the plaid skirt and black halter-type blouse picked out for me. Several male eyes have trailed after me since I've made the clothing switch, and I won't lie and say that it didn't boost my self-confidence a little.

Alicia pats her belly. "I'm starving. Let's get some lunch."

"Sure, where do you want to go?" I ask.

"Let's eat at the food court."

I follow her to the center of the mall where we claim a table next to the two story indoor fountain and put our bags down. A chlorine scent surrounds me, and it feels like a day at the city pool—it reenergizes my body and gives me a new burst of liveliness, despite my aching feet. "Lish, I'll grab our lunch if you stay with our bags."

She pulls out Mom's card and hands it to me. "Get me a really big salad since it's on Mom."

With the card firmly in my hand, and I make my way over to the line for Pinni's—who's known to have kick-ass grilled chicken salads.

I find I'm uncomfortable in my brightly colored—hey look at me—skirt showing off so much skin. Tugging at the material on my hips, I try to get a little more thigh coverage. I wrestle with my personal clothing dilemma and catch the conversation between the two women in front of me.

"I really think you should go," the young blonde woman says as she digs in her designer handbag. "She really helped me."

"Janie, not everyone believes in that stupid hoodoo crap," the slightly older woman replies.

The blonde looks up from her bag with an expression of horror. "It's not crap! If I hadn't gone to Madam Zoë, I'd be married to that cheating snake, Robert. She's totally legit."

The older woman rolls her eyes. "Just because she told you to not trust Robert doesn't actually mean she saw your future. I could've told you he was a loser, and my advice would've been free."

Future?

That got my wheels to turn. What if this Madam Zoë can really tell it? If she can, she could totally help me out with my current crisis—give me a little insight. She might know how long before the demon takes me to hell. This might be what I need—someone to help me out with my future because by the looks of my life lines, I don't have much time to waste.

"Excuse me," I say as I tap the blonde on the shoulder. She turns and points an artificially beautiful smile at me. "I'm sorry. I don't mean to be nosey, but I heard you talking about Madam Zoë."

The blonde puts her hand on my shoulder, which is odd because most people don't think I look approachable. Must be the new clothes. "Oh my God. Have you been read by her, too?" Her eyes sparkle with excitement.

I bite my bottom lip. "Um, no actually, but I want to be. Can you tell me how to find her?"

"Oh, sure," she says as she digs in her bag. "Here." She hands me a yellow business card. "Here's her address—you don't even need an appointment."

"Thanks." I turn the card over in my hand and read 'Madam Zoë. Find the answers you seek.'

Let's hope so.

# Chapter Ten

My cheery sister bursts though my bedroom door. "Come on. Get up. Get up."

I groan and throw a pillow over my face. I'd only been about ten minutes into my nap after our exhausting mall trip when she wakes me. "Go away. No more shopping."

"Screw shopping!" She opens my closet door. "We have to get you ready to see Rick."

"Alicia, it's Saturday." I groan again. She's lost her mind. "We have all day tomorrow to put together my new look."

"You're not getting it, Nat." She throws some clothes on my bed. "He's here. Right now."

My arm flies up quick as lightning, and my fingers snatch the pillow off my face while I gasp. "What?"

"Yeah." She points at the floor. "Downstairs. *Right now*. Didn't you know he was coming?"

My brain scrambles as I throw my legs over the side of the bed and jam my feet to the floor. "Oh my God." For a second, I debate on making a run for it, but I'm not even sure if I'm ready for this. But this is Rick, the guy who saved me from Trevor. He deserves more than that.

Quickly, Alicia grabs a brush from my dresser and goes to work smoothing my long, black strands. After she's satisfied with her handy work, she goes into Picasso mode. She applies my make-up to cover the yellowish tone of the skin on my face. She smiles as she dabs on the last smidge of my lipstick. "Wow. I'm good. Maybe I don't need Grad school. I could just do makeovers for a living."

I lean around her and peer into the mirror and my jaw drops. The girl looking back at me gives Taylor Gee a run for her money as the most beautiful girl I've ever seen in person. My body drifts toward the mirror as I turn my face from side to side in admiration of my sister's awesome work.

"Wow is right," I whisper.

"I know, huh?" she laughs. "Come on. You've kept him waiting long enough."

My palms grow clammy as I stand at the top of the staircase, hesitating. What if he doesn't like the new look? Can my heart handle another rejection? More importantly, what am I going to do if he *does* like the new look? Am I ready to turn our new friendship into more? It's not too late to keep it at just friends. Maybe that would be the best thing because I don't know how much time I have left.

I push those questions to the back of my brain and decide to let the chips fall where they may. After all, Rick is a change for the better. He's nothing like Stew. He could help me transition into another person. A better person. Someone people will actually miss when I'm gone. I don't need to love him to date him. I don't think I'll ever fall in love again.

My fingers wrap around the handrail as I take the first step as the new me. Rick's in deep conversation with my mother. They sit casually on the couch and neither of them notices I've come into the room. Mom's hazel eyes sparkle as she laughs at something he's just said. She fidgets with the tight bun in her hair, like a giddy school girl. I can't help but to notice how striking Rick's profile is when he smiles at her in return.

Suddenly, he turns those gray eyes on me, nearly stealing my breath. I feel my insides turn as I wait for his response to my make-over. A wide smile slowly stretches across his face. He stands to greet me as I step closer. "Hey."

"Hey," I say back. I don't even realize I'm grinning like an idiot until I feel heat flood my cheeks. I avert my gaze from his.

"Nat, honey, why didn't you tell me you had such a handsome *friend*," Mom coos, obviously ecstatic a boy is showing interest in me and lingers on the last word a little to long.

I groan. "Mom..."

Rick chuckles and hides his smile behind his hand, but I'm too embarrassed to yell at him right now. He soon settles his amusement and speaks. "Are you ready, Nat?"

Curiosity engulfs my brain, and I instinctively tilt my head. "Ready? Ready, for what?"

He lifts an eyebrow. "Our date, of course."

Date? What date? Did I overlook the part when I agreed to a date? "I—I didn't—"

"Sweetie, *go*," Mom urges. "Have a good time." She winks at me and leaves us alone in the living room. She's obviously happy. I've changed my looks and now have a country-club worthy guy interested in me. The button down shirt and pressed khakis Rick's wearing practically scream money, not to mention the shiny, black sports car parked out in the driveway.

I turn to Rick as soon as I'm sure Mom's out of earshot. "I don't remember agreeing to a date with you today."

He steps toward me. "You didn't have to."

My eyes narrow. "Pretty sure of yourself, aren't you?"

He takes my hand in his. "Only when it comes to what I want." A grin spreads across his face. "Come on. Let's go."

I peer into his eyes and get lost in the turbulent seas that thrash around in them. Being so close to Rick makes my heart flutter. In the movies, girls always fall for the heroic guy who saves their lives. Is it possible that's all I'm feeling—a false sensation of intensity because he protected me? I'm still not fully over Stew. How is it possible to feel this pull toward Rick?

Ugh. There I go again.

If this is going to work—the new me—I need to put Stewart Masterson out of my mind. A date with Rick might be a step in the right direction.

Interlacing our fingers, I smile. "Okay."

He gives my hand a gentle squeeze and bites his lip, trying to keep his smile from growing wider. "Let's go."

We walk hand and hand out to his car where he opens the passenger door for me. I slide in and allow him to shut me inside. He moves with grace around the front of the car and takes long strides to shorten the time to get to the driver's seat.

Once he's comfortable, I turn to him. "So?"

He laughs and his eyes scrunch from his wide grin. "So?" he mocks.

I try again. "Where are we going?"

He shakes his head. "Don't you like surprises?"

"Not really." I run my fingers through my hair. "I'm more of a straightforward kind of girl."

He tilts his head down as he twists to look at me. "Not about *everything*," he says as he backs down the driveway.

The tires of his car squeal as they make contact with the road.

Where the hell does he get off? I barely know him. Of course I'm going to keep things from him. "What's that supposed to mean?" I demand.

He shrugs and keeps his cool. "I'm just saying, you keep secrets, like Masterson for example."

My arms instinctively cross in front of my chest at the mention of *his* name and the betrayal of my feelings. "Let's not talk about him."

This is not how I pictured this date going. I want to get over Stew, not keep dragging out his name. We ride in silence, and Rick stares straight ahead, like he doesn't want to talk about Stewart, either. After a few minutes, I catch him staring at me, and I quickly look away.

He sighs. "Look, I'm sorry. I didn't mean to piss you off. Not another word about him. Forgive me?"

Not really, but I don't want a long, drawn-out argument over why I don't want to talk about Stew and my secrets.

"Yeah, fine." I need a subject change. Quick. "So where are we going?"

His body relaxes, like he's glad we've changed topics, too. "Can I surprise you just this once?"

To lighten the mood because I feel a little bad for snapping at him, I joke, "Okay, just this once." I grin before I crank his stereo up.

He slips his sleek sports car into an open space at Easton Mall, and I can't help but to let out a little groan. This is the last place I want to see any more of.

He chuckles as he takes in the look on my face. "Yeah, the mall isn't really my scene either, but I thought we could catch a movie or something. Your mom told me about your all day shopping trip."

I roll my eyes. "Yeah. Allllllllll day." He shakes his head and places his hand on his door handle. "Anything in particular you want to see?" I ask, while I open my door.

"Wait!" He scrambles out of the car and runs to my door. "Let me get that for you."

Who says chivalry is dead? "Thanks."

His hand naturally meets mine, and we interlock fingers. The warm skin against mine sends waves of pleasure throughout my entire body. This is nice, someone liking me— wanting to be seen with me. In public.

Rick opens the door into the building for me and then immediately relocks our hands. "You look beautiful, by the way. I like the new look."

"Thanks, but I feel kind of silly, actually. My sister played Barbie makeover with me today."

He smiles. "Well, I think you'd look great no matter what you wore. Hell, even in a moo-moo you would probably turn me on."

I giggle. "A moo-moo?"

Rick shrugs. "You know those old night gown looking dresses old ladies wear."

I shake my head. "I know what they are. I just can't believe *you* do."

The smell of popcorn is overwhelming as we step inside the movie theater. He leads me to the counter. "What do you think? Comedy? Romance? Action? Horror?"

I shrug. "Doesn't matter. You choose."

He rubs his chin and studies the board. "Wow. Nothing like adding pressure on a first date."

"This isn't our first date."

He smirks. "No?"

I shake my head. "No."

He turns to face me—both of my hands in his while he gazes into my eyes. "Care to enlighten me, Miss Sugarman?"

I roll my eyes. "Uh, the diner."

Light pours into his eyes, like he remembers that day. "You said that wasn't a date."

Right. I did say that. "Okay, well, I changed my mind."

His deep laugh echoes through lobby of the theater, and he playfully wipes his brow. "Good to know I can relax a bit then. First dates are nerve racking."

Dancing around the smile I'm hiding only lasts a second or two. I laugh at him and swat playfully at his arm, but he whirls out of my reach. It feels good to have a friend. "Oh, shut up and pick a movie, already."

He finally chose 'Demon Rising' (why am I not surprised by that?), and I convince myself I can handle it. Normally I stray away from anything mentioning demons, but most demonic movies are so far from the truth I doubt it will scare me.

We opt to share a tub of popcorn and a drink after a ten minute debate on what we should order. I hold the buttery tub of goodness with both hands and follow him into theater seven. I'm anxious to see where he chooses to sit. Everyone knows the back row is make-out central—not that I'd mind trying those electric lips out sometime—but I want to make sure he likes me for the right reasons before we go there. Not because he's like Stew or anything. I just don't want to recreate that drama anytime soon.

"Is this, okay?" he asks as he stands about five rows down from the back.

Yes. He is a nice guy. I knew I liked him for a reason. "It's fine."

Relieved, I follow him to the middle of the row and take my seat next to him. I grab a handful of popcorn and stuff a couple pieces in my mouth. When he doesn't immediately dig in with me, I stop and look at him. Steele gray eyes watch me intently, almost studying me.

The popcorn scrapes my throat as I swallow. "What?"

He looks away and runs his fingers through his long hair as he realizes I've caught him gawking at me.

"Rick? If I have a booger or something, you can tell me." In the dim light of the theater, the hearty laugh that comes from him causes me to frantically search in my purse for a mirror. "Seriously. Do I have something on me?"

My face heats up. Oh my God, how embarrassing.

He rests his hand on my arm. "Nat, calm down. I'm laughing because you're cute when you're nervous."

My eyes narrow. "I'm not nervous. I—" I what? I couldn't finish that sentence because I am nervous. There's so much pressure for me to work out my feelings about moving on. I can't let something stupid make me feel silly and self-conscious the rest of the night.

"Really, there's no need to be nervous around me. I like you, Nat. And I'd still like you even if you had the biggest booger in the world."

I bite my lip. This is not good because those three little words make my stomach do a flip. "You like me?"

His lips turn upward and then he licks them before he shoots me a stunning smile. "Of course I like you. Would I be here if I didn't?"

My brain panics a bit. I don't think I'm ready for this. It's too soon to have this conversation with a guy, but I can't resist the nagging question on my mind. "Well...um...why?"

His brow rises up. "Why?" The word sounds like the answer should be obvious to me. But I'm still clueless as to why Rick has all this interest in me. It wasn't like I was a prize in the eyes of the rest of guys on campus or anything.

I nod. "Yeah, I mean, you're practically the only guy who even talks to me." The only human guy that is.

He shakes his head like he's disgusted. "That's everyone else's loss, isn't it? Just means you have more time for me."

My eyes meet his. "But, *why*?"

He sighs as he gently touches my cheek. "Because you're special and I see that."

My heart flops around erratically in my chest. I swallow deeply as I gaze into his gray eyes. The words flowing from his lips sound sincere. He's answered the doubting voice in my mind and it scares me to think that I might actually like him back.

Should I stop questioning a good thing and just go with it?

Before we can dive any further into the topic, I panic, not ready to deal with such a heavy issue. I look down and stuff my face with a handful of popcorn. "Want some?" I offer around a mouthful of kernels.

A faint smile flirts across his face, like he knows I'm running away from this conversation—running away from him, but he doesn't say a word. He reaches in and takes a handful. "Sure."

The movie flickers in the darkness. Twenty minutes into it, the dark-haired lady on the screen is about to go to hell. A demon, who was the woman's boyfriend, smiles as the ground swallows her up. "Another soul collected," the demon character says. I wonder if that's what it'll be like for me. Will I be alone and terrified? My eyes start to sting. I cover my eyes to block the rush of memories that flood my brain. Why did I agree to see this movie? This is the last thing Rick needs to see—the crazy side of me shining through. I don't want him exposed to this part of me because I'm afraid it will rip away all the normalcy I feel when I'm around him.

Shielding my eyes is no longer enough. My head drops to my knees and I shove my index fingers into my ears. A panic attack starts to hit me hard. There has to be a way out of this deal. I just need to find it before it's too late.

A smooth circling motion on my back soothes me—Rick's hand. When I don't look up after a couple of minutes, he takes my hand in his and guides me to an upright position before rushing me out of the theater.

My body relaxes instantly once we're in the cool hallway of the building and I drop my hands loosely at my sides and open my eyes.

"Hey? You okay?" he asks, concern written all over his face.

My lips pull down into a frown. "I'm sorry. I should've known better. Demons sort of freak me out."

He nods, making me feel like he doesn't need any additional explanation, which is great because I'm definitely not ready to share that part of me yet. "Come on. Let's get your mind off this."

Gladly, I follow Rick through the doors into the mall's brightly lit atrium. This is the same food court Alicia and I were at earlier. The mall buzzes with other people trying to entertain themselves on a Saturday night.

I wrap my arms around my body, now hyper-aware I'm not in my comfortable all black-invisible wardrobe that usually helps me disappear from the rest of the world. Numbly, I walk beside Rick down the heart of the food court and take in the scenery. I'm instantly angered when my eyes land on Stew. He's at the table claimed by a crowd of people I recognize from campus with Trevor Humphreys and Taylor Gee on either side of him.

Assholes.

Stew looks up from his sandwich and meets my narrowed stare. Nausea fills my belly. I thought he felt something for me, but after last night, I know different.

I take Rick's hand in an outward show of affection and hope Stew notices I'm moving on.

Oh man, does he notice. Stew's jaw drops, nearly smacking the table, and I feel a flutter of smug satisfaction.

Take that Stewart!

Rick looks down at me and smiles. I give his hand a little squeeze as we near the table. His skin against mine is warm and reassuring. The closer we get to the tables, the more I notice all the pointing in our direction. Trevor quickly turns his bruised face away from us, like he doesn't want to chance another fight with Rick. Stew, on the other hand, has now recovered from shock and looks pissed. He crushes the soda can that's in his hand while he locks eyes with me.

What gives him the right to be mad at me?

As we pass, Taylor, of all people, greets us. "Hey, Rick. Hey, Natalie."

Rick gazes down at me and gauges my reaction before he makes the decision it's okay to stop at the table. After I shrug my shoulders, he answers her casually. "Hey, Taylor."

Her smile stretches from ear to ear, like she's glad he knows her name. "What are you guys up to?" She glances down at our hands and wears a mischievous grin.

Rick shrugs. "Nothing, really. Just watched a movie. Now, we're trying to find something to do next."

Stew's jaw muscle flexes as he watches us from the table.

Her eyes light up like they always do when she thinks she's digging up rumors to spread about someone. "Oooh. What movie did you see?"

"Demon Rising," Rick answers.

Stew's brow furrows and he glares only at me. "But Nat hates demon stuff."

Everyone at the table stares at Stew with puzzled looks. They're all probably curious how Stew knows that personal detail about me.

I can only think of revenge when I look at Stew. Before I realize it, I blurt out, "People change. And well, I like *new things* now." For added effect, I lean my head on Rick's shoulder. Hopefully that stings him a little, knowing I'm with Rick.

Stew shakes his head in disgust and rises from his seat. "Whatever. I'm fucking out of here," he grumbles, before he turns to walk away.

Taylor sees her opportunity to get Stew alone and quickly chases after him. She doesn't even tell us goodbye. "Wait up, Stew!"

Those two stuck-ups belong together.

I know I've hurt Stew but good riddance to that asshole. What gives him the idea that he has any right to control me? He doesn't care about me. Never did, apparently. I'm just aggravated I let myself get involved with him in the first place. I should've known better. We're nothing alike.

The rest of the people at the table ignore us as soon as Taylor and Stew leave, so Rick and I continue walking hand in hand away from the food court. Satisfaction flows through my veins as we step into a little pet shop. I'm still on the revenge high.

"Wow," Rick whispers. "I'm sorry to bring Stew up again, but it looks like you guys had an intense relationship. Are you sure it's over? He looked pretty pissed."

Rick should know, I guess, since we are kind of dating now. It's only fair to be honest about past relationships. "You're right. We *were* something, once, but Stew refused to tell anyone we were together, like he was ashamed of me or something."

Rick pulls me into a tight hug against his chest. The heat from his body radiates off him. Warmth spreads through me, like being wrapped in sunshine. "I figured it was something like that," he whispers in my ear.

Muscles throughout my body relaxes as I snuggle into his chest. It feels good to be close to someone who cares about me even if it's just a friend. Rick makes me feel safe. "How did you figure it out?"

His breaths are even and steady as he strokes my hair. "I'm kind of good at reading people, so I just knew. I'm glad I got to you before you got too serious with him."

I sigh. "Don't worry. Like I told you before, that's over." And I meant it. It was over. The feelings I had for Stew weren't the same anymore. I could handle being ignored, but being set up for major embarrassment was crossing the line. You don't do that to someone you claim to have feelings for.

I hug Rick tighter. He's my only friend in the whole world now and I cling to him like he's my life raft—the one thing keeping me a float in normalcy in this demon madness. It's probably not right to lead him on this way, but I need this closeness.

"Why are we in a pet shop, anyway?" I murmur against his chest.

He laughs. "Don't you like animals? I thought all girls liked puppies."

I shrug, thinking of how Mom never allowed us to have any pets before Rick pulls me down an aisle. We laugh as we pet the exotic birds through the cage wires and try to get them to cuss. Then we move on to admire the puppies behind the glass. Their little, wet noses press against the glass as they attempt to lick us.

"They're so cute." I actually cooed. First pink, now puppies? Who am I?

"Yeah, they are, but you want to know my favorite?"

A smile presses my cheeks upward at the thought of the cussing parrots. "The birds?"

"Nope. Snakes."

"Snakes?" He nods, and a shiver escapes down my spine. Snakes represent evil, or at least that's what I was always told in Sunday school when I was a kid.

"Let's go look." He nudges me down the aisle.

They keep the creepy, legless creatures in the very back of the store. When Rick asks one of the workers to get the slimy, gray snake, I take a step back. I hadn't noticed, until this moment, I'm a definite snake hater.

The store employee brings out the creature all tangled up on his hand. The snake's tongue flicks in and out as it surveys its environment.

Rick takes the snake. It slithers through his fingers like they're a maze. "Nat, don't be scared. They aren't bad. Just because something seems scary doesn't mean it will actually hurt you."

When I take another step back, goose pimples freeze on my skin. The snake wraps its body around his arm and Rick strokes its scaly skin.

"It's just a little snake," he prompts. "Come on. Pet him."

How the hell does he know it's a boy? "Him?"

"Sure, pet Lucifer." Okay his evil obsession is creepy. How can I possibly fall for a guy who likes evil and runs toward it while I rack my brain to be free of it?

My eyebrows draw down with confusion. "Lucifer?" I swallow down the nervous lump that's building in my throat. "As in the devil?"

He smirks, like that should be obvious. "Yep, one in the same. You don't know the bible story about Lucifer becoming a snake?"

My lips are suddenly dry, and I wet them carefully before answering, "Who hasn't?" At the mention of evil, my heart thuds. Throughout my years of study, I've learned Lucifer is the King Demon. The boy demon told me once that's who he works for, collecting souls, and one day I will too after he transitions my soul.

I can't seriously continue to date Rick if he truly is obsessed with demons. "I know you like reading about demons and stuff, but can you cool it with all the evil talk?"

He tilts his head to the side and continues to stare—almost mesmerized—by the snake.

What the hell? Is he a freaking Slytherin snake whisperer? The pet shop door swings open, and for a second, I debate on running out of it. It's not too late to run away from him and go back to being the old me, blocking everyone out again.

"Why does demon talk freak you out?" he asks without his gaze leaving the snake.

I grimace at the thought of explaining my emotional traumas to a guy I might want to become romantically involved with. I practically spilled my guts to Stew, and look where that got me. So instead, I decide for the evasive approach. "It's a long story."

Rick motions for the pet shop worker to untangle the snake from his wrist. Once it's gone, he turns those powerful charcoal eyes on me. "Nat, I've got nothing but time. I want to know everything about you. Let me get to know you. Let me into that beautiful brain of yours."

Some things make life so much easier if you can keep them secret. He's already heard the 'she's crazy' rumors and hasn't run away from me. No one, except Stew, knows why I see a shrink. If I tell him everything, I might push him away. But then again since he likes demon stuff, maybe he'll believe me. He might even know a way to win my soul back. At this point I'm willing to try anything.

His eyes are fixed on me while I debate the situation internally. He's waiting.

With a sigh, I figure what the hell. What's the worst he can do? Ignore me like everyone else. "Okay, but can we go somewhere more private? It's not something I want to share with the entire world."

Like I'm a flower ready to crumble at any second, he gently takes my hand. I quickly realize we're headed to his car. Once we reach it, in what's becoming a routine lately, I swiftly slide my body against the cool leather of his seats.

When Rick's seated in the driver's seat, he turns expectantly to me. "Okay, we're alone now. Talk to me. Please?"

"Well..." I manage to choke out. Fear grips me as I get ready to reveal a huge secret about myself to this guy. "It started when I was five..." I trail off and doubt if I should say anything else. It's still not too late to keep my secret.

"Come on, Nat." His fingers trail across my cheek, and I my skin tingles from his touch. "Talk to me. You can tell me anything."

After a deep breath, I convince myself that if I'm going to date Rick, he needs to know. He has the right to know that the little demon may try to kill him for being with me. He deserves to make his own choice to hang out with me after he knows the truth. I continue, "When I was five, my mom and I were alone in our house eating lunch, and she started choking on a piece of hotdog. And well, she died."

Rick contorts his face in confusion. "But, she's fine. I mean, I just met your mom."

"Only because I made a deal with a little demon boy to save her," I say defensively and automatically regret my tone. This is not some shrink I need to defend myself against. This is Rick. Someone I want to know the truth about me, and believe it.

His eyebrows bunch over his eyes. "Whoa, whoa, whoa. Are you trying to tell me you made a deal with a demon for your soul?"

"Yes," I whisper. My heart pounds as I wait on his response. I knew I shouldn't have told him. Gah. When will I learn to keep my secrets to myself?

We sit in silence for a few minutes before he speaks. "How do you know the deal you made was a bad one? I mean, you're still here—alive—and still you. And your mom is still alive."

What the hell? He's seriously not running away in fear that my craziness will rub off on him? In fact, I think he might actually believe me. Either that or he's going along with it so I don't flip out on him.

I scratch my head. "Oh, I don't know, because he was a *demon*! No deal with a demon is good."

His face tells me he's stunned, yet curious at the same time. "Tell me everything. I want to try to understand." So I do. I tell him all about my life—how the demon randomly appears as a little boy. How he takes every persons soul who shakes his hand—everyone's except mine and how I've been trying to kill the little bastard to get it back ever since.

"You know, I've read a lot about demons," Rick says after a couple moments of silence. "Maybe he wasn't evil or at least he might not have been there to hurt you. Did you ever think of that?"

"No it's worse. He wants me to be his demon counterpart." I shake my head. He doesn't understand the complexity of the situation here. It doesn't matter if the demon didn't hurt me then. He wants to make me his evil sidekick for eternity, and that seems worse than dying. The little demon wants to make me a killer like him. "What part of my soul is damned do you not get?"

He shrugs. "Maybe it's not."

"Yes, it is." Frustrated, I throw my head back against the headrest and close my eyes. "Let's stop talking about this."

"Why?"

I sigh and turn my head to look at him. "Because I hate thinking about it, plus I made a deal with myself to only discuss it with my shrink."

He grimaces. "Your shrink?"

I nod. "Crazy, remember? I'm, like, certifiable."

Rick reaches out and takes my hand. "I don't think you're crazy."

When I look at him, his face is determined, like he needs me to believe him. "Yeah, right," I say. He shakes his head at my reaction. "You're only saying that because you're just as crazy about demons as me. Just in another way."

He throws his hands up. "You caught me. Now we know why we're perfect for each other. We're both demon freaks."

Instinctively, I punch his arm and laugh. "Shut up. I'm serious. I *really* am damned."

"Not if I can help it. I'll help you get off the naughty list." He laughs as he starts the car and then tears out of the parking lot. "There has to be a way to save your soul and I'm going to make sure we do."

My lips pull into a tight line. "And how do you suppose you're going to do that?"

"Don't worry." He steals a sideways glance at me and winks. "I have connections."

I roll my eyes. "Sure. I bet you do."

## Chapter Eleven

I can't believe Alicia left for grad school this morning. The thought of being alone with Mom all the time while Dad spends all his time at the hospital sends a twinge of sadness through my heart. Last night after getting no answers from the demon book I bought online, I'm determined I'm lost on where to look for answers on saving my soul. If only I had more time. It probably wouldn't bother me if I was an old lady or something, but I'm only twenty. I'm not ready to die yet, so giving up isn't an option.

"You look gorgeous, honey," Mom gushes as she stands in my doorway and admires my clothes.

"Thanks. Alicia put it all together." I go to my satchel and fumble through my things. If it were bigger, I could just stick my head in there and hide from her.

The tension between Mom and me gets intense sometimes. She was one hundred percent against my old Emo look and told me constantly that it wasn't healthy for me to look like I was in constant mourning. But who wouldn't mourn for the loss of their soul? So, I suspect the compliments and the look of content spread across her face is genuine. I wish we could really be the perfect daughter she craves. My life would be so much easier if I was normal, but I'm not.

"I'm sure going to miss your sister. I can't believe she's gone, already."

I know she's sad—I'll miss Alicia, too. She's always seemed like Mom's best friend. The loss of her around here may cause Mom to finally snap. They have so much more in common than we do. Alicia is beautiful like Mom. I've heard some of the other doctors at the hospital compliment Dad on his trophy wife. My parents got married while my dad was in medical school. They probably were in love back then, before he went on to become one of the state's best cardiologists, but that's all changed. At least it feels that way.

A couple years ago, Dad began his mid-life crisis or some kind of crazy weirdness. First it was sports cars. Now, he sleeps around with nurses half his age. Everyone knows about his affairs, but Mom refuses to show any sign of distress in the family. I'm pretty sure that's why she's ecstatic I've finally conformed. It helps with the mask of perfection.

Sometimes, like now, I feel guilty for being so difficult with her. The thought of leaving her soon chokes me up a little. With both me and Alicia gone, she'll be alone.

All this drama with Stew and Rick has certainly kept my mind preoccupied lately. I haven't dreamed about the boy demon in a couple of days now, but I know he's out there. Waiting.

Tears sting my eyes at the thought. The emotional realization hits me hard. My eyes trail over Mom and take in every inch of her. Hands clasped in front of her as she lingers in my doorway. She looks worried.

This could be the last time I ever see her. I turn my hands over and stare at my palms. My life lines stop in the middle of both hands. Rick has distracted me so much lately I'm not really sure how much they've changed. My hands ball into tight fists in front of me and my body shakes.

Mom wraps me in an embrace, and I bury my face in her neck. She misunderstands my tears, but I don't care. I need her close. The smell of her lilac perfume surrounds me as I breathe it in. "Don't worry. She'll be home for Thanksgiving." She soothes my hair. "Come on. I'll make you some breakfast before you head out to school. Just like when you were a little girl."

I nod and let her believe these are tears for my sister. She releases me and scoots from my room. I blow out a breath between pursed lips. It's probably best she thinks that. No need to trudge up the demon issue with her after we've had this nice bonding moment, because those conversations never go well.

Once I'm through with breakfast, I step out of the house in my new, prepped-up outfit. My heart does a little flip when I see Rick's car parked beside mine. He gets out and grins as I approach. "Hey, you."

Rick looks really good today in his dark washed jeans and his long sleeved black shirt. His gray eyes sparkle against the morning sunlight while his brown hair hangs loosely around his face. He could easily pass for a movie star, looking as good as he does.

I'm glad he's here, but I'm a little hesitant. Is this too much too soon? "Hey. I'm surprised you even want to hang out with me again."

"You know, Natalie, you don't have to worry about that. It takes a lot more than a little secret to scare me off." His fingers lightly trace my forearm, and I smile. It's a simple touch, but it feels so intimate and caring. "Actually, I couldn't wait to see you. One day away was enough, so I wondered if you'd ride with me to school." The slight resistance I felt a second ago when I approached him leaves me. His charm makes me melt a little.

My eyes shoot to the ground. I want to say yes, but I think this feels too soon. I don't want to get serious with him.

He takes in my silence and frowns. "It's okay if you don't want to."

I look at him. "No. I mean, I want to, but I can't."

"Can't, huh?" His head whips toward Stewart's house and narrows his eyes.

I frown. I don't want to seem weak when it comes to Stew, but I would be lying to myself if I said I wasn't a confused, emotional wreck right now. Still, I don't want Rick to think I'm still into Stew. Honestly, since Stew blew me off at that party, I don't feel as attached or strongly for him anymore. "It's not what you think, Rick. I have an appointment after school."

He seems to accept that and nods. "Can I follow you then? We can at least walk in together."

The gossip wheel about Friday's party is bound to turn today if the people from the party spot us together. I nod, and hope a show of solidarity with Rick cools the rumor flames of what the cause of the fight may have been. "Sure."

Butterflies tickle my stomach as I pull into my normal parking spot by the football field. My hands slightly shake as I gather my things. I can't believe I feel this nervous. Maybe, this is a mistake. Are we an official couple now? I mean, I've never had a boyfriend-boyfriend, other than Stew, but I don't count a relationship that never went public.

Rick taps on my window and then opens my door. "You ready?"

No.

"Yeah, just getting my stuff," I say as I hop out of the Focus.

He twists his lips. "So..."

I have no clue what he's about to say. "So?"

He gestures to my clothes. "Are you ready for this? I know this is a big change for you."

I sigh as I look down at my outfit and shrug. "I guess. What choice do I really have? I'm already here, plus my sister tossed most of my old ones."

He laughs. "Tell you what, we're in this together—demon deal thing and new clothes alike. You already know I'm okay with kicking some ass over you, right? Someone gives you a hard time, just let me know." He sticks out his right hand. "Deal?" I stare at his outstretched hand.

Shaking hands is usually a no-no for me, but this is Rick. I trust him. It's nice that I finally have someone to be there for me. "Deal." I shake his hand.

Our skin touches, his grip firm in mine. A static shock passes between our hands and I quickly jerk my hand back. "Damn." I shake it to rid the left over tingles. "Did you feel that?" It felt oddly familiar, almost like—never mind, I'm thinking crazy. There's no way that shock was the same as the little demons.

He rubs his hands together and laughs like it was no big deal. "You shocked me."

My palm rubs against the cotton fabric of my skirt. "*That* was a little more than static electricity, Rick."

The grin on his face stretches. "I think you're overestimating my electrifying personality."

I furrow my brow and shift my eyes to my open palm. Is it possible that I am overreacting? "You seriously didn't feel a huge shock?"

He laughs at me again, like I'm making a big joke. "Come on. We don't want to be late for your big reveal day."

All morning long I see the stares and hear whispers as I walk around campus. Not everyone is receptive to my new look, but the one person who is—Taylor Gee—alarms me. She smiles and waves every time she sees me, like we are fast friends, which is messed up considering she's the one who started all those rumors about me being crazy. She made my life a living hell back then. Why the hell does she want to be friends with me now?

I shake my head and try to think about something else.

The scene with Rick in the parking lot replays in my brain. Maybe, I'm being paranoid, but that jolt I received from his handshake this morning reminded me so much of the one I receive from the little sadist. Could everyone else be right?

Maybe I am crazy. It's not like Rick is a five year old who steals souls.

My morning classes fly by without much incident, so I hope lunch follows the same pattern, A third of the students in the cafeteria ignore me, which is a good thing. I'm blending in. I'm no longer the freaky looking Emo chick who everyone thinks is mental.

I head outside to the quad. Rick's under the tree and stashes his book in his bag as I walk toward him.

He grins and then speaks loud enough for others to hear. "Hey beautiful."

Such an outward display of affection, here, in the middle of the open courtyard, in front of everyone, causes my stomach to knot. But I kind of like it. The feeling of being admired is one a person should cherish. It's something I've craved for so long, but I've only known him a week, and two dates doesn't mean we're on the pet name stage yet. We didn't even kiss after our date Saturday night, merely a polite hug good night. He needs to slow down.

"Hey," I simply reply as I toss my bag to the ground and fold myself onto the ground next to him.

"So? How's the big change going?"

I shrug. "Okay, I guess. I think I actually have a new BFF."

He tosses his head back slightly letting the sun skip through the leaves and shine on his face. I stare at him openly as I can't help but notice how amazingly attractive he is. "And who is that?"

"You're admirer." A grin stretches across my face. "Watch this."

My eyes scan in the jock table's direction. I spot Taylor. Her attention zooms in as our eyes meet. I wave. Her unnaturally white teeth gleam from across the quad as she waves back.

Never far from his minions, Stew takes in our little exchange—his eyes fixed on me while wearing a serious scowl—and my heart crushes. How could I ever fall for someone like him? He's an asshole of epic proportion.

The urge to stick my tongue out at Stew and flip him off surges through me, but I won't give him the satisfaction of acknowledging his presence. Instead, I inch closer to Rick and turn my focus on him just to piss Stew off some more.

"Wow." Rick laughs. "Who knew clothes would make such a difference."

Stew still has his eyes on me. I know it's wrong to use Rick like this. He's going to get the wrong impression, but I don't care, hurting Stew like he hurt me is all I care about.

I kiss Rick's cheek. "I don't think it's just because of the clothes."

Rick slowly licks his lips and gazes into my eyes. "Glad I can help," he whispers as he reaches up and strokes my cheek. His touch is familiar, and for a second, I forget this is just a show for Stew's benefit.

My heart thunders in my ears, and I nervously bite my bottom lip. He leans in so close that I can feel his breath on my lips. Inching forward, I actually find I crave his kiss which surprises me after I've spent the past couple of days warning myself to take things slow with him. My motion halts when I feel a tickle on my right hand. This moment can't be ruined by a stupid itch. I move my hand, and it lands on something slender and slimy. Instinctively, I pull away and jerk back from Rick. My eyes snap to the ground and my mouth gaps open. I jump to my feet like I have superpowers. A blood-curdling scream rips from my throat as I stare wide eyed.

"Whoa!" Rick yells as he rolls away from the brown snake who has settled next to us. "Was not expecting that."

Our commotion causes heads in the quad to whip toward us. My Statistics professor, Monkey Man Miller, who happened to be walking by at that moment stops abruptly. "What's going on over here?"

Words won't leave my tongue. My whole body shakes as the adrenaline pours through my veins. I just touched a snake for God's sake.

The professor stares at me, like I'm nuts. I still can't bring myself to speak, so I lift a shaky finger and point at the coiled up snake in strike mode.

Dr. Miller's eyes flash with panic. He locks his gaze on the snake, and then he yells, "Everyone inside the building!" No one moves until he adds, "Now!"

Students scamper inside. Everyone goes—everyone, but me and Rick. My legs won't budge. I'm frozen in fear and still at a loss for words.

Rick turns to me. "It'll be okay. It's just a little snake. They can't hurt you, remember?"

Dr. Miller rubs his chin and mumbles, "How am I going to get rid of this? Maybe I should call maintenance."

"I can do it." Professor Miller and I stare at Rick with wide eyes. "I can get rid of it. I'll take it over to that empty grass lot and let it loose so everyone can come back out."

The teacher grimaces. "Son, I don't think it's wise—"

He cuts himself off when Rick swiftly picks the snake up by its head and holds it away from his body. The tail wiggles back and forth. Nausea rolls through me, and I fight the urge to pass out. This is no pet snake. It's wild and dangerous. Rick could get really hurt if that thing bites him.

With unfathomable grace, Rick runs out of the quad—snake in hand—and across the parking lot. He reaches the empty grass lot and kneels down. Rick releases the slimy creature back into the wild, safe—like he's protecting *it* from the student body instead of the other way around.

Within the seconds, he's back in the quad, which most of the people have repopulated. Rick dons a triumphant smile as he looks at me.

"Thank you, Mr. Steele," Monkey Man says.

"No problem. I had to." Rick gives me a sad smile. "Nat hates snakes."

"Whatever." Professor Miller scratches his head and mumbles to himself before heading back into the building.

No guy has ever tried to prove they would protect me against anything like Rick has. In only the short time I've known him, he's saved me twice. A grin threatens to expose how flattered I am by one little statement. Our eyes meet, and his travel down to my lips, causing me to lick them. It feels like he wants to kiss me. I mean, really kiss me. Intensity flows between us, like there's an invisible rope pulling us together. My face heats up, reddening my cheeks, giving my feelings away.

"Rick?" Taylor calls as she makes her way over. "That was amazing. How could you stand touching that thing?"

Her presence totally changes the vibe between Rick and me. He directs all of his attention to her and explains how snakes are merely misunderstood creatures. Whatever. They are just as bad as people think—possibly even worse: snakes and evil go hand and hand, especially when Rick refers to them as Lucifer, God's archenemy.

"Well I think you're really brave." Taylor swoons.

Gag.

Taking Stew away from me isn't enough? She has to go after Rick now, too?

All that waving crap earlier wasn't for my benefit. I see that now. Taylor is so fake.

"It was nothing, really, just looking out for my girl here." He wraps his arm around me and gives me a little squeeze.

Her smile widens. "Oh, Nat. You have such an awesome boyfriend."

"He's *not* my boyfriend." I answer a little too quickly and instantly regret it.

Rick's smile fades as Taylor raises an eyebrow. "No? Oh. I thought—"

Quickly, I try to recover. I didn't mean to hurt Rick's feeling. "I mean, not like officially, or anything."

Taylor shrugs. "Okay. Whatever. So anyway, I'm having a party Saturday night—you two should come."

Before I have chance to reply, Rick answers, "Sounds good."

"Great." Taylor smiles. "See you there. Natalie, you know where my sorority is, right?"

I nod, and she turns on her heel and heads back to where she came from.

Taylor takes her throne next to Stew, no doubt to fill everyone in about Rick's triumphant bravery. Stew seems unimpressed as he picks at the fray on the bottom of his tee shirt. He hasn't made any attempts to speak to me since we agreed to meet at Morris's party. Probably for the best. I can't imagine what I'd even say to him. There would most definitely be a lot of cussing involved.

"Can I walk you to your next class? I want to tell you about some of the possibilities I found on the internet about saving your soul." Rick breaks me out of my delusion of all the evil things I'd call Stew, given the opportunity.

His arm is still draped around my shoulders. It's nice he's trying to help me, but he hasn't figured out the internet doesn't have any real legit information about demons yet. I smile at him and will pretend to be interested in all the possible angels he found just to appease him. "Sure."

# Chapter Twelve

Dr. Fletcher enters the room, and her mouth draws into a lopsided grin. "Natalie, you look beautiful."

I knew she'd notice.

"Thanks." There's no way I'll tell her why I made the change. I don't want to go into detail about my social life with her, yet.

The little doctor smiles. "Does this new look mean you're working on your outlook on life and death?"

I shrug. "A little, I guess."

She's pleased with herself. I know when I leave she'll pat herself on the back and tell her office staff about how much she's helping me.

Dr. Fletcher pulls my chart out of her desk drawer and sits in front of me. "So, what would you like to discuss today, Natalie?"

"Well...I, um." I stumble over my words, not sure where to begin because I really hate being here. The good doctor puts her hand on my arm.

A vibration rips through my bones.

Oh God. He's here. Either Dr. Fletcher or me is about to die. My pulse quickens, and tears pool in my eyes. I'm not ready for this. I mean, I don't want it to be me. The doctor isn't exactly my friend, but she's got a family. I focus my energy on the photo in front of me. Bile rises in my throat. The guy in the picture is familiar, *very* familiar.

It's Rick. Lilim is too young to be his mother, but still she's obviously very close to him.

My leg bounces uncontrollably as I try not to puke. I have to save her. Warn her somehow. He's my friend. I have to break my personal rule about not interfering because I can't allow that little monster to take away someone Rick loves.

The vibration intensifies, much thicker than I've ever felt before. My brain rattles in my skull, but I push through it and yell as loud as I can. "Lilim, you have to run!"

"So, it's true." She gasps and jerks her hand away from me and the noise stops instantly.

What the hell?

My breaths are rapid, and I tremble all over like I'm sprinting a mile. I choke out, "He's coming for you."

Dr. Fletcher sits back in her chair and has regained her composure. "Who's coming for me, Natalie?"

My palm rubs my forehead. Of course she's calm. She didn't hear anything, but she did say 'it's true', which makes me think she believes me. "I've never stopped him from killing someone before, but I can't let him take you." I tip my head in the direction of her family photo. "Rick's my friend."

Her eyebrows lift. Instead of being fearful for her life, she looks at me with pity. "No one is out to get me, Natalie. Trust me. I'm not going anywhere." She flips through my chart and then pulls out a prescription pad from the pocket of her white lab coat. "How do you feel about medications?"

My scalp itches, and I dig at the crown of my head. At this point I'm desperate for any help I can get when it comes to the demon, but medications aren't going to fix me. "I'm not really into taking medications."

She gives me a smile that's full of sympathy. "I think medications will work wonders for you. They can help combat all that fear you have inside your brain."

"Fear?" I echo her words.

The pen in her hand taps the prescription pad. "You want to be normal, don't you? Let me give you a prescription to help with that. Maybe, that demon will be out of your life once and for all."

I finally nod, and my stomach rolls. God knows how much I wish that little beast would just disappear. I take the prescription from her just to let her feel helpful, but I don't intend on using it.

Another thought flits through my mind as she writes out the medication order. "You won't tell Rick about this will you? I don't like for people to know what happens when the demon comes."

She smiles. "Of course not. I won't tell my...*nephew*, anything about this. Everything in my office remains confidential, including that you even see me to begin with. I never tell him about any of my patients. Especially one he has a special bond with. He talks about you often, you know."

That's a relief. At least Rick won't know who my shrink is. That would be all kinds of embarrassing.

I say my goodbye's to Dr. Fletcher and make an appointment with her secretary on the way out.

As I reach into my purse to put my appointment card away, I find Madame Zoë's business card. I'd forgotten about her with everything that has been going on in my life. Maybe she'll give me some answers about my current demon situation. She may know a way to save my soul if she's a real psychic and not one of those con-artist fakes. I've tried every other form of research about killing demons, might as well try a new method.

The girl at the mall said no appointment is needed, and it's on my way home. I crank my Focus alive and pull onto the main drag of Grove City. Four blocks down from Dr. Fletcher's office, I pull onto Columbus Street, and start counting house numbers—looking for 996.

After passing it a couple times, I pull up to the address. The numbers are kind of old and have lost a couple of nails, so they read 666. Creepy. The little blue house doesn't show any sign that a fortuneteller lives here or that anything weird goes on inside. The house is kind of cute, actually, with its white picket fence and neatly trimmed lawn.

When I open my door, I hesitate. Maybe I'm in the wrong spot. But what the hell, I'm already here, might as well go check it out. The gate attached to the fence groans under my hands as I undo the latch. Chills spread through my body and goose bumps erupt all over my arms. My footsteps thud, even though I try to be quiet, as I step up on the tiny concrete landing in front of the door. That's when I see it, a handwritten note that reads: *Madame Zoe's, always open.*

She must live here, too.

I swallow, reach for the lion head knocker adorning the entrance, and knock with three quick raps. For some reason, I kind of expect the door to open on its own after I finish the last knock, like they do in scary movies. I roll my eyes. I'm thinking crazy.

It takes a couple seconds before I hear a little frail voice call to me from the other side of the door. "Comin'."

She must be pretty old, because it takes her a good minute to make it to the door. The dead bolt clicks, and then she opens it. The door remains chained, so it doesn't open very wide. I gasp a little when she pokes her face between the cracks. Her eyes are milky white. The color they once may have had is lost in a cloudy haze. The odd contrast of such white eyes set in deep brown skin causes my skin to crawl. It's probably a medical condition or something, but the effect is freaky.

At first, I almost turn around and run off her stoop, but she's just a little old blind lady with some kind of exotic looking bird on her shoulder. It's not like she can hurt me or anything.

"Come child. Don't be scared. I know what you seek." Her deep Southern drawl startles me. She's definitely not from here in Ohio.

Curious as to how she knows what I want, I start to ask that very question, but I'm too late. She shuts the door in my face.

Okay. I guess, no reading today. As I turn, the door opens. She emerges and beckons me inside.

I follow her in and let my obvious question slip. "I'm sorry, Madame Zoë? But how'd you know what I wanted?"

My vision takes a second to adjust to the dark room. The large green bird on her shoulder—I've seen its kind before. I think it's a parrot or something, but I'm not really sure. It seems too big for her frail shoulder. The living room is crowded with seven birdcages. All of them house a different bird, except for one empty cage, which I assume belongs to her shoulder accessory. They squawk simultaneously as I stand in the middle of the room. A mixture of rotten food and dirty bird smell makes my stomach churn in disgust. I pinch my nose shut. It's hard to imagine such an upscale lady, like the one who gave me Madam Zoë's card, in this filth-infested room.

I wrap my arms around myself to avoid touching anything. This was a mistake. There has to be a polite way to get out of this room.

The rest of the house is blocked from view by the thick drapes hung in the living room. There are rows of tiny little cloth dolls, all in the shape of people with button eyes, hanging from the ceiling. Large pins protrude from the sack-like figures, many of them stuck in the heart. Dried blood stains the dolls, like it oozed from the hole the needle made. What kind of evil voodoo goes on here?

Motionless—and soundless—I stand, waiting. I want to run, but I can't force myself to be rude to this old lady.

She cackles as she sits and motions for me to join her at the makeshift fortunetelling table located in the center of all the cages. A crystal ball in the middle of the table would complete the setup, but it's merely covered with a modest burgundy cloth. Madam Zoë places a large clay bowl on the table. I take a seat in the rickety folding chair across from her and fold my hands in my lap.

"Go ahead, child. Tell me what you seek," she rasps.

There's no way this lady is truly psychic, so I decide to not spill my demon problems and just ask about my man dilemma. That seems harmless.

I hadn't really thought of how to pose my questions, so I stumble around. "Um...Well...I want to know—who's the right guy for me?"

She smirks. "Child, you have bigger things to worry about than matters of the heart. I see what you've done."

What *I've* done? "No offense, but how can you possibly say something like that? You know nothing about me."

Her lips draw into a tight line. "I don't need eyes to see. Your aura's marked. Tainted. Which means it's no longer your own."

This lady's crazy. There's no way she knows my soul is bound to the demon child. I have to get out of here before this lady fills my head with ideas and causes a panic attack. "Look, I think this was a mistake. I'll just go." I rise from my seat.

"Sit down," she orders firmly. Her frail voice turns authoritative.

With a huff, I slam back down. This was a shitty idea. She's out to scam my money and scare the crap out of me.

"Like I was sayin'—I know what's comin' for you. Give me your hand," she says in her gravelly voice.

I hold out my hand. The calluses on her fingertips scratch at my skin. Is it possible this old lady knows about the demon? No way. This is probably her line to get her clients roped in, but I'll play along so I can get out of here.

She takes my hand in both of hers and gently strokes the life lines in the palm of my hands. "Let me study you."

Ice crystals form in the wake of her fingertips against my skin. My breath goes still as I watch in amazement at Madam

Zoë's power. This woman is for real. Fear would have been the response in a normal person, but I'm desperate for answers even though I'm scared out of my mind.

I'm lost in a trance. Lost in the possibility I've finally found someone to help me. The ice numbs my palm, but my fingers feel surprisingly warm. I'm so mesmerized by my own hand I don't see her grab the silver knife until it's too late.

She slices my finger with the razor sharp tip of the blade.

"Ouch! What the hell, lady?" I snarl as wrench my hand back.

She grabs my hand and continues to massage my finger. "Shhhhhh. This is necessary to see." Her voice is calm and soothing—like she's trying to soothe a frightened animal.

"To see what?" I ask as a perfect round blood droplet forms on my right index finger. Madam Zoë milks my finger into the clay bowl on the table. Thick, red liquid slides down the side of the bowl and finally settles in the center.

She smiles. "Your future, of course."

After she's satisfied with the amount of blood she's squeezed from me, she releases my hand. Instinctively, I shove my finger in my mouth to stop the bleeding. With insane quickness, she yanks four feathers from the green bird on her shoulder and tosses them in the little scarlet pool. I'm awestruck when she throws in three black rocks and sprinkles a fine powder over the bowl's contents.

The powder clings to the air and floats around my face. Madame Zoë chants some sort of voodoo words that I don't understand as she strikes a match.

The feathers engulf in flames. Smoke whirls around the bowl. The stench of the burning feathers assaults my nose. I close it with my hand. She sticks her face in the middle of the smoke. As it swirls around, she closes her eyes and inhales deeply through her nose like it's a breathing treatment. Without warning, her eyes pop open. The white eyes that I saw when I first came in are now the color of topical waters in a thrashing in a hurricane. Blue light streams from her eyes and spotlights the fire in the clay bowl.

"Holy shit!" My breath whooshes from my lungs as I scramble out of my seat. The chair lands with a hard thud. I should run. I know I should. But she might be my only hope at saving my soul.

"Sit, Natalie!" she commands. Her stern voice takes me by surprise.

"How the hell do you know my name?" My voice quivers. I turn the chair upright and grasp it for support.

"It's clear that your soul is damned. It happened so long ago when you were just a little girl. Your time is almost up. The countdown has begun. Look at your hands, child. When your life lines disappear, so shall your soul. Be careful, the one who seeks it—the one you fear—is closer than you think." Her eyes roll back in her head as she takes a deep breath of smoke. "Soon...dark things will appear as a sign the very end of your human life is near. It's only a matter of time until your one of Satan's minions."

Satan's minion? Me? A soul collector?

Cold unfolds through my whole body, and I shake. Dying I can handle. I don't look forward to it, but from what I've seen, it's over pretty quickly when a demon takes your soul. Being like the demon child, taking people's lives, well that's a new twist I wasn't expecting. One I don't want to be true.

My knees buckle and I drop to the floor. Fear grips every pore in my body as tears stream down my face, and flashes of the five-year-old soul stealer sear my vision. I'll be just like him.

A killer.

On my knees in a bird-poop infested floor, I squeeze my eyes shut and begin to rock back and forth while sticking my fingers in my ears and block out the possessed Madam Zoë. She keeps chanting, "Time is near" over and over.

I can't handle this. I want to put all this behind me, not confirm what I've feared.

When I look up to Madame Zoë, a muffled sound hums into my ears through my hands. Her glowing blue eyes light up most of the table as she holds up her hands and screams out her chant. The smoke swirls and expands from the bowl and covers the table, and my whole body quivers in fear.

I need an escape. I rise to my feet and stumble toward her door. My hands pull free from my ears long enough for me to hear one last thing. "Child, come back. I can tell you where to find him."

"I just want to be left alone!" I cry, as I blast through her front door.

My feet thunder across the pavement until I reach the security of the Focus. I shove my key in the ignition and tear down the street. My body rocks back and forth while I drive home. My teeth chatter uncontrollably.

What just happened back there? I sure as hell didn't expect that freak show.

The tears continue to pour from my eyes. I wipe them with the back of my hand and smear my make-up all around in the process. My heart floods with relief when I pull onto my street. Home never looked so good. Anxious to get inside, I throw my car into park, fling the door open, and nearly tumble out of it. Still trying to recover from my fall, I run, half hunched, toward the house. I probably look like I'm on crack, but I don't care. After all, people are used to me being crazy.

Just as I reach the door, I hear Stew call my name, but I don't dare turn to face him. My triumphant argument cannot happen while I look crazy. My hand turns the knob, but the door doesn't budge. A growl escapes my throat and I kick the door as hard as I can.

"Natalie?" Stew's voice is hesitant. "Everything all right?" His hand touches my shoulder and I shrug away from his touch. "Tell me what's wrong."

My throat constricts. I couldn't tell him even if I wanted to. I shake my head.

"Did something happen? Are you hurt?" His words have a little panic in them. "Is it Steele? Did he do something? I had a bad feeling about that guy."

Tears thicken in my eyes and cloud my vision. I blink them away and let them fall down my face. I sort through my ring of keys to gain entry. My hands shake like a withdrawing junkie. I find the right one and finally manage to slip it in the slot. The door shoves open and I bolt through to seclusion and slam the door in Stewart's face.

Stew pounds on the door and yells, "Come on, Nat. Talk to me!"

My back presses against the door, and I close my eyes.

"Please, Natalie." When I don't answer, he yells out my name again. "Let me fucking help you!"

I can't fathom dealing with him right now. Stew and his bullshit will have to wait.

I sprint up the stairs and lock myself in my room, then throw my exhausted frame on the bed. My clothes are drenched in sweat, and my legs feel like Jell-O. All these years I've questioned my sanity, and now I know there is someone else who *knows*. If people could see what I just saw, they would stop doubting me. Madam Zoe is definitely the real deal. It probably wasn't the wisest decision to run out of there before she finished telling me all the information she had, but I couldn't help myself. Those neon blue eyes freaked me out. It was just too much for my brain to process at once. If I would've stayed, I'm sure a squad would have had to come and pried me out of that house, and then dropped me off at the nearest padded cell.

I curl into a ball as Madam Zoë's words replay in my mind, and I feel ashamed of running out on her. She seemed like she was only trying to help. After all, she even offered to tell me where to find the demon boy. It would be nice to know where he is, that way I can go to him and plead for my soul.

Tomorrow, I'll go back, and explain. Apologize, even. I'd do it now, but I'm a mess, and it's getting late. Stew might still be out there and I can't face him right now.

Tomorrow is definitely a better plan.

# Chapter Thirteen

"So what the hell was going on with you yesterday?" Stew's words startle me as I grab my bag from the car, and my whole body stiffens.

I tuck a loose strain of hair behind my ear, trying to play it off, and throw my bag over my shoulder. "Nothing was wrong with me."

Stew shakes his head. "You forget how well I know you. Just tell me. You were crying. Did that freak, Rick, do something to you?"

Where does he get off calling my friend a freak? I clamp down hard on the meaty flesh inside my cheek to keep from screaming at the top of my lungs and turn away from him.

Fingers grip my elbow. "For God's sake, just tell me what happened."

I jerk away from him. "Leave me alone, Stew. I don't have to tell you anything. We are not together, remember?"

Stew's nostrils flare and his mouth draws into a tight line. "Fine. Whatever."

My chin tips up. "Good."

I stalk away from him, and a small part of me wants him to stop me. When he doesn't I wrap my arms around my body and head into school.

I decide I need to apologize to Madame Zoë for freaking out yesterday. Now that I know what to expect, I think I can sit through the whole reading and find out more about this boy demon. Maybe she can tell me where exactly to find him and how to cut a deal to get my soul back. Obviously my methods of killing him aren't successful. Thoughts drifted all around last night, trying to pinpoint exactly where the demon might be. She seemed to know a lot about my situation, and she said he was closer than I thought. He could live right in my neighborhood. Madame Zoë is the only one who can tell me where he is. Hell, at this point I'd do anything to not become a killer.

When my last class for the day ends, I scoot out the door.

Rick yells for me as I fly down the hallway. My pace slows, and I whip around to face him.

He eyes me suspiciously. "You weren't going to wait on me?"

I chew on my bottom lip. "I'm in a hurry. Sorry."

He nods. "Hot date?"

I sock him lightly in the ribs. "Whatever."

He holds his hands defensively. "Hey, I'm just checking. I mean, you could at least tell me where you're running off to."

I shrug. "I told you, it's no big deal. Just something I got to do."

He looks around. "It doesn't involve Masterson, does it?"

I roll my eyes. "Don't be stupid."

"Okay," he says as he leans in and kisses my forehead. "Call me tonight."

I nod and back away from him. "I will."

A couple minutes later, I'm in the Focus, zooming toward Madam Zoë's. Mentally, I've prepared all day what I'd say to her.

When I pull up to the blue house, it appears just as innocent as yesterday. I wonder if the neighbors have any clue about the freaky stuff that happens inside this place? The absolute filth is probably a health code violation.

The thought drifts away when I get out of the car. It only takes a few seconds to get on her little stoop. The lion knocker stares me in the face. There's no nervousness in my body today because I know what's on the other side of the door. After three knocks, I wait.

Nothing.

Yesterday it took her a couple of seconds to come to the door, but at least she'd yelled to let me know she was coming. I press my ear to the door. The birds squawk and their cages rattle, but I don't hear Madam Zoe.

I try again, knocking a little harder this time. This time I hear footsteps behind the door. It opens. My eyes almost bug out of my skull. It's not Madam Zoe. Taylor Gee stands in the doorway, mouth open. She doesn't say anything. She stares at me expectantly with big chocolate eyes.

I swallow deeply, and then ask, "Is—is..Madam Zoe in?"

Taylor stands a little straighter. "Natalie? What are you doing here?"

I scratch my head. It's not like I can tell her that I'm here to get help tracking down a demon. No way does she needs more information to back up my crazy-chick status. Life has been a little more bearable the last couple of weeks since I've gained her acceptance again. "Um...I came back to finish my reading."

She frowns. "Listen, Natalie. You can't tell anyone about what Grandma does here. If this got out, people would treat me like..." She looks me up and down.

That look says it all. The last thing Taylor Gee would want is to be like me. If it got out that her grandma was a freaky fortuneteller, her reputation would be ruined. She'd be out-casted like me. So, I understand why she's worried. "I won't say anything. You think I need to give people any more ammunition against me."

Her mouth tilts sideways. It's kind of a sad smile. "Good. But, you have to go. Grandma got really sick last night and I've got to get things cleaned up around here while my mom watches over her at the hospital."

My mouth feels dry, like I haven't had a drink in years. I wet my lips and open my mouth to speak, but nothing comes out.

Could this be my fault for involving her in my demon madness? Had he come here and hurt her?

I nod and step back as guilt rushes over me. "I'm so sorry." My breath catches, and I can't get anything else out.

Taylor shuts the door without saying goodbye or telling me what exactly happened to her Madam Zoe.

When I flop into my car seat, my brain wanders. She was really old. I'm sure telling a fortune the way she does is hard on the old ticker. That was probably it. A heart-attack. Nothing I did. My hands grip the steering wheel, and my knuckles turn white.

My breath comes out in ragged spurts. I try to calm myself down and convince myself this has nothing to do with me. I rest my forehead against my hands and breathe deeply. How the hell am I going to find that little bastard now? The one person who can help me is out of commission. Now that his visits have become so frequent I just know something is about to go down. I can feel it. I need some major help with this. But who can I turn to? Rick hasn't exactly been a great resource. He romanticizes demons to much and never gets down to business about how to kill them every time we talk about it.

My four-cylinder starts up and putters down the street. Things never work out for me. Whenever I want something, it never happens. Stew is a prime example of that. Finding the demon is never going to happen. It's funny because I never thought about searching for him until Madam Zoë brought it up. Maybe that's what I need to do? I could gain the upper hand.

She did say he was close to me. I bet that creeper lives in my neighborhood somewhere, pretending to be a regular kid. If I keep my eyes peeled, maybe I can find him on my own. After all, I'd never forget his little face.

After I make it home, I peek through the blinds, looking for any dark-haired male suspects. There's a couple of blonde kids playing across the street, but they don't fit the profile, no sense in checking them out any further. Next door is where Stew lives. I know the demon doesn't live there, so I move on to the neighbors. None of them have kids. At least I don't think so, anyway.

Frustrated, I flop down on my bed. Where do I even start?

The rest of the week drags by, the soul-sucking depression returning to drain the last bit of life from me. Rick—the ever-attentive guy—constantly asks me if I'm okay. Lying to him is kind of hard. The way he looks at me, like he truly cares, works on my conscious. I want to trust him, tell him things, but I don't think I can be that real with anyone. Things tend to work better for me when I shut people out. Eventually, they leave me alone, but I don't want to lose Rick. He's the best friend I've ever had, and I know he wants more. I want to give him more, but this whole demon situation won't let me lead a normal life.

Sitting under our tree, I stare at Rick's profile while he reads one of his evil books. Do I even have time to have a real relationship with this guy? Is it even fair to him? And it seems crazy that I am even worrying about this to begin with considering.

I sigh, my heart heavy.

"Natalie? What's wrong?" Rick looks up from his book. His eyes trained on me.

I shake my head and avert my eyes from him.

He exhales noisily. "Please, talk to me. Something has been up with you all week."

He doesn't need this dumped on him, too.

"Nothing's wrong. Just bummed about Monkey Man's class. I'm not ready for the exam he's giving today," I lie coolly.

He tilts his head and draws his brow deep over his eyes. "Are you sure, that's it? You can talk to me, you know. You can tell me anything."

Not this. "I know. Seriously, it's just school stuff. No big deal."

"Okay." He doesn't sound so convinced. "We're still going to Taylor's party tomorrow, right? Would that cheer you up?"

Crap. I forgot about that. Taylor is the last person I want to hang out with. The thought of going to her house doesn't thrill me, but Rick's expression tells me he wants to make me happy. For him, I'll go.

I smile. "Sure. Are we riding together?"

He laughs. "Of course we are. You're my unofficial girlfriend, remember?"

"Right. I forgot."

He throws his hand over his heart. "You don't know how deeply that wounds me."

"Oh, my God. You're such a drama queen!"

He puts his best falsetto on, and says, "Shhhhh. That's a secret!"

We laugh together. It feels good to be happy in the moment. If only I wasn't about to become a demonic killing machine, there might have been a chance of having a real future with Rick. But the luxury of time is something I don't have.

He wraps an arm around me and pulls me tight. I don't try to fight him on the closeness. It actually feels pretty nice. He has one arm around the small of my back and brushes my hair away from my face with his free hand. "You are so beautiful. Do you know that?"

Blood rushes to my cheeks, and they burn. I drop my chin down, embarrassed by his compliment. Two fingers slide under my chin and angle my face to look at his. Lips light as feathers brush against mine. I thought it would feel wrong to kiss Rick, like I was being slutty for jumping from one guy to another so quickly, but it doesn't. It feels right, like I belong here—with him. My face tingles, and the taste of his lips sends a rush of heat through my core. When he pulls back, I smile.

"I've been thinking about doing that for a while, now," he whispers, his lips inches from mine.

I bite my bottom lip. "Have you, now?"

"Oh, yeah." He smiles before leaning in again.

He kisses me—once, twice, and then the third time he stays—crushing his lips into mine. His warm tongue parts my lips and enters my mouth. He tastes like mint while his spicy scent swirls around me. He cups my face and rubs my cheeks with his thumbs. After he's satisfied he pulls back and gives me one last peck.

"Wow." He grins and closes his eyes, clearly delighted. "Just like I remembered."

I laugh. "We've never kissed before."

"In my dreams we have." He sighs. "That was pretty amazing."

Rick leaves me at Art class at the doorway. I watch him walk down the hallway. He's pretty wonderful—absolutely perfect. A giddy feeling consumes me as the butterflies whirl around in my stomach. My recently kissed lips spread into a wide smile and I sigh happily. Rick is a nice distraction.

"Ugh. Can I get by now since Mr. Wonderful is gone?" Stew sneers.

Unmoving, I stare him down. How dare he say something like that to me? Anger rolls through me, and my body shakes. I square my shoulders and huff. The middle finger of my right hand shoots up in his face. His jaw drops, and he grunts. Instead of giving him time to say something, I leave him stunned and whip around. Stewart Masterson no longer has any power to make me keep my anger quiet. He's an asshole—

one that doesn't deserve my time. Feeling empowered, I throw my satchel down on the table and saunter over to get my supplies.

Out of the corner of my eye, I notice Stew slip a piece of paper into my bag. What the hell is that? Probably some evil hate letter to get back at me for flipping him off. He's not going to see me get upset. I refuse to read it in front of him.

Stew already has our painting laid out on the table. It's funny that the title we settled on for this project is *Trust*, which is the furthest feeling I have for him. It was the only issue we both had on our individual idea list, so we went with it.

He's not very artistic, but he tries. Most of the work falls on me because I don't want a pathetic grade just because he can't draw.

I load my large, round brush, and slap some midnight color onto the canvas. Painting calms me. It's the only place I can let my emotions fly without judgment. Art doesn't need an explanation. Everyone interprets it differently. I really don't have a plan when I work. The flow of the piece usually guides me, but working with Stew puts me in an artistic funk. The vibe he omits isn't exactly conducive for creating a grand masterpiece.

Stew sits with one hand tucked under his chin as he doodles on his canvas. He couldn't look more bored if he tried. How could I have ever fallen for him? I shouldn't have been so stupid. He never even apologized to me for standing me up.

Ugh. He makes my skin crawl.

My pent up rage comes out on my work. I press the brush harder than necessary into the canvas.

"Damn, Nat. Easy," Stew says.

Anger floods my brain. Easy? How dare he even speak to me, let alone try to tell *me* what to do. My nostrils flare and I take a calming breath, but it doesn't help. Out of spite I dig at it harder, practically obliterating the brush.

His eyes narrow. "What the hell is your problem?"

Through clenched teeth, I growl, "You! You're my problem."

"Me? I didn't do anything to you."

I set my eyes on him. Is he really that stupid? "Oh, no?"

"No," he answers, his eyes hard. "I should be the one pissed. You keep flaunting Steele in front of my face like you have no heart."

*Me* have no heart? Before I realize what I'm doing, I fling my brush at his chest. Black paint splatters across the front of his white Polo shirt. He throws his hands out in a 'Stop' motion and stares at me, surprise written all over his face.

"Fuck you, Stew! What do you know about heart?" I yell as I stand and grab my bag.

His face turns white.

"Miss Sugarman!" Dr. Woods yells.

The Art doors swing open. I run my fingers through my hair and take a deep breath. My pulse races as the adrenaline flows through my veins. The satisfaction of finally screaming at Stew fills every inch of me. Dr. Woods probably thinks I'm a raging bitch now, but whatever. It was worth it.

I detour into the girl's restroom. The dampness here chills me to the bone and the smell of a recently snuffed cigarette still lingers in the confined space. Sometimes I like to study in here. This is a place I can breathe, far from prying eyes because no one ever comes in here.

I toss my bag to the water-speckled floor and grip the gleaming white sink with shaky fingers. The warm water in my haven doesn't work, so I twist the cold knob. My cupped hands fill with water and I splash it on my face. The person in the mirror peering back at me looks weak, not powerful like I'd felt a few minutes ago when I told Stew off.

Thoughts buzz in my brain. Would Rick eventually treat me the same way?

My heart aches with the loneliness I'd feel if Rick walked out of my life right now too. He's all I have. Alicia is gone. Stew makes my skin crawl, and Mom and Dad don't want to hear about my problems. In such a short time Rick, and I have grown so close. The pull between us was instant, way back to the first day in the parking lot. He accepted me, no questions asked. Stewart and Rick are polar opposites, but I'm drawn to both. One pushes my commitment away, while the other can't wait to be together.

The water drips off my chin, and I notice my make-up is smeared. I crank out a large piece of scratchy paper towel and methodically dry my face.

My stomach bubbles with dread as I throw my paper towel in the trash can. I snatch my bag off the floor and remember the paper Stew slipped in there. Curious, I dig through it until I find a little two by two folded piece of paper. With my bag snuggly on my shoulder, I unfold the note. I smooth out the creases, and read his tiny, very guy-like writing. "We need to talk."

Like hell we do. I don't care what he has to say. The anger I just stomped down returns and the paper instantly gets wadded into a tiny round ball. My fingers squeeze so hard they turn white. Stew and his bullshit can kiss my ass. I've got more important things to focus on than him—like a kindergarten demon that's out to kill me.

After slamming the note in the trash, I head out. The empty dank hallway echoes with each step I take, filling the atmosphere with dread. What the fuck is happening to me?

# Chapter Fourteen

A tap on my bedroom door nearly scares me to death. I was zoned out, worried about all possible scenarios that could happen tonight at Taylor Gee's party. I've tried talking to Taylor a couple times about her grandma, but she always brushes me off and tells me "not at school."

I stare at my door through my dresser mirror. "Come in," I call.

Rick steps into my bedroom with his hand behind his back. His tall frame fills my doorway. He looks good—dressed to kill in a navy blue shirt and dark-blue jeans. The tattoos on his right arm are the only thing about him that screams I am a bad boy. Well, that and the little smirk he does that makes me swoon a little every time. His dark hair hangs loose and frames his handsome face. He wears the bad boy, surfer hair look well.

I turn to greet him. "Hey."

He smiles sheepishly. "Your mom said I could come up. Hope you don't mind."

Of course she's fine with it. The idea of me with a guy like Rick is a dream come true for her. "No. It's fine."

He closes the door behind him and pulls out a bouquet. "These are for you."

Wide-eyed, I take the flowers from his grasp. No one has ever given me flowers before and yet the gift feels quite natural. I'm drawn to the purple color of the flowers, like they are my favorites and I never knew it. "Thank you. They're beautiful."

"I thought you'd like those." He grins. "They're called forget-me-nots."

Forget-me-nots, how subtle. My lips turn up into a natural smile. "They're great."

"Can I at least get a hug in exchange?"

Instinctively, I wrap my arms around him. When I pull back, we are nose to nose. I search his face, and I get lost in his eyes. They're warm and inviting, and the way they stare into mine sends a tingle all the way to my toes. He leans in and places his lips to mine. He threads his fingers in my hair. The sensation of him so close stirs a hunger I have never felt before. Our bodies press together tightly and my hand rubs his neck.

I don't want him to stop, which is completely wrong. I can't believe I'm so into him. I can't explain it.

With a groan, he pulls away and leaves me breathless.

"You drive me crazy. Do you know that?" he whispers and gives me a little peck on the lips.

The desire to be near him gnaws in my gut. It's crazy that I feel this kind of connection with a guy I barely know. The more time I spend with him, the more I need him. I've never been one to depend on people, but Rick makes it so easy. He's not like anyone I've ever known. He accepts me for who I am, never tries to change me.

"So, are you about ready?" he asks.

"Yeah. Let me put these in some water." I gesture toward the flowers. "I'll be right back."

Without thinking, I leave him in my room, alone, while I scamper off to the kitchen. Mom greets me as I step into the kitchen with a huge smile on her face.

Oh God, please don't say anything about Rick.

"Aren't those beautiful, Natalie? Rick is such a nice young man."

My face inflames as blood rushes to my cheeks. I turn my head away from her, grab a vase from under the sink, and fill it with water. No way do I want to talk boys *with my mother*.

Thankfully, she doesn't say another word while I'm in there. I turn on my heel and head back upstairs. I startle Rick when I walk in. He's sitting on my bed, thumbing through the sketchbook I left on my night stand.

My eyes narrow into little slits as my private images are being pawed through—being judged. "I usually don't show those to anyone."

"Sorry. I was a little bored." He closes the book. "These are really good. You should change your major."

I roll my eyes. "Please. Have you met my parents? Art is not a real major to them. Besides I don't think I'll be around long enough to actually finish a degree."

"Ah. That's right. The demon-has-my-soul-and-wants-to-kill-me-thing." He pushes himself up from my bed. He takes my hand, pulling my knuckles to his lips. "I told you I'm working on that."

I pull my hand away. "This isn't a joke, Rick. What I told you about the demon boy is real."

A strand of hair falls against my cheek and he tucks it behind my ear. "I know."

The way he looks at me makes my insides knot. Either he believes me or he's a great actor. There's so much I want to tell him. Maybe he can help. "He came to see me again, you know."

Rick's eyes narrow. "Who? Masterson?"

I shake my head and roll my eyes. "No. How many times do I have to tell you, that's over."

His face relaxes a little. "Yeah, I heard about the paint today."

A groan escapes my lips as I bury my face in my hands. Rick pulls me down beside him on the bed. "Stew is an asshole. He's lucky it was just paint and not a fist to the face."

That makes Rick laugh. "Let's hope I never piss you off."

"I highly doubt that would ever happen. You're not like all the other jerks around here. You'd never lie to me."

He frowns. "Natalie..." The way he says my names sounds bad. Like what he's about to tell me isn't good news. "There is something I am keeping from you."

I knew it. He is too good to be true. "You have a girlfriend or something, right?"

"What?" The bewildered look on his face speaks volumes. "No. Why would you think that?"

"Because, Rick. Nothing good ever happens to me. People always let me down when I peel back their layers. They're never who they say they are. You have become my best friend. The one person I can trust. So, what is it then?" Tears sting my eyes, but I refuse to let them fall. Hopefully whatever he's hiding isn't something that will make me hate him.

He's quiet for a second while he searches my face. "I'm..."—he swallows like he's getting choked-up, but then he gives me a sad smile—"It's—it's nothing, really. I mean, I can't dance, and well, I was worried you wouldn't want to be my date for this party if you knew."

My right fist connects with his shoulder. "Dancing? You let me worry like that because you can't dance? Maybe you are a jerk after all."

He laughs. "I'm sorry. I just wanted you to know before we got to serious. No dancing is sometimes a deal breaker." I shake my head at him, but he just grins even more. "So, are you ready to go to your new BFF's party?"

I squeeze my eyes shut and sigh. "I dread seeing her, actually. There is something I need to talk to her about, but I don't want to go to another party."

"We don't have to go. You can just talk to her at school, right? We can do something else if you'd rather. I have her cell number. You can text her and tell her we aren't going to make it." He pushes a lock of my hair off my shoulder and his fingers linger on the exposed skin where my shoulder and neck meet.

"Okay, sounds good." I bite my lip. "No movies, though. Okay?"

"I think I've learned my lesson there. What do you have in mind?"

Rick's staring at me expectantly, waiting for my solution. My gaze shifts to his lips and the only thing flashing in my brain is kissing him again. I know the demon said no loose ends, but maybe a little fling with Rick can keep me happy for the rest of eternity. Dying a virgin has crossed my mind a time or two. How lame would that be? Rick obviously has no problem with getting close to me. And even though I'm not exactly in love with him, more like of a serious like, maybe getting close to Rick would be okay.

Sheepishly, I smile at him. "Well, you've been to my house a few times, but I don't even have a clue where you live. That's something a girlfriend should know, right?"

He raises an eyebrow. "So, are we official now?"

It seems less slutty as long as we are a couple. "Yeah. I mean, if you want."

My heart pauses on a beat for a millisecond until a grin stretches across his face. "So that's a yes?" I ask, probing him for answers.

"Yes. It's a definite yes." I bite my lip, fighting my elated grin. He grazes my cheek with his fingertips. "I've wanted this more than you know."

His lips press to mine, and butterflies twist in the pit of my stomach. The feeling of belonging to someone engulfs me, and the desire to be close to Rick pulsates through my veins. If we had more time, I think I could love him. I mean, *really* love him. He's practically the ideal guy. A girl would have to be completely insane not to fall for him.

Rick pulls away. His charcoal-gray eyes stir with need. "Come on. Let's go to my place. There's no one there."

Once in his car, he steals a glance in my direction every couple of minutes. My hand rests in his while he shifts gears. A smile tickles my lips when I meet his eyes. My body fills with nervous anticipation when Rick slows and turns down an alley. It leads to a private driveway, which then turns into an empty parking lot. I gawk at the sign on the building.

My left eye brow lifts. "Um, Rick? What are we doing at Fletcher's Funeral Home?"

He turns toward me. "You said you wanted to see where I lived."

A shudder runs down my spine. "Seriously? You live here?" Creepy.

He shrugs his shoulders. "It's not as bad as you think. Actually, I don't live in the funeral parlor. I live there." He points to the second floor above the three-car garage. "It's a small apartment and my family owns the funeral parlor so I don't even have to pay rent while I'm in school."

"So, you live alone?"

"Awesome, huh?" He waggles his eyebrows. "Come on. I'll show you my bachelor pad."

We make our way up the outside staircase leading to Rick's place. He unlocks the door, turns on the light, and leads me inside. "It's not much, but it's better than living with a roommate or with my family."

"You don't like Dr. Fletcher?" I ask before I realize I've just let it slip that I know her. That was one secret I didn't want him knowing.

Rick stops mid stride and tilts his head. "You know Lilim?"

The back of my neck stings with tension, so I rub it. "Yeah. She's sort of my shrink. I've been going to one since I was a teenager and got caught with a deadly weapon trying to protect myself from a demon. It's nice to talk about the demon stuff with someone who will keep it confidential."

He chuckles. "You were really going to shoot him, weren't you? I can tell you don't like him."

A humph escapes my lips. "Hate him is more like it." Then I stop dead in my tracks. I don't remember ever telling him I got caught with a gun specifically. I referred to it as a weapon only. "I never said anything about a gun to you before. How did you know?"

Rick shrugs. "You must have told me." The he quickly tries to get us back on track of our original conversation. "Hate is such a strong word, Nat."

My eyes search his face, but he's relaxed, not a hint of tension in his face. So, I decide to relax. I must've told him about the gun and forgot about it. "Not strong enough to truly describe my feelings toward him though."

His fingers rub my shoulder. "He might just grow on you. You have a whole eternity to get to know him, right?"

I push his hand off me. "Ha. Ha. Very funny, Rick."

He smiles. "You never know."

"It's nice in here," I say as I take in the dark green walls and white-carpeted room. "Very manly."

He sits on his black leather couch, which takes up most of the claustrophobic room, and pats the cushion beside him. Without question, I fold myself onto the seat next to him. He throws his arm around me. It feels natural. Cozy. I turn my face toward him.

His eyes are smiling more than his lips when he whispers, "Hi."

I smile back. "Hi."

My hair drifts into my eyes, and he brushes it away from my face. His thumb traces my cheek. Electric tingles zing deep into my bones. I turn my head into his hand and nuzzle it. Rick tilts my chin up and kisses me deeply. The smell of him swirls around me as my fingers find their way into his long hair. He crushes me to him, yet it still doesn't feel close enough.

He traces my bottom lip with his tongue and runs his hand down my back, stopping at my waist—testing the waters. Warm fingers slide under my shirt, and my whole body starts to tingle. My bones hum with need as I squeeze myself tighter against his chest. He kisses me so deep, I'm not sure I'm even living on air anymore. The very essence of Rick seems to be enough to sustain my very existence.

I lie back on the couch and pull his body on top of mine. We lay there, pressed together like magnets, as I trace the waistband of his jeans with a light touch. A moan reverberates in his chest as his fingers knot in my hair.

My fingers need to explore. They find their way underneath his shirt and onto his muscular frame. The ripples of his abs glide under my hands, and I memorize every inch of him by touch. My insides burn with intense heat, one I've never felt before. A flame only Rick can extinguish. Gentle kisses trail down my neck, and I toss my head back and let a little groan slip.

He has no idea how much I need this—how much I need him.

Panting a little I realize I've never wanted someone more than I want Rick at this moment. Not even with Stew have I felt such a connection.

There's so much heat between us—going all the way seems like a natural step. A step I need. I reach for the buttons of his jeans, a little unsure if I should take the lead on this. I need him to know I want to do this with him. Rick's eyes grow wide as his hand grips my wrist.

"Not here." His breath is hot on my lips.

My hands freeze as confusion floods my brain. A flash of rejection zings my brain. "What? This seems like a perfect time."

Without answering me, he rolls off the couch and cradles me in his arms in one motion like I weigh practically nothing.

"It is a perfect time. I just meant not on the couch." He kisses me while I'm pressed against his sculpted chest. "My bedroom has an actual bed and I need to sprawl you out and explore every inch of you."

Oh. He scared me for a second, but the thought of being tangled up in some sheets with him excites me. One corner of my lips turns up. "A bed would be good."

It's like a scene from an old movie. The one with the bride being carried over the threshold and for some reason it doesn't even feel cheesy. How could it? The only thing in the air is pure romance and lust.

We enter his dark bedroom. My arms encircle his neck, and I strain my neck to place a kiss on his lips. There's a large bed filling up most of the space in the room. He lays me down, and instantly I'm surrounded by the smell of him. The thought of lying in the very place he dreams brings me to another level of closeness with him.

The moonlight streams in from the only window in the room and illuminates Rick. He's beautiful in this light—nearly perfect.

He pulls his black tee shirt over his head and tosses it to the floor. His body is sculpted like a Greek statue with tattoos covering his right arm all the way up to his shoulder. He looks even better shirtless than I had imagined a thousand times before. A little sigh breaks out from behind my lips. His body is amazing. No wonder I'm not the only girl around campus that's noticed Rick's a hottie.

Directly over his heart, there's a circle of snakes inked into his skin. Three snakes in the tattoo form a perfect circle, nose to tail and polishing off his devilish handsome look.

The rest of his clothes come off just as quick until he's down to his boxers. I study the contours of his body. The defined muscle that cuts in from his hips tells me he's toned everywhere. My lungs suck in a quick breath as he climbs onto his bed beside me. It's like he's about to devour my body, and I'm going to love every second of this.

Once the deed is done, there's no going back. We'll never be just friends again. We'll be so much more and for a second I hesitate.

Is it fair to him to do this? I mean, he probably believes we'll have a lifetime together. Will it make me totally selfish to do this when I know I'm about to become evil and may never see him again?

Before I can change my mind and ask him to stop, he kisses my neck and whispers, "You're so beautiful."

My heart skips a beat as I melt. Maybe it's better this way. I won't be around long enough to screw things up. We can have this magical, short-lived romance before I die and he'll be left with the memory of the girl he once loved.

I search out his lips. Honestly, I didn't have intentions on sleeping with him so soon, but right now that's the only thing I want to do. It's the only way I'll be able to get the closeness I crave and free my mind from all the craziness even for just a little while.

Rick caresses my shoulder, then my arm, and pauses at the hem of my shirt. All I can think about is his fiery touch and how much I want his skin on mine. One by one, he slips each button from the hole in my Polo shirt, never pulling his eyes away from mine as he starts to undress me. There's pure lust in his eyes and just staring into them causes an intense tingle between my legs.

After what feels like an eternity, he slides the shirt over my head. A soft moan escapes my lips as his breathtaking body covers mine. He rolls over and pulls me on top of him. His fingers glide up and down my spine. My eyes drift shut and I lean in for a kiss.

In one swift motion he sits up and forces my legs open until they wrap around his waist. His hard cock presses against me.

The only thing separating it from my moist flesh is two thin pieces of fabric. Rick reaches under my skirt and grabs my ass with both hands and encourages me to ride him with our clothes still on.

The sensation of him rubbing against me causes me to tingle, and my panties feel wet. Rick unclasps my bra and then tosses it to the floor. In a normal situation, I would feel shy about having my body on display, but with Rick, I want him to touch me.

I keep working my hips against him and soon a feeling builds up taking over every sense in my body. I wrap my arms around his neck and moan in his ear.

Rick rubs his thumb over my pebbled nipple. "That's it, baby. Come for me."

I bite my lip as he sucks my pink nipple into his mouth. My fingers find their way into his hair as I explode into full body tingles. My legs quiver below me as I ride the wave of intense pleasure.

Rick lies back, pulling me down on top of him, once I settle down. "You are so fucking hot when you come. I can't wait to do that again with me inside you."

I lean in and kiss him hungrily. I never knew talking in bed was such a turn on. My lips part, and his tongue snakes its way into my mouth as I try to show him how much I want him. His dick jerks under me, and I can tell he's getting my message and is ready to have his way with me.

I reach down and try to reposition myself. A gasp slips out of my lips as I break away from Rick's kiss as my hand slips into nothingness. All my weight is concentrated on my right arm and when my hand goes down, there's nothing but thin air to lean on. I nearly topple off Rick, but claw at his chest to keep from falling over. Where the fuck is the bed?

My eyes spring open. A scream rips up from my throat when I realize we are a good three feet higher than the bed. Panic springs from every cell in my body. I scramble to get away from Rick, and I slam onto my right side when I make contact with the hard-wood floor. Air whooshes from my lungs, and I'm stunned by the fall for a second, but quickly regain my bearings. Something's not right. He's not right. Who just randomly floats during sex?

Someone that's not human.

My mouth gapes open in shock as Rick levitates above the bed. I can't move. All of my limbs just quiver like a heart out of rhythm. Humans can't float like that and there's only one thing I know of that has supernatural abilities like that. My soul crushes at the thought of his deception. My hands cover my mouth and I shake my head violently. No! This can't be.

This whole time he's been keeping secrets from me, trying to make me fall in love with him—listening to my secrets, pretending to be concerned, when he was one of them this whole time. Everything was just a lie. What kind of person, no scratch that, monster does that?

An evil, sick freak—that's who does that.

"What the fuck?" I yell out loud in anger as I frantically search for my shirt with my hands, but never taking my eyes off him. My stomach rolls. This was one twist I didn't see coming. Isn't my life screwed-up enough?

He sits up and meets my glare with pained eyes.

How could he? How could he do this to me? Why? Why me? Why does this crazy shit have to happen to me? My fists ball up and I want to scream. I'm losing it. I can feel the crack forming in my brain. There's not enough air in the room and it's smothering me. I have to get out of here.

My sights never leave him as I try to buy some time to figure out how to get out of here alive. "Why did you bring me here? Are you going to try and kill me, because if so, get in line asshole."

He grimaces like I've just smacked him in the face. "Nat, I can explain."

Explain? I don't want him to say another word to me ever again, let alone explain why he's such a liar.

The top I had on somehow lodged itself under his bed. Both of my hands grip it hard and I growl while I tug it free. I jerk it over my head and peel myself from the floor. Slowly, I back away from him. The pulse in my neck is pounding so hard I can feel it in my face. Who knows what he is capable of?

"What *are* you?" I demand firmly, desperate hear him say what I already know.

The sea in his eyes thrashes violently. "I think you know."

My hearts pumps wildly, and sheer panic envelopes me as my fear is confirmed. "You're a demon?" My voice squeaks a little as I say it aloud. A flash of the small dagger in my purse flashes in my brain. If I can get to that, I may have a shot of making it out of here alive. A shake overtakes my hands as adrenaline flows through my veins while I work out my plan.

He nods. His mouth pulled into a tight line.

He lowers himself to a standing position in front of me with ease. "Not just *a* demon, I'm *your* demon."

My skin crawls as his snake tattoo comes to life and slithers around on his skin. My insides churn as the contents of my stomach threaten to expel. I grab onto his dresser to keep upright on my wobbly legs. "That's not possible." I can hear the quiver in my voice. The fear I always try to hide from my boy-demon cracks through my veil and the room starts to spin like I'm about to pass out. Tears sting my eyes. "My demon is a little boy!"

He shrugs and holds up his hands like he's guilty. "I can take on whatever age or form I need to help me make deals. When I first met you in *this* life, you were five, so I appeared to you as a boy to earn your trust. I can change forms at will. It's one of the few perks of being a demon. I've appeared to you in different forms throughout your life—to stay close to you. Whenever I need to collect a soul or remind you of our deal, I choose to show you my childhood form. But this"—he grabs his chest over his heart—"is my true form. The true me—the me that loves you." His torso moves forward, like he's getting ready to come toward me.

"Stay back!" I hold a shaky hand out, attempting to stop him. "Just stay away from me. You tricked me—all this time. I thought I could trust you."

"You can trust me." He steps forward. "I'm still the same person. Nothings has to change. Things will be so much better now that you know."

"Just shut up!" My vision blurs before I blink away the tears. "I told you things. We almost..." I almost had sex with him. The thought causes my stomach to lurch.

He reaches for me, but I swat his hand away as I take another step back. "Please, Nat. Give me a chance to explain."

A chance? Is he serious? "Stay away from me. You evil bastard!"

He steps closer. "I can't. You belong to me. We have to stay together. It's more important now, than ever."

"Screw you! I don't belong to anybody!" I sprint into his living room. The shaggy carpet trips up my foot but I manage to keep my balance. The purse I carried in is still on the couch and relief floods me. One good thing he taught me over the years is to always be prepared for his arrival and a possibility of a fight. Scooping up my purse, I reach in and feel for the blessed knife. The hilt of the dagger meets my palm. With a tight grip on my weapon, I spin to face him.

Rick's leaning against the frame of his bedroom door, unfazed by me, and he's smirking. This is no game to me. That smug bastard is going to have the fight of his life if he wants to take my soul. "I'm not dying without a fight."

He shakes his head and steps in front of me. "I'm not going to kill you."

"Then you won't mind if I leave," I say as I sprint toward his front door. I thrust my hand toward the knob, but he grabs me from behind before I can get the door open.

Damn.

He spins me around and pushes my back against the door.

The knuckles on my right hand are white as I raise the dagger up. The snake tattoo on his chest is the perfect target. I lunge forward with as much force as I have in me. Like always, he catches my wrist before I can make contact.

He stares me dead in the eye. I jerk my arm, but his grip is too tight. My left hand shoves at his chest. "Stop, Nat. Just listen."

I go still but hang on to my weapon so tight my fingers go numb. He tries to turn my face to look at him with his free hand, but I whip away from him, disgusted.

He sighs heavily as he removes the knife from my hand with ease and takes a step back. His left hand rubs his forehead while he holds the dagger in his right. "This is not how I wanted you to find out about this." He looks at me, and I wonder if I can somehow get my knife back. "But, you know, Natalie, rules are rules. We made a deal, remember? We can't change that. You knew I'd come for you. I made sure you wouldn't forget me. That's why I stuck you with that dream every night and collected every soul I possibly could near you. So you'd know I'm real, and I'd be back."

"You bastard!" I scream in his face and my bottom lip trembles. "You're the reason my life's been so fucked up. I was just a little girl, damn you. I had no idea what I was agreeing too and have been working my ass off to figure out how to get my soul back from you ever since then."

"So, you'd rather have your mother dead then?" My jaw drops. Of course I didn't want Mom to die. I'm no monster.

He takes in the expression on my face and his eyes soften. "I'm sorry. I shouldn't have said that. I know how much family means to you and I am sorry that your life has been so crazy. But it will be so much better once you're with me. Things will be different. You'll see."

"I'll *never* be with you," I growl through clenched teeth.

"Is it because of him?" Rick's eyes narrow. "Stewart doesn't love you. He's proven that time and again. You need to forget about him. He's no good for you."

"At least he's human!" I practically scream.

"He's not who you think he is. Trust me." He takes another step and reaches for my hand. I recoil away from him, but he snatches my wrist and forces my hand open—palm up. "You can't fight it, Nat. It doesn't matter how you feel about me or him for that matter. The deal's already made. Look at your life line." He shakes my hand, drawing my attention to it. "Time is almost up. When your life line fades, if I don't transition you into a demon, you'll die and your soul will go to hell for eternity." His voice softens. "Please don't make me send your soul there. I can't bear it. You have no idea how bad it is down there."

Waves of nausea roll through my stomach as I stare down at my open hand. He's right. The line has faded more. It's almost nonexistent. Clenching my fist, I jerk away from his maniacal grip and bump my elbow against the door. Being trapped causes my breath to hitch.

My mind reels with the realization that Rick is my demon tormentor all grown up and he knows my deepest secrets. Things he could use to hurt me. Bile rises into my throat, and I turn my face away for fear of puking in his face.

He wraps a tentative arm around me and I don't fight him. His breath comes in spurts on my cheek. "Look at me."

My eyes squeeze shut and let tears slick down my face. Looking at him is the last thing I want to do. He's finally got me in his clutches, and I am completely defenseless. "Please. I just want to go home."

He attempts to wipe my face, but I sway from his touch. "You need to trust me, Nat. I can make you happy. I know I can."

The thought of just kissing and nearly loving the very thing I hate with every cell in my body causes my head to spin. Dizziness washes over me. I need to get out of here. The weight of the information is so heavy it's difficult to breathe. "I want to go."

"This is a lot, I know, but you need to believe that I love you. You mean everything to me. I'd never hurt you."

What a lie. My face whips around and the sadness of being tricked turns back to anger. It nearly bubbles right through my skin. "Oh, no? Then why the hell did you trick me? Turning me into one of Satan's minions isn't hurting me right?"

He gnaws his bottom lip, and his eyes search my face. "Natalie, please. I have my reasons for doing that if you'd just calm down and let me explain."

I glare at him. Loves me? Never wants to hurt me? I think I'd rather take my chances in hell than to spend an eternity with a lying demon. Hate courses through my body and all I want is to get away from him—far, far away. Screw his explanation.

His face twitches, almost like he's nervous under my heated gaze. I nearly laugh. A demon confessing love for someone he's stolen a soul from is so unbelievable. It's probably another ploy to damn me further, but what the hell, maybe I can use that angle to get away. "I don't want your explanation, Rick. I *just* want to leave. If you love me, you'll let me go." Even I can hear the pleading tone in my voice.

He rocks back on his heels and furrows his brow. "This is not how I intended for you to find out. Go home. Think this through because we will have to talk about this. You can't run away from me."

When I nod in agreement, he steps back and drops his head. His hand motions me to go.

As soon as he clears the space between us, I fly out his front door, taking the stairs two at a time to put more distance between us. Gulp after gulp of cool night air burns my lungs. Just when I thought my life couldn't get any worse, my new boyfriend turns out to be the person—thing—I hate the most.

My pace slows to a brisk walk, and I fold my arms firmly over my chest as I walk through the tight nit row of houses. My eyes dart around, searching for any signs of danger, or worse, Rick.

Why do I always fall for untrustworthy guys?

My whole body is numb, so the cold doesn't even bother me. My heavy legs weigh a ton, and it takes everything I have inside to keep going. All I want to do is quit. Lie down and give up. What's the point of trying anymore? He's everywhere, always has been—watching—waiting to collect me when the time came. How am I ever going to win against him? He's so strong.

I can't fight it anymore. I fall on my knees, and the concrete sidewalk scratches my bare legs. My head feels like a twenty pound bowling ball in the palms of my hands. Can I bring myself to try and kill Rick? I need my soul back. The only options he said are I have are to die and go to hell or collect souls. I just want to be normal. But, Rick was my friend. He's wormed his way into my life. It wasn't as big of a deal when he was a nameless little demon. One who killed people right in front of me. It'll be hard to look him in the eye and kill him now.

Why didn't I figure out there was something wrong with Rick? All the signs were there. The demon obsession, the shocking handshake and some of the weird comments he made. Instead, I overlooked all that, glad to finally have a friend.

Some friend.

My make-up smears on my hand when I run the back of it across the rims of my eyes.

He said I belong to him. What the hell am I going to do? I know he's right. Every inch of me knows it's the truth, but there has to be a way to be free of him.

I need answers but I'm sure as hell not going back to the demon's lair to get them. I need someone to tell me what to do. There's no one I can turn to.

Madam Zoë is still in the hospital, so I can't exactly go to her for help.

There's only one other person who might be able to help me.

# Chapter Fifteen

I grab my cell phone and search through until I find the number I texted Taylor Gee at earlier. My fingers pause over the call button. She's going to think I'm insane. This will just give her confirmation that I'm nuts, but it'll be worth it at this point if I can convince her to take me to see her grandmother.

The tone chirps as I press the button. It rings twice before Taylor's happy voice answers. "Hello? Party Central."

I was half expecting to get her voice mail, so I'm a little stunned when she picks up so quickly. "Hey, um, Taylor. It's me. Natalie."

"Natalie? Where are you guys. Are you going to bring that hot-ass man of yours over or not? You're missing all the fun." She sounds drunk—happy, but drunk. This could work to my advantage. If she's that drunk, maybe I can talk to her about my demon issue and if she refuses to take me to Madame Zoë then I can pretend this conversation never happened. Drunk people are notorious forgetters.

"We aren't going to make it over tonight," I say while I sit on the cold cement. "I was actually calling to ask you for a favor."

The line is silent for a couple seconds, and I'm afraid she's hung-up on me. "Taylor?"

She exhales nosily into the receiver. "What kind of favor?"

"Can you take me to see your grandmother? I really need to talk to her. It's sort of an emergency."

"Tonight?" Her tone starts to sound really put-out, and the phone gets some interference, like she's walking around.

"Well, yeah, if you can take me." I pray she doesn't ask me to explain myself. What could I tell her that wouldn't already make me seem like a crazy freak?

I hear a click of a door on Taylor's end and her surroundings are suddenly very quiet like she's locked herself in a room somewhere. "Is this about the demon thing?" My jaw nearly hits the ground. That was the last thing I ever expected to come out of her mouth. "Grandma told me you were a marked soul and that I should help you because she's too weak to save you."

"Save me?" Her words stun me. "You know about that?"

She lets out a sarcastic little laugh. "Yeah, I know lots of things that I wish I didn't. You're little problem with your soul is just one of them. This seeing the future and past thing isn't all it's cracked up to be, you know. Grandma said it's a natural gift to see and that I should embrace it."

"I never knew..." I'm bewildered and at a loss for words.

"Of course you didn't know. You think I want to go around telling everyone that I may be a bigger freak than Natalie Sugarman? Hardly. No offense."

I sigh. "So, you're going to help me then?"

"Maybe," she says.

"Maybe?" I echo. "What do you mean maybe? I need to know what to do about this demon."

"You mean Rick?" I swallow hard as she lets out a little laugh under her breath. She must be telling the truth if she knows that. It would've helped if she'd told me yesterday about this though. "I thought you finally came to terms with your fate and were getting used to being with him. I mean, come on, you threw Stewart Masterson away like a piece of trash when Rick came along."

Me leave Stew? Taylor must not be too good of a fortune teller if she can't see that Stew ditched me, not the other way around. She might just be saying that to get me to spill the beans, but I'm not biting into that. I know she likes Stew, and I'm not giving her any information that she could twist and use to get closer to him. "Whatever, Taylor. I don't want to get into my relationship issues about Stewart with you. You wouldn't understand, anyway. Can you just please tell me what to do about Rick? I have to get my soul back."

"No." I start to argue with her again and tell her maybe she should just take me to see her grandmother anyway, but she recovers quickly. "I mean, I don't know off the top of my head. Grandma gave me a book to go through to help you, but I never looked at it because frankly, I didn't think you needed any help. I thought you looked happy. But since you're obviously not, I'll take a look and then give you a call when I find something."

Having a partner on my side in this demon deal makes me think there may be a chance to get my soul back. The only thing is I don't know how longer I have. Who knows what he has planned next for me. But, I'm really in no position to argue with her. I'm positive that'd just piss her off and then she'd never help me. "Sounds good."

Finally after walking another hour, I round the bend to my neighborhood. The flats on my feet barely make a sound as I walk up the steps to my front door. My fingers shake from nerves as I pull my hand away from the protective cross-armed pose and suck a deep breath down my lungs. Air blows out through my pursed lips and I twist the knob.

Locked.

Damn it! Can nothing in my life go right? Reflexively, I search for my hip pocket, but tragically skirts don't really have them and I didn't really think about grabbing my purse during my escape.

Where the hell is Mom?

"Why did I leave my purse?" I mutter to myself, defeated.

My fist bangs on the door, after multiple pushes on the unanswered doorbell.

Still nothing.

I throw my head back and sigh. "Perfect. Can my life get any worse?"

The window in my second floor bedroom is typically unlocked, so I head around to the back of the house. Moonlight dances across the well-manicured lawn and shines on the love nest I'd shared with Stew.

Assholes—human and demon guys alike.

The trellis leading to my window intimidates me tonight. It's looks a million miles high. I reluctantly make my way over to it, unsure if I can muster one more ounce of energy to get up it. The sole of my right foot screams in pain as my leg quivers with exhaustion when I apply pressure to climb. Quickly, I jerk my foot down and peel off my shoes. Tiny blisters coat the soles of my feet. Climbing the trellis to my room is out of the question. I just don't have it in me to climb that high.

Tired, depressed and numb, I turn toward the tree house, eyeing it with trepidation. Ugh. I don't want to go in there, but I don't seem to have a choice at the moment. It's only five stairs high. A hell of a lot better than twelve feet of tiny lattice strips. I think my feet can bare it.

Bare footed, I walk across my yard and let the cool, dewy grass soothe my throbbing feet.

Painfully I make it up the five-foot ladder and get inside the tree house. The wood is rough under my fingers as I grab onto the floor and hoist myself inside. A beam of light blinds me, and my body stills. My heart jumps into my throat, and I think about jumping down to the ground to flee the scene. I am not alone. I take a deep breath and wait.

# Chapter Sixteen

"Natalie?" His voice trickles through the darkness.

A white spot from the flashlight shining in my eyes speckles spots my vision until Stew lights a candle. "What are you doing up here?"

He shakes his wrist to put out the match. "Waiting for you."

For a second I debate on taking my chances with the twelve foot lattice instead of bunking in the tree house tonight, but I'm too exhausted—both mentally and physically to make it much further. Stew stretches out his hand to help me inside. Reluctantly, I take it. His touch is warm and familiar, but his closeness irks me.

"Why would you be waiting on me? We hate each other now," I say as I sit as far away from him as I can on the comforters we once snuggled on. The dim light helps to hide my post tear-ridden face.

His brow furrows. "Why do you hate me?"

Is he really that dumb? "You know why."

I can't face him. It just hurts too much. How can he not know why I would be so angry with him?

I gaze around the tree house, and my stomach ties into a knot. I hate the memories this place holds. Those nights with Stew feel a million years ago even though he's right next to me.

Stew sighs. "Maybe that's our problem. I really don't know why you're mad at me. After you threw your paintbrush at me, it's obvious you think I did something to you. But I don't understand why you get to be the one mad one here." He waits for a response and when he doesn't get it he huffs. "You know what? I'm sick of trying to forgive you, when you do nothing but bitch at me every time I try."

My nostrils flare as I squeeze my hand into a tight fist and think about punching his face. "Forgive me? I can't believe you have the balls to even talk to me after what you did."

"Me? I didn't do anything to you!" he growls.

"Oh, so I suppose you were being Mister Nice Guy when you stood me up at Morris Well's party?"

He leans back in his elbows and tilts his head. "Stood you up? I didn't stand you up."

My eyes narrow and my heart pounds like a jack rabbit in my chest as I look at him. "Then where were you while Trevor Humphreys tried to rape me?"

While his jaw hangs open, I run my fingers through my hair and turn away from him. I'm so done with this conversation and him. All I wanted was a little peace after what I've been through tonight. Not face down another one of my demons, so to speak.

The weight of the day crashes down on me. Every part of my body shakes. I'm cracking. Right here in front of Stew. The last person I ever wanted to see me cry, but I can't help it. No one soul should have to go through so much.

Stew wraps his arms around me, and I don't push him away. I don't have the strength to fight against anything else. Tears fall from my eyes as everything hits me hard.

"I'm going to kill him," he growls.

I don't even realize I'm balling hysterically until he wipes away my tears and tries to calm me down. "I'm so sorry, Nat. Please. Look at me." He turns my face to his and cradles it in his hands. "I didn't stand you up at Morris's party. I wanted to come—I swear—but I got into a major argument with my dad...over you. He took my keys and practically barricaded me in the house."

That only makes me cry harder. "Why didn't you call me, Stew?" I choke through the tears. "I wouldn't have gone."

"I couldn't. Dad's an asshole. Like I've told you, he's crazy. He broke every phone in our house, including the cells when I told him you were my girlfriend. He forbid me to ever speak to you again. Dad said..."

"Said what?" I prompt him.

He pulls away from me and takes my hand. "He said he'd kill me first. He'd rather see me dead than to be with you."

I'm flabbergasted. "He wouldn't actually kill you, Stew." I squeeze his hand tight. "I'm sure he's just being dramatic. I mean, I'm not that bad."

"That's what I thought too, until I pissed him off by saying I was going to be with you whether he liked it or not." He twists away from me and pulls up his shirt. I gasp as I take in the site before my eyes. It's like something you see in a movie. Thick red scars line the length of Stew's back. It looks like he's literally been beat within an inch of his life. My heart crushes. I can't believe his own father would hurt him like this...over me.

"Oh my God. Your dad did this?"

He nods and puts his shirt back down, taking the scars out of my line of sight. "Now do you understand why I needed to keep us a secret? He's insane. For some reason, he's got it in his head that you're completely evil—that you can change me. Make me into some sort of monster. I swear to you, Nat. I had every intention of coming to that party, but I really thought he might kill me. You should have seen him. He completely flipped out. He's never gotten that violent with me before. Sure, he's hit me, but never beat me like he did. I couldn't bear to hit him back. He's my father for crying out loud, but I didn't want to push him any further, so I didn't try to leave. When Trevor stopped by to pick me up that night, I asked him to tell you what happened. I wanted you to know that I wanted to be there."

I rub my forehead as tears flow from my eyes. "That's how he knew."

Stew nods. "Trevor lied to me." His fists balled up in his lap. "I was pissed at you because he told me you and Rick where making out at the party, and when he tried to confront you about it, Rick beat him up. I heard all the rumors going around about the fight between Rick and Trevor, but I believed Trevor. He's supposed to be my friend. I should've come to you for the truth. I never knew...I've been so crazy jealous over you guys—I've been a complete asshole. I understand if you hate me. But I swear to God, I will take care of Trevor. I'm so sorry, Nat."

As he gets choked up, I wrap him in a hug. "I forgive you."

We cling to each other like we'd be lost if we let go—pulled apart forever. Desperate sobs flow between us.

I bury my face into his solid chest. Leaving him will be so hard. Rick is out to take my soul and force me to leave everyone I've ever cared about.

I kiss him through the tears. "I'm so sorry."

He gives me a sad smile.

We lie down and hold each other tight. The moment wrapped in silence. The only sound is two hearts beating in sync. Guilt washes over me for nearly sleeping with Rick as I lie in Stew's arms. The pull I feel towards them both is crazy. When I'm close to one there's always a pitting desire to get closer, which is crazy considering one of them is one hundred percent pure evil.

Is it possible there was never really any connection to Rick at all, just merely the initial attraction followed by the false sense of security I felt around him? He knows everything about me, so it's possible he just filled my head with exactly what I needed to hear. Whatever the cause, he's still evil and the key to my salvation.

I make a silent vow to get my soul back from Rick. There has to be a way, and I'm going to find it, even if that means killing him.

# Chapter Seventeen

The hallway is completely empty as I enter the building fifteen minutes before the start of my 8:00am class. I allow my fingers to run along the handle of the knife I threw in my bag last minute for protection. It's silly, really, to carry it because I can't over power him. He proved last night that in any form he takes on he can take me out if he wants. But the knife makes me feel a little better. Like I'm doing something to stay alive versus just cowering in my room all day and go along with whatever plan Rick has in store for me.

My boots echo off the scuffed, white floors with each step I take. When I get to my first class I lay my bag on the desk and reach inside to grab my books. A perfectly folded note falls to the floor, landing near my right foot.

Uneasy, I look around and then pick it up. I unfold the note after I clear the lump from my throat. My eyebrows rise in surprise. All it says is "Turn around."

A gasp swoops out of my mouth while my eyes focus on the writing. My heart pounds as I slowly turn. The tips of my fingers turn cold while they cling to the strap of my bag. I didn't even hear him walk up behind me.

Rick stands there, eyes focused, not more than a foot from me. I swallow hard and it makes an audible gulp noise. My back thumps against the desk as I try to put distance between us and my blood runs cold. Trapped. There's nowhere to run, so I lift my chin and meet his stare and hope he can't tell how much I actually fear him.

His lips part, like he wants to say something, but he quickly closes them as he takes in my face. He can tell I'm still pissed.

I ball my fists up at my side and wonder if it'd even hurt if I punched him square in the face. "Stay away from me."

"Not an option." He shakes his head. "We need to talk."

I throw the bag back on my shoulder and curse the fact that Taylor still hasn't called to tell me how to get rid of Rick yet. "I have nothing to say to you."

"Fine." He folds his muscular arms. "Then I'll talk. You listen."

I roll my eyes. "Don't you get it? I don't want *anything* to do with you. I just want you to give me my soul back and leave me alone."

He sighs heavily. "You know it's not that simple. You've seen enough soul collections to know a deal is a deal. Please don't make this hard."

"Hard? That's a laugh. What about this is hard for you? You're already evil. You're not losing anything. I'm the one with everything to lose."

His eyes narrow. "You don't know a thing about losing something."

"Whatever," I growl and try to push past him, but he snatches my hand, bringing me to a halt. "Let. Go."

He grips my hand tighter. "Not until you hear me out. You have to come with me. You're not safe unless you're with me."

He's right. I'm not safe. Every second I stay close to him is like a crazy death wish. I try again to get away from him without success. "I don't have time for this."

"Make time," Rick says as he pulls me toward the exit doors.

Jerking my arm in a wild frenzy, I grumble, "Okay. *Okay!*" He stops and releases my hand. "I'll meet you."

"Where?" he asks flatly, his eyes stern.

A place with a lot of people would be best. His ability to stop time only happens when there's a need to collect a soul. That much I've figured out over the years. He can't kill me in front of a ton of witnesses. "We can talk at lunch—in the quad."

Rick shakes his head. "No. It's too crowded there. Meet me at my car."

"Hell no!" I bark. "There's no way I'll agree to that."

"The other alternative is your bedroom...tonight." A smirk flashes on his face. He knew that would get under my skin.

Yesterday afternoon the thought of Rick and me alone in my room would've made me giddy, but now it just makes my skin crawl. Partly because of fear, but mostly the idea of being close with him makes me feel crazy. I have never gone that far with anyone before, and I hate the fact he's given me the first orgasm I've ever had with another person. "Fine," I lie. I have no intentions of being alone with him ever again. "I'll meet you at your car."

My arm burns from where his skin met mine. I rub my hand on it to get rid of the tingling sensation.

I take a step away from him. "Natalie," he whispers, his voice thick with malice. "Don't make me come after you. I've chased you long enough. The time for games is over."

The threat reverberates in my ears. I can tell he means what he says by his tone. Without answering him, I turn on my heels and bolt away from my desk. It's almost like he can read my mind, and that's fucking creepy.

I look over my shoulder, and Rick just stands there, unmoving. His eyes trained on me while I retreat.

My shoulders sag once I round the corner out of his line of sight. I rub my forehead. How am I going to get out of this?

I dig in my bag for my cell. Taylor has to have some answers by now. Even if she doesn't, maybe I can bribe her to take me to see her grandmother for some help. There has to be a spell or something to get my soul back.

My face crushes into a broad chest, and it bounces me back a little. "I'm sorry." I try to apologize without looking up while

I scroll down my contact list on my phone. Rick has me so distracted.

"Well, well, well, back for more? I knew you were into me before." That voice. That cold, slithery voice makes my skin crawl.

Our eyes meet. I haven't been this close, or alone, with Trevor Humphreys since the party. His thick cologne wafts around me, and memories of what he tried to do rush back. My stomach turns and I fight the urge to vomit all over his gleaming white sneakers. I take a step back and hold my breath as I try to step around him. I'm not giving this asshole one minute of the precious time I have left.

Trevor steps in front of my path. "Aw, come on, Nat. Don't be like that. You know I was only playing around with you before."

Playing around? An image of him smacking my face repeatedly assaults my brain. Instantly, my eyes narrow. "You're psychotic," I say. "Get some professional help already."

He laughs in my face. "That's rich coming from the town's very own violent psychopath. Tell me, do you have your doctor's number handy. Maybe we can be padded-cell roomies. That could be fun."

My fists ball up at my sides as anger pulses through me. If I thought I'd have a chance of landing a couple good punches, I'd already be swinging. But the last time we fought, Trevor got the upper-hand on me quickly. I decide to play it off like it doesn't bother me and try to get by him. "Shut up, Trevor. You don't know shit."

His nostrils flare. "Look, you little bitch. I'm done fucking around with you. I know you told Stew I tried to rape you. He left me fifty messages this morning telling me he's going to beat my ass." Trevor closes the gap between us and shoves me back against the wall. "You're going to tell him that it never happened. I'm not going to let a little freak like you ruin my reputation."

I stare into his face. "Go to hell you piece of shit. I'm not lying for you. I hope the whole world finds out how demented you are. You *did* try to rape me. I'm just glad Rick came in and kicked your ass before you had the chance."

Trevor's eyes narrow, and he shoves his forearm against my throat and pushes. Hard. I claw at his arm, and my fingernails dive into his flesh. My temples throb and my head feels like a balloon ready to pop. "Oh, you're going to tell him and anyone else who'll listen, because if you don't..." He presses harder to prove his point and black spots speckle my vision. "I won't take no for an answer next time. Rick won't be around to protect you forever."

My knees start to buckle below me, and my lips go numb. I'm fighting to stay awake. The last thing I want is to pass out near someone who is literally trying to kill me. For a fleeting second I wonder if this is how I'm going to die—at the hands of Trevor Humphreys. It would be a convenient time for Rick to come and collect my soul.

Unable to look anywhere else but Trevor's face, I stare into his eyes. Once again, I see the rage in them as he takes pleasure in assaulting me. There's something evil in them, more evil than the actual eyes of the demon I once stared into. What could drive Trevor so crazy? What would make him want to kill me so badly?

"Trevor!" I hear Stew's angry voice in the fog of my brain, followed by the sound of running footsteps toward us. "Let her go!"

Trevor releases me, and I slide to the ground, gasping for air. My hands clutch my throat as I watch Stew shove Trevor back and then blast him with a punch square in the nose. Trevor stumbles back and his hands fly to his face.

"What the fuck, dude?" Trevor questions while wiping the blood from his nose with the back of his hand. "That bitch is lying! Why the hell are you taking her side? Come on, man. You should know I would never try to rape someone!"

"She wouldn't lie to me, Trevor." Stew growls and then charges after him. Trevor doesn't get a chance to say another word before he's tackled.

Trevor flies back into the trophy case across from the gym doors. The sound of screeching metal and breaking glass assaults my ears. My bones begin to hum, just like they do when Rick collects a soul. I swallow deeply, now desperately afraid that Stew has killed Trevor.

Trevor lays there, unconscious among the broken glass on the floor beneath Stew. I look for signs of life as my heart pounds away in my rib cage. Finally, I see Trevor's chest rise and fall but I'm still on high alert because the buzz in my bones is still there, growing in intensity. Rick's obviously close. I only feel this sensation whenever he's around and using some of his demon powers.

Stew's back is toward me as he rises up from the ground. He casually dusts himself off and looks in Trevor's direction. He stands over Trevor's limp body and freezes. Stew stares down at his own hands, flexing his fingers in and out and my heart stops.

"Stew?" I wait for him to turn toward me. I want to know that he's alright and that Rick's not coming after him. "Are you hurt?"

"My hands," he says. "They burn like fire."

Oh no. Did I miss it? Did Rick just freeze me in time?

"You didn't make a deal, did you?" I blurt the words out before I realize I'm about to blab my entire history with demons to the boy I love.

"A deal?" He turns to face me "What are you talking about?"

I suck in a quick breath before scrambling to my feet and gripping the wall to steady myself. "Oh my God, Stew! You're eyes! They're...they're glowing!"

Stew tilts his head and furrows his brow. His hand gingerly touches his face. The white glow still emits from his eyes. "What do you mean my eyes are glowing?"

"Did you make a deal with Rick?" My voice rises while my mouth goes dry. "Are you like him now?"

"What deal?" He takes a step toward me, and my heart leaps into my throat.

I should tell him to stay back until I know exactly what's going on here, but this is Stew, the guy who owns every piece of my heart. Rick did say he could change forms and for a split second, I wonder if Stew is really Rick. My brain scrambles in my skull.

"Stop right where you are," Rick's voice echoes down the hallway and Stew freezes in his tracks. "If you get any closer, I will end you. I won't let you kill her."

"Kill me? Can someone please tell me what the hell is going on! And why are his eyes glowing like that?" I shout at Rick while I point my finger at Stew. "Did you make a deal with him just to keep everyone I love away from me?"

"I didn't make a deal with him." Rick shakes his head. "Like I told you before, Stew isn't good for you. He isn't who you think he is. He's not even human."

"Well, tough guy, what exactly am I?" Stew takes a step toward Rick his eyes hard. "You've done everything you possibly can to keep Natalie and me apart since you've got here. Now you're just trying to freak her out by lying. I'm sure she's told you she believes in demons and all that crap and you are just using that to drive the wedge further between us."

Rick steps closer to Stew. "I don't work that way. Besides you're the one trying to come between Nat and me. She was mine long before you ever came around."

I want to jump in here and say I don't belong to anyone. That I am my own person and make my own decisions, but since I'm not exactly sure what's going on, I keep my mouth shut and train my eyes on the exit door.

Rick's eyes narrow as he starts circling Stew. "I have to admit. You aren't like any other demon I've ever met. You're really good at hiding yourself from your own kind." Rick glances at me and raises his eyebrows. "And that's virtually impossible to do. It's kind of a turf thing. We always have the capability to detect one another." He pauses and turns away from me and stares at Stew. "At times, you seem completely normal—human. But obviously, you're pure demon, like me. I've never come across another demon with an ability like that. But I must say, you've got quite a temper. You can't even control your power long enough to make a fight look human. Messiness like that can get you discovered by a hunter and I can't have that kind of attention brought near me or Nat."

"Stew?" My voice shakes. "Please tell me he's wrong. Tell me you're not a demon and you haven't lied to me this whole time."

"Natalie, I'm no demon. I mean, come on, this guy is obviously Loony Tunes." Stew shakes his finger at Rick. "Demons aren't real. This is all some kind of sick joke. Quit trying to scare her."

I dig in my book bag and pull out my compact mirror. He's in denial. Is it possible he doesn't know what he is? I take a step toward Stew and toss my compact into his open hands. "If demons aren't real, then why are your eyes glowing?"

"My eyes aren't—" He stops mid-sentence as he looks into the mirror. The light from his eyes reflects back onto his face. "Oh my God. What the hell..."

"Well you got the hell part right," Rick says, his voice thick with sarcasm. "The question is, did you really not know? I can recall the exact details about the moment I sold my soul to a demon and was transitioned. Are you telling me you honestly don't remember that?"

Rick's right. My deal with him haunts me every minute of everyday. How could Stew forget something like that?

"I'm telling you." Stew rubs his face. "I don't know. I've never made a deal with a demon, the devil or an angel for that matter. I'm just me. It must be you. You!" He walks over and shoves Rick. "You did this to me, didn't you?"

"Calm down." Rick shoves Stew back and then they stare each other down. "You would remember if I made a deal with you. Just ask Nat."

My hand burns at the thought of promising my soul to Rick. I dig my nails into my palm to take my mind off the memory bubbling in my brain. "He's right."

"What?" Stew stops and snaps his head toward me. "Are you telling me you believe this asshole? That I'm a demon?"

I nod and I feel my body tremble. "Yes."

Stew backs away from Rick. "Not possible."

"Oh but it is, my friend. You are a demon. This makes you extremely dangerous to Natalie, especially if you don't know anything about your powers like you say. She's marked, and when I activated her life line, her soul became ripe for the picking. This also explains the pull you feel toward each other." My eyes burn, but I fight back the tears. The question of why someone like Stew would want to be with me finally comes to light. It's not love, he's merely drawn to me because of my marked soul.

"No." Stew shakes his head and looks at me. "No. I love her."

"You think you love her. The call of a soul is a powerful thing. The pull you feel toward her, you may have mistaken for love, but that's because you don't know it's just her soul calling for you to collect it. It's like a Siren calling you with its seductive song. So, until you learn to control your powers"—

Rick points to Trevor who still lays unconscious on the floor—
"you need to stay away from her."

Stew closes his eyes and nods, before taking a deep breath,
and appearing utterly defeated. When he opens his eyes, the
glow has erased, and they've returned to the beautiful gray that
I'm used to. He appears completely human again, all traces of
his demon power gone with a blink of an eye. Stew frowns at
me. "You know I'd never do anything to hurt you."

I couldn't peel my eyes off Stew. He runs his hand through
his hair—something I've learned he does when he's frustrated.
I'm lost for words and really not sure who to trust. Before me
stand two demons who both have the power of killing me with
ease.

Chatter from down the hall catches my attention and panic
envelopes me. "We have to get out of here before someone
comes."

Rick nods and turns his head toward the gym. "Hold those
doors open, Natalie," he says before grabbing Trevor's limp
body by the ankle. "I'll stick him inside there. He'll be too out
of it to remember much of anything."

"What should I do?" Stew asks with a little panic still in his
voice. "I can't get caught fighting in school. I'll get kicked off
the football team and lose my scholarship."

Rick rolls his eyes and pulls Trevor into the gym. "Get out
of here. I've got this."

Stew glances from my face to Rick's and then back to me. I
can see the struggle in his eyes. I wonder if he's waiting on me
to come with him, to run away and fill him in on everything I
know. But I can't, plus I'm, not sure if he might kill me if we
are alone.

I can't look at Stew, so I stare at the cracked tile by my feet.
If I look at him I might lose it. The one guy who I thought I
might still be able to trust is something I can't stomach being
around—a killer; a demonic soul collector.

Who knows if his feelings for me are even real? After what Rick said about my soul calling out to demons, I don't think I can really trust either one of them.

I look up to face Stew, but he's gone. No trace of him insight and all I'm left with is uncertainty.

# Chapter Eighteen

Hopping in my Focus and just taking off to avoid my little scheduled talk with Rick keeps sounding better and better. I would love nothing more than to leave all this craziness behind. Knowing my luck, he probably has some creepy demon radar to detect his victims and would catch me before I even made it off campus.

I sigh heavily. Looks like I don't have a choice in the situation.

I open my bag and double check that I have the canister of salt I ordered from a demon hunter's website in there. The site said that salt burns demons and if Rick gets too out of hand or makes any sudden movements, I won't hesitate on dowsing his ass with it.

The professor dismisses us, and I push myself out of my seat. I turn in the opposite direction of the cafeteria and head for the exit doors. Sunlight gleams brightly in my face as I step outside. Squinting, I dig through my bag to find my sunglasses. Standing on the steps I search the gleaming sea of cars under the fall sun. Finally, I set my eyes on Rick's black car.

Waves of nausea roll in my stomach. The thought of being alone with him in such a confined space brings bile from my stomach into my throat. Screaming won't help and asking Stew for help *definitely* isn't a great idea either until I can figure out where he stands.

Rick's probably going to tell me again how I'll die if he doesn't transition me into a demon. I'm not sure if I'm ready to just tell him to piss off and let me die yet, but I am so tired of not knowing what my future holds.

Could I really endure an eternity in hell?

I lean against the trunk of Rick's car, hoping we can just talk outside.

He rolls the window down after I stand there a few seconds. "Get in."

It's an order, not a question. I will my body forward and hate every step I take. My jittery fingers grip the door handle and pull it open. Hugging my bag like a protective shield, I slide onto his leather passenger seat. The smell I'd come to love—spice and earth, the scent of Rick—permeates the interior space and makes me sick to my stomach. Instead of facing him, I stare straight head, looking through the windshield.

I don't have to look at him to know his eyes are fixed on me. "I'm glad you came."

I grunt. "Like I had a choice?"

"Look, I know you're pissed at me—"

"Pissed?" I hiss, cutting him off as I turn to glare at him. "I'm more than pissed, Rick. I *hate* you—you and Stew both. You both lied to me."

"I can't speak for Stew, and I'm not entirely sure he even knows what he is, but I can tell you I am sorry for what *I* did to you—so sorry. I'd take it back if I could." He lays his head back and pinches the bridge of his nose. "But you saying you hate me...do you know how much worse that makes me feel?"

A demon feel worse? That's a laugh. He has no feelings. If he did, he wouldn't be able to kill all those people and take their souls while he smiles about it. He deserves to feel bad. "Good! I hope you rot in hell for tricking me like you did. God knows how many innocent people you've done that to."

He bites his bottom lip as it starts to tremble and takes in a jagged breath. He looks heartbroken, like I've crushed him. "You're right. I deserve eternal torture for what I did to you. I had no right to take you like I did. It was selfish. Being a demon means we lose the resistance against doing the wrong thing. We just go after what we want. It's not like there are consequences for our actions anymore. We're already damned to hell. It can't get any worse than that. I knew it was wrong, but when I saw you, I knew it was *you*. My actions, they're unforgivable, I know that. I have to explain myself to you. You have to know *why* I did it. You're the only thing in this world that I care about."

My eyebrows bunch over my eyes, and I draw my lips in a tight line. "What do you mean, 'It was *you*'?"

"For nearly sixteen years, I've been trying to convince myself you'd be happy once you knew why I did this to you. Lately, I've even tried using my power to unlock your brain to help you remember your past. I'd hoped I could make you remember, but nothing I've done has brought any memories back to you."

Unlocking my past? Is that what he was trying to show me before? "What are you talking about? Memories of what?"

"Our life together," he says matter-of-factly.

Drawing my bag in tighter, I meet his eyes. They look a little red, like he's fighting back tears, and suddenly I feel bad for him. Memories of the moment he touched my forehead and showed me those strange images of a time long ago flood my mind. The images were just part of a puzzle—one I couldn't figure out.

The hell he's put me through is pushed to the back of my mind when I search his face for further explanation as the curiosity in me bubbles. I can't help myself from asking. "What life?"

A faint smile flirts across his lips. "I wasn't always a demon, you know. I was human, once, with you."

"With me?" I whisper, baffled by what he's trying to tell me.

He smiles at me. "Yes, back in the 1800's. We were the happiest couple. We were young and we'd been married for a couple of years. That's how things were done back then." His eyes stare off in the distance, like he's remembering something a million miles away.

He sounds sincere, but I'm not sure I buy it. "What happened?"

A heavy sigh and a moment of silence later, Rick continues. "You died."

That takes me by surprise, hearing someone talk about your own death is morbid and twisted. "I...I died?"

He nods.

My mouth is dry, like I just drank a cup of sand. "How did I die?"

"You were murdered. That's why I became what I am."

I gasp. "You *killed* me?"

His eyebrows lift, and he holds up his hands, palm up. "No! How could you assume that?"

My fingers scratch my scalp. "But you said that's why you're a demon."

He shakes his head. "I didn't kill you, but all of your murderers got pumped full of lead thanks to me. Those men—the ones I showed you in the memory—they killed you. They rode to your father's farm and took full advantage of the fact that you were a young girl left alone. They tortured you, Natalie."

I stare at Rick with my mouth agape. This is some far-fetched story.

Rick clears his throat and continues. "Your little sister, Sarah, found me working out in the field and told me to come quick. I ran four miles as quick as I could to get to you, but I got there too late. You were already gone. Those bastards drowned you in the water trough and back in those days an eye for an eye was the way things were settled. I wasn't going to let them get away with killing you. I rode into town and dragged Sarah along. She was a great help. You would've been proud. She was able to point them out immediately."

Things start to click. "So, the memories you showed me of the cowboys and the little girl named Sarah, those were true?"

He nods. "Don't worry. I made them pay for what they did to you. I shot them all down in the street like dogs. Of course, nobody knew why I killed them because it happened so fast. The sheriff and his men became my judge and jury and decided I needed to die for gunning down three men in the street in cold blood. The townspeople strung me up and just as the noose tightened around my neck, a demon, Lilim, came and offered me a deal. A deal that promised I could find you again in another life if I agreed to help her collect souls. I was desperate to get you back and would've agreed to anything, including my eternal damnation."

"You mean Lilim, my shrink?"

"Yes. The one and only. She made me what I am and if she's in town it's more important than ever to transition your soul. Quickly. You can't be alone with her, Natalie. Ever. Her or Stew. They're both demons, and that makes them dangerous to you. A soul bound for hell is a highly sought after commodity by all demons, and Lilim is one of Hells biggest collectors. She's ruthless. And until we know what they're after, you need to stay away from them. I don't trust either one of them."

I run my fingers through my hair and then lay my head back against the headrest. Is there no one I can trust? I just want a normal life. "Why did you damn me?"

I meet his gaze and wait for his answer. His eyes search my face. "When I went to collect your mom's soul I knew I'd finally found you the second I saw you. I couldn't pass up the opportunity to mark your soul—to tag it as mine, making it untouchable to other demons. It put a safe guard on you until you were twenty-one—old enough to choose between right and wrong and choose the course of your soul. I couldn't take the chance of losing you again. I had to make you mine."

"Found me? But you said I died."

He cocks his head to the side and fixes his eyes on me. "You did, in a past life cycle."

"So what? You're saying I'm reincarnated or something?"

He sighs. "All souls are reborn until they make a deal with a demon and commit themselves to do Satan's work. If you don't make a deal then you just keep getting reborn over and over."

I swallow deeply and think about how freaky that is if it's true. "How many times have I been reborn? How come I don't remember you from the last time we met?"

"I don't know how many times you've been reborn and neither will you." Rick's lips turn up into a sad smile. "That's the beauty of being a pure, unbargained soul. You have the advantages of having your past memory wiped out and starting over every time you are born. We demons—that's part of our punishment, along with doing Satan's work, we never forget. We live with our pain."

My face grimaces at the mention of killing people. I'm going to be just like him soon. "Satan's work? So is that what I have to do, now? Collect souls?"

"Yes. You'll be what I am—a demon—once your life line completely fades and I transition you."

I shake my head. "That's why you damned me, isn't it? You wanted me to be like you, because you think I'm your old girlfriend or some crazy shit? You didn't want to be alone any more remembering her and think I can fill that void for you."

The stormy seas in Rick's eyes thrash. "Not, like. *Are.* I knew you from the time we were babies. Your face isn't one I'd ever forget."

My stomach turns. He's never going to let me go as long as he thinks there's hope that I'll go along with his dead girlfriend theory.

"Natalie? Talk to me," he whispers after I sit there for a few minutes staring out the windshield.

"I'm sorry, Rick, but I don't want to be a demon. And I don't want to be with you. I don't love you, and I feel nothing for you. Keeping me prisoner as an eternal demon won't change that." My voice is barely audible. "I just want to be normal."

He rests his head against the leather headrest again. "What will it take for you to trust me? To realize we are meant to be together."

My pulse quickens. Here's my chance. "You could start by giving my soul back." He grimaces, so I throw in a little bargain of my own just like one of the internet sites I read said to do. At this point I'd agree to just about anything to get my soul back and have a chance at a normal life. "If you give me my soul back, we could start over as friends and maybe one day I could fall in love with you and then maybe you could make me a demon after I choose it."

He smiles a little. "You think you could love me?"

He needs to believe me. I touch his cheek and stare into his eyes. "I think so, but only if I'm able to make that choice while I'm free. If you make me become a demon, I'm afraid I'll always resent you, and I don't want that."

His eyes search my face. "There is a way. I've only heard of it, never done it myself, but it might work."

My interest perks up. "A way?"

He nods and runs his fingers through his shoulder length brown hair. "You can trade your soul for three others."

My eyes narrow. "What do you mean, trade?"

"You'll have to convince three willing souls to commit themselves to hell in your place. And you have to actively help me collect them."

A sigh purges from my throat. I'm not evil like him. There's no way I can ask someone to go to hell. An eternity of torture isn't something I'd wish on anyone. "No way will someone volunteer to trade places with me, let alone *three*. I can't ask someone to do that. I'm not a killer."

"I'll help you."

"You'll...help me?"

"Like I said, I made a mistake. Taking advantage of your innocence wasn't right. I knew you wouldn't refuse to help your mom, and I used that to get what I wanted. I owe you this. The opportunity to choose, I mean *really* choose, not just make the deal because you feel guilty about your mom. I want you to love me the way I love you, and if this is what it takes, I'll help set you free with the hope that you'll come back to me."

Relief floods every pore of my body at the thought of ridding my life of the demon plague I've been cursed with since I was a little girl. I can't even imagine what freedom will taste like.

The slight joy I feel is short lived. How can I damn three other people to take my place? I want out of this deal, but I know in my heart it's wrong to even consider damning another soul. "I don't know, Rick. How can I live with that?"

"Relax, Nat. The souls I'll find you will have sinned so greatly, sending them to hell will be a good thing. Think of it as doing the world a public service. And the only thing I ask of you in return is promise me you'll stay away from Stew and Lilim until we can get your soul cleared. I can't allow them to take you away from me."

Closing my eyes, pictures of how normal my life can be once this is all behind me zings in my mind. The whole situation with Mom embarrassing me at Taylor Gee's would've never happened. Life would be a whole lot easier without the possibility of hell lurking around every corner. My hands grip my back pack harder as I bring it closer to my chest. This is it. My way out. I open my eyes and slowly release my fists, palm up, and peer down at my almost nonexistent life line.

Three souls don't sound so bad, especially if he picks out some really evil ones to damn. I've seen some of the creeps he's taken over the years, and he's right, some of those people seemed evil to the core. Maybe I can get through this. "Okay. When can we start?"

# Chapter Nineteen

In true Rick fashion, he has his nose stuck in a book while sitting under my tree in the quad. Probably learning tricks on how to be more evil from his demonic reads.

As much as I hate it, if I want my freedom back, I have to learn to work with him and make him believe I trust him.

The deal Rick offered me yesterday seems to be my only option. Taylor won't take my calls and she avoids me every time I see her around campus, so it doesn't look like she's going to come through for me.

Pushing through the double door, the crisp fall air nips at my skin. Tightening the belt around my black sweater, I go to face my demon.

He snaps his book shut and smiles at me as if he hadn't conned me out of my soul sixteen years ago. "Hey. I was hoping you'd come. I saved you a seat."

I throw down my bag and plop on the cool ground. The urge to snap at him about not having a choice in the matter fills me, but it seems pointless to voice that now.

Across the quad I spot Stew. He looks distracted, but otherwise like his old self. When he turns toward me, our eyes meet, and he gives me a subtle nod. I return his gesture with a faint smile of my own, and he begins to gather his things.

"Great," Rick grumbles as Stew walks toward us. "Didn't I tell him to stay away from you? Maybe I need to make it a little more clear this time."

"Be nice," I hiss. "I think he's more confused about what he is than we are."

"Oh, I'm not confused." Rick stuffs his book into his backpack. "I just wish I knew how he hides himself from other demons. Like now, he's not giving off one evil vibe that I'm able to detect. That would be a great trick to know."

Stew drops down beside me and sits his books next to him. "I wanted to talk to you guys about the other day. I know you said to stay away, but I need your help. I want to know exactly how I got this way."

"We got bigger issues to worry about other than the mystery of who owns your soul," Rick growls.

I raise my eyebrows. "We do?"

Rick nods and leans toward me, close enough that his cinnamon scented breath wafts around my face. "I found your first assignment."

I blink slowly, and my stomach twists into a humongous knot because of the way he enunciated the last word of his sentence. "You did?"

He stares into my eyes. "You sure you're ready for this? We could always transition you, and then you could take your time learning how to collect a soul while getting to know me. Once I clear your soul, then it's back up for grabs to anyone who wants to take it if you make another deal."

My voice has a hint of panic in it. "I'll never make another deal."

"Wait," Stew interrupts and holds his hands out in a stop motion. "Are you saying there's a way to get my soul back?"

"Not yours," Rick sneers. "You're already a demon. Natalie has an opportunity to get hers back. A marked soul can renegotiate the terms of their soul's contract with the demon that marked them."

Stew narrows his eyes when he faces Rick. "I've told you already. I didn't make any kind of deal for my soul."

I shake my head. "I don't believe you, Stew. I've seen Rick collect more souls than I can count. Meeting a demon"—I look at Rick—"isn't something you forget. Ever."

Rick rubs his face. "If you truly don't know how you got this way, it makes you even more dangerous than I thought. Until we figure out exactly what's going on with you, I'd rather keep an eye on you myself."

"What do you mean?" Stew asks.

"I'm saying you need to go home and pack your bags. I need you to stay close."

"Stay with you? Hell no," Stew says.

"It's either that, or I kill you." Rick shrugs. "I have to make sure Natalie stays safe."

"Stop it. Both of you," I say. "I trust him, Rick. If he was going to hurt me he would've done it already."

Rick leans in and eyes Stew. "All the same. I'd feel better if I knew where he was at all times."

"Fine," Stew says. "To prove to you I'd never hurt her, I'll stay with you until you clear her soul. Then will you tell me how to make this go away?"

"Deal." Rick extends his hand to Stew.

The second Stew and Rick's hands meet my bones shake inside my skin. I close my eyes as the incessant vibration rattles my brain around in my skull. My palm burns like fire, and I try to breathe deep through my nose. The air feels so thick and it's hard to suck it down into my lungs.

The sheer power these two demons exude in a mere handshake makes me lightheaded and nauseous. My head drops as I will them to stop, because I can't collect enough strength to voice how much pain I'm in.

"Oh my God." The rattle stops, and I open my eyes and look upon Stew's face. His brows nit together as he reaches his hand toward my face. "You're bleeding, Nat."

Before Stew's fingers reach my face, Rick slaps them away. "Don't touch her."

Stew's eyes narrow as he looks at Rick and then drops his hand into his lap. "I wasn't going to hurt her."

"All the same, I'd rather you not touch her. It's not worth the risk," Rick says as he hands me a tissue. "Our bargain overwhelmed her. We have a physical effect on marked souls. We need to be careful when the two of us are together. No more deals around her. Sorry about that, Natalie."

Scarlet stains the tissue as I wipe my nose. "I'm fine. Seriously. Can we please just get back on track for this soul collection? I'm already freaked out enough without adding the possibility that the combination of the two of you simply shaking hands can kill me."

"You're right," Rick agrees. "We all need to meet at my car at the end of the day so we can get started."

I swallow hard. I can't believe I agreed to this.

"You want me to come along?" Stew asks and seems surprised. "You just said it's too dangerous for us to be around Nat at the same time."

"No." Rick shakes his head. "I'll be able to keep you in check. I'm older and stronger than you. That much I can tell about you, so for your sake, don't try anything."

Stew squeezes his lips into a tight line, and it looks like it's taking everything he has not too smart off to Rick.

We all sit awkwardly in silence for a couple seconds. I'm still not sure if I can trust Rick and I wonder if Stew is really that dangerous.

I study Stew's profile. He still looks exactly the same to me. The same gray eyes and smooth, tanned skin still compliment his haphazardly styled brown hair and dimples. He doesn't look like a killer.

Then I look at Rick. I take in his chiseled cheekbones and soft, shoulder-length brown hair. He doesn't look so scary either. They both look like ordinary guys. No hint of evil at all.

My heart does a double thump in my chest with the thought of my attraction to both of them.

I'm in so much trouble.

# Chapter Twenty

Rick leans against his car as I approach him. His arms are causally folded across his torso and jet-black sunglasses cover his eyes as he stares off in the distance. I follow his gaze and spot the Capital's football team practicing on the field. My eyes instantly search for Stew's number—40—in the mass of purple and white jerseys.

Tucking my black hair back for a better look, I distinguish Stew from the rest. He's throwing passes to the guys as they run one by one to make the catch. Sunlight bounces off his helmet, and even from a distance, I feel the power he exudes on the field.

With sunglasses on, Rick's eyes are unreadable. "You ready?"

I swallow hard. "Ready? I thought Stew was coming with us."

"I don't think having Stew around is the best idea. After what I saw with Trevor the other day, I don't think he can keep his power in check. The combination of my power and his may kill you, Nat. And I can't have that. I told him what he needed to hear today just to appease him."

My insides churn. Even though Stew is a demon, I still feel a lot safer with him with me instead of being alone with Rick.

The thought of riding in this car alone with Rick makes my pulse race, but I want to be free. Plus, I have a canister of salt in my bag. If he tries anything funny, I won't hesitate to use it.

"Let's just get this over with," I say, walking toward the passenger side.

Rick dashes around me and grips the door handle before I get the chance. "Do you want to eat first or anything?" he asks as he opens the door.

Sliding in the car, I answer, "I think I'd prefer to send people to hell on an empty stomach if you don't mind."

He shrugs. "Suit yourself, but eating helps."

"Helps what?" I ask, completely clueless as to what he's talking about.

"Making deals takes a lot of you. It drains practically all of your energy and eating helps balance that out a little."

I shake my head. "I already feel sick to my stomach. Eating now will just make me puke."

Rick shrugs. "Suit yourself."

After he's seated in the car, he rips through the parking lot, flinging gravel everywhere. Once on the main road, he glances over at me and smiles. Ugh. I roll my eyes. Dream on asshole. He has about as much chance of me liking him now as he did when he was in his little sadistic five-year-old form.

When he turns into Dublin Methodist Hospital, my eyebrows shoot up. "Um, why are we here?"

Steering his car into a visitor's parking space, he answers, "The soul is here."

Chewing my bottom lip, I clench my bag tight against my chest. Rick gets out of the car and shuts the door behind him. When he comes around to the passenger side and opens the door, my pulse speeds. I can't move. My feet are stuck against the floorboard of his car. I can't do this. I can't possibly kill someone. I thought I could, but now I don't think so.

"Ready?" Rick asks.

"No," I whisper.

"Have you changed your mind?"

"No, but I don't think I can go through with this." Tears fill my eyes. "I can't be a killer."

Rick squats beside me and rubs my arm. I should pull away, but his touch seems caring and that comforts me a bit. "Don't think of it as being a killer. Once you get in there, your soul will take over since it's marked. I haven't collected a soul near you since I started your lifeline countdown for a reason. You'll feel the evil in these souls now and be able to see what I see when I look at them. It's not pretty most of the time. Some of the crimes these people commit can sicken you to the very core. A revenge feeling will take you over and push you to do things that right now you believe are unthinkable. It will get easier. I promise." He stands and then holds out his hand. "Trust me."

Not even realizing I've been holding my breath until now, I blow it out through pursed lips. This sounds like it's about to be the roughest soul collection I've ever seen.

I put my hand in his. "Okay."

Rick leads me through the automatic doors of the hospital entrance. I let go of his hand once we are inside and shove mine deep into my pockets while the mixture of rubbing alcohol and sickness floods my nose. Like most people, I hate hospitals, so I stay close to Rick as he stops at the elevator.

When we reach the fourth floor—The Oncology Ward— the hustle and bustle of the nurses and assisting staff is like a whirlwind, as we walk down the hall. My bones shake under my skin. We're close now. That familiar vibration I always get around the damned zings through me, and I'm not afraid. I welcome it. This time the hum brings me closer to my freedom.

I'm relieved we aren't in the Cardiology Wing. I'd hate to have to explain to my father why I am here. I never visit him at work, so this would totally look suspicious.

The staff must not notice us because no one stops us as we walk past the patient rooms. They have no clue we are here to murder one of their patients.

Rick leads me down the long corridor containing the patient rooms and finally stops at 214.

He turns to me, and says, "Just follow my lead, do exactly what I tell you, and this will go very smooth. You've seen enough of these to know how this works, right?"

I nod stiffly while my heart thumps hard against my ribs. Just because I've seen a ton of soul collections doesn't mean that I'm ready to actually participate in one.

Rick gives his hands one solitary clap.

Out of the corner of my eye, I notice a nurse frozen in mid step as she pushes her big green medicine cart. Turning my head to get a full view of the hallway, I see all the people on this floor appear to be standing statues, stuck in the moment Rick clapped his hands. Time's frozen. Just like when my mom was dying. Just like the first time I met Rick and all the other times he's collected a soul near me. A ragged breath fills my lungs and I freeze, too. Not because of Rick, but because I can't will my body forward.

"Come on." Rick takes my hand and opens the door. "This will be over before you know it."

The evening sun shines through the large double pained window and illuminates room 214. The strong stench of urine fills the room and I pinch my nose shut and breathe through my mouth.

I gaze upon a sleeping old man in the hospital bed before me. His silver hair is thinning on the top and only a few strands still remain, covering his scalp. Age spots cover his forearms and hands. The long plastic hoses hooked to the opening in his neck fog up with each rhythmic breath the ventilator pumps into his lungs. The multitude of tubes attached to his right arm flow with an array of clear liquids.

"Who is he?" I ask, never taking my eyes off the man we are here to kill.

"His name is Floyd Jackson," Rick answers.

The name doesn't ring a bell, but that doesn't make this any easier. My eyes search around for a chart or something. "How do you know that?"

Rick looks at me. "Part of the job perks. It's like developing a sixth sense. We can tell a lot about a dying human just by being close to them."

I watch the man's chest rise and fall. "You mean, you can tell who people are just by looking at them?"

He nods. "Along with what sins they've committed."

Running my fingers through my hair, I stare at the old man I've been sent here to condemn. I knew this would be hard, but looking at him now, in the flesh, I'm not sure I can go through with it.

What if this man has a wife, and kids, or could be the grandpa of someone I know?

My arms snake in front of me, creating a cross like barrier. "I don't know about this, Rick. It feels wrong. I can't just kill him."

"The first one is always the hardest. Besides, this is an easy one. This man has murdered eleven children and doesn't feel a drop of remorse for his actions. The world will be a better place once he's taken out of circulation. He won't be able to be reborn and commit more heinous acts against innocent kids ever again."

I gnaw on my chapped lips hard and soon taste a slight hint of metallic.

"Kids?" I whisper.

Rick nods and holds out his hand. "Let me show you."

My arms stays crossed in front of me. "Show me? I don't want to see him kill people," I say.

"You have to know what he's done so you can make the deal with him. You have to learn his weakness to get him to agree."

Tears well-up in my eyes. How could this feeble man kill so many kids? He doesn't look like a killer or a pedophile. He reminds me of the rich old guys that hang around the country club. My whole body trembles, and I feel the sudden urge to bolt from the room. Run away and never look back.

Rick pulls my hand down and threads his warm fingers through mine. "It's going to be alright. Trust me." He gives my hand a little squeeze. "Close your eyes."

Reluctantly, I shut my eyelids. My palm starts to burn as my bones begin to hum. Electricity passes from Rick's skin into mine. My insides quiver as an image of a little girl flash in my brain. She's wearing a pink sundress with matching shoes and her hair in two perfect brown pigtails. Her jump rope swings in perfect time while she sings. The girl can't be older than seven. My breath catches as I see a man I recognize as a younger version of the old man from the hospital stalking the child. Panic fills me as I watch him creep up behind her.

The jump rope smacks the sidewalk once more before he grabs her from behind. His massive hand covers her face and muffles her screams. Her green eyes are wide and terrified.

The homicidal maniac drags the little kicking body into his white van that's parked along the street corner. He jumps inside the van with the girl in his arms and then slams the door shut. Inside, the windows are covered over with cardboard boxes and the tools he uses to help him with this crime are strung around the floor.

The girl bites his hand, and the man grunts in pain.

"You little bitch," he says before he punches her in the face.

Her body goes limp, and he lays her on the van's floor. He grabs the roll of duct tape and rips off several strips. His large hand smacks one piece over the girl's tiny mouth and then bounds her arms together. He reaches under her sundress, and my stomach lurches.

"No more!" I shout. "I can't watch this."

Rick grips my shoulder and the vision morphs into a series of flashing pictures. I see the faces of several different little girls. They are all screaming and crying.

My nerves scramble under my skin.

Rick's right. If anybody deserves a lifetime of hellish punishment, it'd be this guy. This man, Floyd Jackson, has never been caught. The girls' faces sting my vision and I think about all of the innocent lives he's taken. All of the families he's ruined and my blood runs cold.

Hate courses through my veins. No longer do I feel any remorse for taking this man's life. I want to hurt him—punish him. I want him to feel scared and weak, just like he made those kids feel.

My fists ball at my sides. I can do this and I will.

"What do I have to do?" I whisper as I open my eyes and glare at my victim.

Rick nods—his eyes hard. I can tell he feels like I do, that this dirty old man deserves to go to hell. "This one's easy. He's in a coma, but he'll be able to hear and respond. The dying can always communicate with us when we've come to make the deal." He extends his hand, like an open invitation to move close. "All you have to do is whisper in his ear. Tell him what he needs to hear if you must. We are not above lying to get what we want. Convince him what he's done deserves punishment. Make him say yes, so we can make him pay."

A chill runs down my spine. I focus on his large hand. The same hand I saw cover that little girl's mouth, and I begin to tremble.

"It's okay. I'll walk you through it," Rick coaches while he stands right behind me. I feel his hand on my shoulder, and I nod.

Kneeling beside the old man's bed, I grasp the bedrails for support as my frame wobbles. I strain my neck and look at Rick for direction. He smiles and stoops down beside me.

I frown. "I don't know what to say."

"Lie to him. Tell him that you know about the kids, and you're here to make all the pain go away—to help him. The secret is too big to handle alone and all he has to do is give you his soul, and it will all go away."

Make this sicko's pain go away? What about the pain he's caused all the kids and their families? No. He needs to feel pain. He needs to suffer for what he did.

Crouching there in silence, I debate on what to do. I can't let him get away with murdering the innocent—I just can't.

Anger flows through ever cell in my body. Leaning in close to the old man's hair covered ear, I whisper, "Floyd Jackson, I know about the children, you sadistic fuck. I can help you with your secret. Just promise to give me your soul, and I will make it all go away. You won't have to carry the pain alone anymore. But first, you need to pay for what you've done. Don't you agree?"

The old man nods his head.

My hands shake, and I grab the bed's railing so tight my knuckles turn white. That was easier than I thought. I never thought the old man would agree so easily. I never thought I would be that excited about taking someone's life, especially killing someone so that I can live.

The entire ride over here I didn't think I could do it. I'm not a killer, but condemning this man to death came so easy to me. It was almost fun in a sick twisted way that I was able to avenge all of those little girl's deaths. I'm riding the world of evil, kind of like a superhero. No doubts enter my mind that I'm doing the wrong thing.

Rick wears a crooked grin as he gives me an encouraging nod. "Perfect. I told you the soul will call to you. Your soul kicked in and guided you through the bargain process like a pro."

I swallow hard. My soul guided me to be cruel? Does that make me evil too, like Rick and Stew? I look upon Floyd Jackson's face and I wonder if I need to shake his hand to seal the deal. "Do I have to collect him, too?"

"No. You're not ready for that yet." Thank God. My shoulders sag slightly as a little of the tension dissolves. "Back up."

Gladly resigning my post, I stand, leaving Rick plenty of room to finish up the soul reaping.

He leans in, and the corners of his lips turn up while he whispers, like he's enjoying a private joke. The old man nods, and mouths the word yes with crusty, cracked lips while Rick stands and shakes his hand.

My hand burns the moment they connect, but this time I welcome the pain.

"What did you tell him?"

"What he needed to hear." Rick narrows his eyes at the mechanically breathing ventilator. "Natalie, you need to pull the plug."

My eyes widen and I shake my head. "I can't do that."

Rick's voice softens. "You have too. You have to be part of his death in order for it to count."

Cold overtakes my hands, and they start to sweat. I look at the frail man in the bed in front me. In order for me to live, he has to die.

Rick's hand gives my right shoulder a little squeeze. "You can do this. Don't think about it too much. Just detach one of the hoses."

There's a pounding in my head from the constant beat of my heart. I take a deep breath and fixate my gaze on my target. The old man closes his eyes and waits on the inevitable as I make my way toward him.

The numbers on the vent flicker with the rhythmic beat of his mechanical breaths. My hand shakes as I reach for the hose attached to the old man's neck. The hoses tugs free with ease, exposing the open trachea hole in his neck. The air whooshes from the exposed tubing as the machine continues to breathe. The man's eyes pop open after about a minute without air. Quick gasps of air spew from the little plastic spout as he struggles to breathe. His skin goes from pale to blue, and his hands clutch the blanket on the bed but he doesn't attempt to reconnect the hose I lay at his side. Finally, after what seems like an eternity, he stops breathing, and everything goes still.

My mouth hangs open. I basically murdered his man so that I could collect his soul. I stare at the dead man in front of me, and I feel numb.

What have I done?

Rick reaches in his pocket and pulls out the black, glass vial. The cap twists off with ease under his fingers. My heart thumps against my ribs and I close my eyes. I've seen this enough to know what comes next. The familiar demonic chant streams from Rick's mouth.

I look at Rick. White light pours from his eyes as he stays transfixed on the old man in the bed. The soul whooshes through the opening in the man's neck and then hovers above the lifeless body.

Rick chants some more, and the soul morphs into a ball. It floats in the air until it grows still over the opening of the vial and then slams down into it. Rick caps the soul, and his eyes immediately stop glowing.

Guilt gnaws at the pit of my stomach. That could've been me. My soul sealed up in Rick's pocket. I don't know whether this new deal is a blessing or a curse.

"We have to go," Rick says, giving my arm a little tug. "I can't stop time forever."

I don't budge. I can't believe I actually went through with it. I helped Rick kill another human being, and I have to repeat this two more times to save my own skin.

Bile rises in my throat. I'm becoming a monster just like him, something I swore I'd never do.

Rick tugs my arm again. This time I follow him while I fight back the sick feeling in the pit of my stomach. Once in the hallway, Rick claps his hands one time and everything restarts. The chaos of the daily hospital routines continue around us. No one has any idea I just helped kill the man in room 214.

The alarms from the room behind me start going off and the nurses look in our direction.

"Come on," Rick urges. "Let's go."

He wraps his arms around my waist and leads me down the hall. I begin to shudder as we step into the elevator—the emotion of the situation hitting me hard. A tall brunette woman enters with us and stands about one foot from me in the tiny enclosed space. Her face softens as she peers at me over her wire framed glasses, and she gives me a half smile. The kind you get when people feel sorry for you. She kind of reminds me of a younger version of Mom—very professional in her beige suit with her hair tied back.

"Are you cold?" Rick rubs the goose bumps on the bare skin of my arm. He looks at the lady in the elevator with us. "Why do they always keep these places freezing?"

The woman chuckles at Rick's attempt to play off my unshakable shivers. "I've always wondered that, too—probably something to do with germs."

The elevator dings, and the doors slide open on the second floor. The lady steps out the door and then waves her arm. "Hey, Derek."

Dad? I shove my arms in the path of the elevator door to keep it open.

"What are you doing?" Rick asks. "We need to get out of here."

I don't answer him. Instead I step into the white hallway. I haven't seen Dad for more than an hour in the past few weeks.

He's practically been living here at the hospital. My eyes spot him immediately. He leans against the wall of the reception area, his elbow resting on the flat surface of the chest high wall. Dad chats with the brunette woman from the elevator, wearing an easy smile, completely unaware I am merely ten feet away from him. He laughs as she touches his arm, and he pushes a lock of hair away from her face.

Alarms go off in my mind after witness that simple gesture. Their body language suggests they know each other well—a little too well.

I'd always heard rumors of Dad's infidelity, but had never witnessed it first-hand. Mom would shit a brick if she saw this.

I need to stop this. Dad needs to be reminded he's a married man. Mom may be frigid, but she doesn't deserve this.

"Don't do it, Natalie." Rick grabs me by the wrist and tries to tug me back into the elevator. "This is not the place or time."

Gah, I just want to punch Rick in the face for trying to reason with me. Of course he wouldn't care that my father is being a complete jerk-off.

I shake him off. "This is the perfect time."

The hallway lights glare in my face. I squint as I make eye contact with my dad. "Natalie?" Dad calls my name—his voice an octave higher than normal. I've surprised him. "What are you doing here?" Rick steps out of the elevator. Dad's eyes bounce from me to Rick. "Who is this?"

I raise my right eyebrow. "Dad, this is Rick. My, um...friend."

"I didn't know you had a *friend*. You're mom never told me." Dad says while he eyes Rick.

"Well, maybe you'd know that if you spent a little more time at home. You know, with your wife." I glance over to the brunette and then back at Dad. "Who's *your* friend?"

Dad frowns at the woman. "Excuse us, Angie. Tell the board members I'll be late to the meeting. My daughter and I need to talk."

Angie smiles at my dad and tells him no problem. She pats his arm and I roll my eyes. She has quite the nerve to act so flirty right in front of my face.

He makes me sick.

Dad rubs his face and then stares at Rick. The tension hanging thick in the air smothers me.

Rick clears his throat and touches my shoulder. "Meet me at my car when you're done."

I nod. Rick gives me a sad, empathic smile before he turns to leave.

When I hear the elevator close behind me, I meet Dad's gaze with narrowed eyes. The pit of my stomach churns when I see the look on his face.

"Let's sit." He gestures to the empty waiting area.

The plastic chair has a crack in the seat and it pinches my leg, but I welcome the pain. It's a good distraction against whatever excuse Dad is about to give me.

I stare at the cheap, wooden coffee table across from me and count the deep gouges in the wood and wonder if that's what the scares on my heart looks like—deep and permanently wounded—after all the betrayal I've been through.

I don't want to hear what Dad is about to say. I can't possibly handle another bad thing in my life right now. I just want him to tell me it's not what I think and that I've got things all wrong. But the creases etched in his face tell me things are about to get ugly.

"Natalie, you're old enough now to hear the truth about your mother and me. We haven't gotten along for quite some time, which is why I don't spend much time at home. We tried to keep it together for you girls, but you both are grown now, and you've been doing well lately. The demon hallucinations haven't happened in a while, so I think you're strong enough to handle the truth." He pats my knee, and I move away from him.

A bitter laugh escapes me. He doesn't know me at all. None of my family really does. But can I expect them too? My parents don't even really know each other. "How would you know if you and Mom get along? You never even try to come home. I guess you're too busy with *Angie* to come around."

"Angie isn't the only reason your mom and I are splitting up," He says, his voice has that sharp tone in it that he uses when he's angry.

"What?" My heart drops into my feet. "You're getting divorced?"

I cover my face with my hands and my right leg bounces. They can't get divorced. Can't they work this out? Can't they find a way?

Dad rubs my back. "Sweetie, I'm sorry to spring this on you. Your mom wanted to wait to tell you. She says you've been overly stressed lately, and she thought telling you right now would only make things worse for your condition. But now that you know about Angie, I can't keep it from you. It wouldn't be right. I'm not good with keeping secrets."

I bite my jaw hard, but it doesn't stop the emotion from overtaking me. Tears fall from my eyes and land on my pants. "I can't fucking believe this. Does Mom know about *her*?"

He doesn't answer, and I feel my heart crack apart.

My family is going to shit. What happens if I can't save my soul? What happens if my lifeline fades first? I know Mom wants everyone to think she's tough, but I've heard her cry when she's alone in her room and she doesn't think anyone is listening. Dad can't leave her now. Mom's going to need him if I die. "How could you? You're timing sucks, Dad."

I jump up from my seat because I'm done with this conversation. I don't want to hear another word out of Dad's mouth. "Natalie, wait!"

But I don't wait. I keep running.

# Chapter Twenty One

Riding through Grove City in Rick's car I let the tears roll down my cheeks. How could Dad do this to our family? Doesn't he care that this will ruin what little bit of time I have left to be human? I cover my face with my hands and cry harder. I don't see how the fiery pits of hell can be much worse than the way I feel.

Rick reaches over and rubs my shoulder. I want to push him off and tell him to leave me the fuck alone, but I don't have the strength. "It'll be okay, Natalie. They both will still love you, even if they aren't together."

No they won't. They never really loved me that much to begin with. They'll never love me back as much as I love them. I wish I had more time—time to try to get them to see how much they need each other. How much I need them.

"Are you sure you're up to another collection tonight? We can wait," Rick says.

I dry my face and look down at my palm. My life line has nearly faded away. There's no time to waste. Crying in my room all night won't save my soul. "I can handle it."

Rick gives me a sad smile then turns his attention back to the road.

The trip to our next victim's place takes us to the outskirts of town. Vast farmlands surround the city and there is nothing but corn fields as far as the eye can see. Our drive feels like it's taking forever. I risk a glance at Rick and it makes me cringe. He looks content, like condemning the child murderer back there is a daily thing and that scares me. I can't imagine this being my eternity.

"So..." I trail off and look away from him. "Do you do that everyday?"

"Damn souls?" He shifts gears and glances in my direction before turning his attention back to the road in front of us. "Yes."

The images of the murdered children flash in my mind. "Are they all murderers like that?"

Rick shakes his head. "No, not all of them. I do try to condemn the truly evil souls to hell, though. It helps me to feel...less evil."

"Mr. Jackson deserved to go to hell for what he did."

"Yes. I agree."

Leaning my head against the headrest, I turn in his direction. "How do you get to see their sin?"

He shrugs. "I just can. I've never really asked too many questions about my powers—why we can do the things we do. I try to stay as far away from other demons as possible. Some of them take this job pretty serious. It's best to just stay out of their way to avoid a fight. The whole turf thing gets can get ugly very quickly if another demon wants to challenge for it. I claimed this area the day I found you." He smiles at me. "But to answer your question, sins are easy to see. Whenever I look at someone, it's like their soul opens up to me. I can see the sins they've already committed or will do in the future if I allow them to live. It's a natural ability for a demon. It helps us with our job."

"How many times have you been to hell to take the souls you collect there?"

He bites his bottom lip. "I've never *actually* been to hell. You're guess is as good as mine on what it looks like down there. I'm kind of like a mail man. I collect the souls from the body and stick them in the vile and then I deliver them to the drop off point."

"And where's that?"

"Can't tell you." He grins at me. "Only demons are allowed to know that."

We ride in silence for a few minutes and I pick at my thumb nail. Thoughts fire in my brain. Maybe Rick is able to read my soul and know exactly what's on my mind. That would explain how he knows me so well. "What do you see when you look at me?"

He sighs. "You...I can't read. Demons can't judge a soul once it's been damned."

My brow furrows. "Why?"

He shrugs. "I don't know. Maybe it's because you and I are the same."

"But we're not the same. Not yet. You said I have until my life line fades," I hiss.

"You do, but you still made a deal with me and I marked your soul. You might not be one of us yet, but you aren't purely human anymore either."

I close my eyes and let out a heavy sigh. "How much time do I have?"

The car slows and I open my eyes. Rick pulls into a sparsely covered gravel driveway in the middle of nowhere and stops the car beside a rickety picket fence. A leaning, white farmhouse sits perfectly in the middle of the property. Shin deep grass hides the front yard, giving it an abandon, spooky look. The windows on the top floor are all broken and the siding is cracked and peeling. It doesn't look like it's been painted since the 1920s.

*What are we doing out here?*

The curtains move in one of the downstairs windows and my mouth goes dry. "The soul is here?"

Rick nods and a shiver rips through my muscles.

We're here to work.

After putting the transmission into park, Rick reaches over and takes my hand. He holds my hand, palm up, in his and trails his warm fingers over my fading life line. Tingles burn on my skin, like an invisible fire exudes from his fingertips as he traces the patterns.

"You have two days left," he murmurs.

I gulp down the lump in my throat. "Two days? Today being one of those days?"

I peer up at him, and his charcoal gray eyes soften when he nods. "I'm sorry."

Tears form in my eyes. The sting is overpowering. My vision blurs just before the tears glide down my cheeks. Two days? I bury my face in my hands. My entire life is falling apart and I only have two days to make everything right.

If he cares about me like he says, he would've told me about all of this sooner. We could've made this new deal sooner to find three willing souls. Instead, he let me believe he was just a new boy who wanted to be my friend while my time ticked away. It's almost like he wants me to fail. Maybe he isn't as sincere about letting me go as he claims to be.

I jerk my hand from his grasp. "Well let's get this done since *I* don't have much time."

He clears his throat, almost like he's getting choked up too, but I don't know if I buy his sad act anymore. "Yeah. Let's go."

Following his lead, I open the door and place my feet onto the rocky driveway. A fowl stench of rotten food crams into my nostrils and my stomach lurches. I pinch my nose shut with my fingers and breathe through my mouth. Garbage heaps, almost as tall as my five foot two frame, surrounds the front door. I'm not sure if it's my nerves or the filth that's getting to me, but suddenly I can't fight back the vomit.

I make it as far as the large oak tree in the middle of the front yard. I cling to it for support as I bend at the waist. A thick green liquid spews from my mouth. It tastes bitter and sour at the same time and it makes me vomit even harder. My nose runs with clear mucus and my eyes sting.

Rick holds my hair back as he rubs my back—the same calming circular motion my mom used to do when I was a little kid and got sick. I try to shove him away between heaves, but he doesn't budge.

When there's nothing left, I straighten my posture and take a deep breath. Rick holds out a napkin and bottle of water for me. I take them with a shaky hand.

"Thanks." I wipe my lips and then take a swig of the water. "You just randomly carry napkins and water around with you?"

He smirks. "I keep a supply in my car. Sometimes deals can take a lot out of you and I wasn't sure how you'd react, so I brought extra." He rubs his chin and watches me drink. "Doing deals kind of makes me hungry."

I raise an eyebrow. Hungry? That's just a morbid thing to say after I puke my guts out. I shake my head and think back to the first day I met Rick. "So the time we went out to Drakes and you wolfed down your hamburger in record time..."

"Just got done with a deal." He answers me and then winks.

I finish the last bit of water and then turn to him. "Okay, so let's get this over with. I don't know how much longer I can stand being out here in the stink pit."

He nods and starts toward the front entrance. We step around all the trash and make it to the stoop. Rick knocks on the faded blue door, and gives me a quick glance before he knocks again. This time when he's done knocking, Rick gives his hands one firm clap. When the door doesn't open, Rick gets this annoyed look on his face.

"What is it?" I ask.

Rick doesn't answer me. Instead he bashes in the door with his foot. It flies open and slams into the inside wall. The dust covered pictures on the wall rattle and a couple fall off. Glass shatters all over the dirt covered floor.

Without an invitation, Rick marches inside the door. Glass crunches under his heavy black boots with each step he takes. I follow behind him and stop in the doorway when I spot a body slumped on the staircase.

The man has shoulder length red hair and a Grizzly Adams beard that matches the color on his head. Dried leaves poke out from his beard and oil stains cover his wife beater shirt. He looks homeless. And he fits the definition of a dirt bag precisely.

I stand silent not sure what to do next, waiting on Rick to make the first move. Rick tilts his head from side to side as he glares at the man and a charge stirs in the air.

Rick takes my hand without breaking his gaze. The contact of his skin on mine sends images of the sins of this man into my brain. My body sways and I squeeze Rick's hand tight.

This deal isn't like the last one. This man, Jeremy Phillips, is an alcoholic-druggie who abuses his wife and keeps her chained in the basement when he's tired of looking at her. Jeremy beats his wife daily just to see her suffer. He enjoys power and the euphoric rush he gets from others pain.

An image is of Jeremy knocking out his wife's tooth because she refused to eat a dead rat, sears my brain and I flinch at such an act of cruelty.

The last vision shows Jeremy taking enough drugs to kill himself. He's going to die tonight, with or without my help. No sadness for the loss of this man's life enters my conscious.

To be honest, I'm glad this man will be damned to hell. No one deserves to torture another living soul the way Jeremy does his wife.

Blood boils in my veins as I see the woman chained in the basement behind my eyelids.

Rick lets go of my hands and I glare at Jeremy Phillips. "We know what you've done to your wife," I hiss.

It's almost like it isn't me speaking. The tone in my voice is dark and menacing and it scares me for a split second that I am becoming true evil myself.

The red-headed man opens his eyes and stares at us. He rubs his eyes and grabs the stair railing to pull himself upright.

Jeremy backs against the wall, his eyes wide. "Who are you people? What the fuck are you doing in my house?"

I shrug. My soul pulls toward this man like a chain yanking me forward. A familiar hum zings through my bones. Now I know why my body always seeks out the damned. Their souls call to mine, reaching out to me.

It's easier than I thought giving into the call. All these years I fought the feeling—fearing it, because I knew a death was inevitable and the demon was close. I never thought about the possibility that I was feeling the victim's energy, too.

I assume Rick wants me to take the lead on this soul collection, like I did the last time.

I push away from the doorway and take a step toward Jeremy. My heart thumps so hard my pulse pounds in my fingertips. The urge to wrap my hands around Jeremy's neck and crush his windpipe is hard to resist. When a damned person's soul caused my bones to hum before, I never knew their sin. But now that Rick has shown me what this man has done, anger comes very natural to me.

A severe need to punish this man flows through my very core and my bones vibrate even harder. "It doesn't matter who we—" Rick grabs my wrist and stops me mid-sentence.

"We want to make you a deal." Rick cuts me off and shakes his head.

My face twists. What are we waiting for? Let's nail this guy.

Jeremy scratches his scraggily red beard and narrows his eyes suspiciously. "What kind of deal?"

Rick stretches out his hand. "Just shake my hand, promise me your soul, and you'll be set free of all your financial burdens."

Financial burdens? You've got to be kidding me. This guy is worried about money? I shake my head and let out a huff.

Jeremy eyes me. He's not buying it.

Rick's head whips in my direction. "Tell him." He jerks his head Jeremy's way. "We can guarantee all of his problems will go away."

I hold Rick's gaze and take a breath. He raises his eyebrows and mouths 'do it'. I roll my eyes. I can't believe Rick has to be nice to this guy and pretend to be an Angel of Mercy instead of the Demon of Death I know he is.

My gaze drills into Jeremy. I want to unleash the anger I feel inside on him. The need to right the wrongs he's committed fills me. After looking at Rick's face, I know I can't. This collection will require me to be nice and a bit of finesse. "He's right." I nod in Rick's direction. "He has the power to make anything happen."

"All you want is my soul?" Jeremy asks. "If I say yes, you'll give me all the money I need?"

"I'll give you more than you'll ever need." Rick stretches out his hand further.

My eyes bounce between Jeremy's face and Rick's outstretched hand. The tension in the air swirls around the three of us. If he doesn't choose to take the deal, I'll still be short two souls.

I bite the inside of my cheek as beads of sweat form on my upper lip. A drop rolls into my mouth and I taste the saltiness. Jitters roll through my body when Jeremy starts shaking his head.

Oh my God. He's not going to do it.

Shit.

My eyes burn and I fight back the tears.

Jeremy reaches out and firmly grabs Rick's hand. What the hell?

"Deal," Jeremy mutters. "Now when do I get my money?"

Rick's lips turn into a smug grin. The same evil grin I've seen numerous times from him during deals. "Oh you won't be getting any money."

Jeremy's face twists with anger. "No, money?" Rick shakes his head. "What do I get then?"

"This," Rick says, as he snaps his fingers.

A noose appears out of thin air tied to the banister on the second floor. It dangles over top of us from the second floor balcony.

Jeremy's dark eyes turn hard as he looks up at the noose. "I didn't agree to this."

An evil smile stretches across Rick's face, and his eyes dance with cruel intent. "Yes you did. Your soul is mine. Therefore I'll take it whenever I want too."

"No! You can't do this!" Jeremy pleads as he turns away from us. "I change my mind."

Rick cocks his head to the side. "Too late. Nat, I need you to put that noose around his neck."

My job as killer was pretty well defined earlier, so this time I don't hesitate. The thick ropes are rough against my skin.

Pointing his index finger at Jeremy, Rick whips his wrist and our victim hovers in the air just inches from me. Jeremy thrashes his feet wildly, trying to break free from the invisible demonic grip.

"No!" Jeremy cries. "I'll do better. I'll be better."

I glide the noose around Jeremy's neck and give it a yank to tighten it. With another flick of Rick's fingers the rope squeezes even more.

Tears and snot pour from Jeremy's face. "Please, God. No!"

Rick snorts. "God? You should've asked him for help when you were hurting your wife."

"I'm sorry." Jeremy's cries are pathetic. He's begging, asking for mercy while he showed his wife none.

"I'm not," Rick growls before pointing his finger up toward the ceiling.

The noose yanks on the man's neck, and a loud audible snap echoes throughout the house. His legs hang freely, swinging slightly from side to side. His tongue protrudes from his mouth, and his eyeballs practically bulge out of his skull.

After I watch Rick collect the soul, he turns to me and says, "Come on. We have to go."

I can't tear my eyes away from the dead body swaying above me. The thought of leaving him here, hanging like that, seems cruel. But he doesn't deserve any sympathy. Deep down I know that.

I turn toward the door, but stop dead in my tracks. His wife is still chained to a wall in the basement. If I don't set her free, it might be a while before someone finds her. She could die down there.

Rick touches my hand, urging me outside.

"We can't leave, yet," I say.

He shakes his head. "I know what you're thinking, but she's not the one we came for, Natalie."

"To hell with that. I know you're not opposed to breaking the rules when it comes to deals."

"I can't hold time much longer. She can't see you and tie you to Jeremy's death."

I shake out of his grip and dash down the hallway. I find the door from my visions, the one he'll never force her into again, and fling it open. I flip on the light switch and tear down the stairs. Jeremy's wife sits on the floor, frozen in time, surrounded by her own excrement.

Frantically, I search for the key rack that I saw in the images. I finally locate the pad lock key, hanging on a nail on the opposite side of the room. The woman jars and I freeze. Crap! Rick's losing his hold on time. She stops moving and I run over to place the key in front of her. Hopefully she'll see it and assume he just dropped it. This isn't ideal, but it'll have to do.

I quickly climb the fourteen steps to the first floor and sunlight from the open door to the outside shines in. Rick leans against the doorframe. A faint smile dances across his lips, almost like he approves of my good deed before he waves me to come on.

Once outside, Rick claps his hands to restart time and we bolt toward the car.

My legs fly beneath me and my feet pound the dusty path, stirring up a cloud of dirt behind me. When I reach the safety of the black sports car, I sigh heavily. Sliding into the car, my body quivers with the aftershocks of another intense adrenaline rush.

Even though the normal reaction when someone dies is sadness, I can't help but to feel relieved. Not only am I doing the world a service by ridding it of those evil men, but I'm helping myself as well. Two souls down. One to go.

Rick cranks the car alive and asks, "Are you okay?"

I nod, speechless for once. Awkward silence fills the car's interior as Rick turns his car around.

"You did good back there," he says as he pulls out onto the road.

Still shaking, I wrap my arms around my body and stare blankly at the dash.

He steals a glance at me. "Some deals are more difficult than others."

The evil grin of satisfaction he had on his face back there makes me shake harder. "You creeped me out back there. It's the first time I've seen you..."

He grimaces. "What? Look like a demon?"

"In this form, yeah," I whisper. I'd seen him look plenty evil in his boy demon form, but this Rick I know doesn't always seem so bad. It's easy to forget he is the same person that tormented me with evil all my life.

Taking a deep breath. I run my fingers through my hair and try to refocus my energy. "That asshole made me nervous. I started to wander if he was going to take the deal."

"Me too. They always have a choice. That's the beauty of free will."

Free will? I guess I had a choice too, if you count my mother dying in front of me as an option. "But you lied to him."

He looks me in the eye. "I didn't say I played fair."

I hope he's playing fair with me.

Not wanting to continue this conversation with Rick any further, I turn my head, and gaze out the passenger window. The nature outside zings by as we head back into town. My body feels weak, like I've just finished running a long distance marathon, so I close my eyes and allow the blackness to blanket my mind.

It takes another fifteen minutes to reach campus. Rick parks his car next to mine and cuts the engine. His dark gray eyes fixate on me and a weak smile plays on his lips. He opens his mouth, like he wants to say something, but then quickly shuts it. He scratches the back of his neck and sighs.

Before he has the chance to say another word, I fling open the door and hop out of the car. Clutching my bag to my chest with one arm, I dig in the pocket of my jeans for my car keys. I hear a car door behind me open, and two seconds later, Rick stands beside me.

"Everything okay?" he asks.

I drag my eyes up to meet his face. "Fine. Just getting my keys."

"Aren't you hungry? We could go get something."

I shake my head. I need time away from him to process everything I've been through today.

Not only did I participate in two murders, I found an evil part of me that actually enjoyed it. Delivering vengeance to the men that caused so many others pain made each heartbeat pound with pride. Maybe I am evil.

Waves of nausea roll through my stomach as I think back on the men's faces. Disgusted with the sick pleasure I got out of our activities today, I dig deeper for my keys, seeking an immediate escape from Rick.

Finally, I retrieve my keys. I unlock the car and throw my bag in.

"Natalie, if you want to talk about today..."

"No!" I whirl around to face Rick. "I don't want to talk about it. Let's just get one more soul, so I can be done with all of this."

He drops his head and rubs his thumb over his key ring. His long, dark hair masks his face. "This isn't easy. Doing the things I do...it's a lot to accept. I know. I'm trying to make this as easy as possible for you, Nat. I really am. I want you to trust me."

I sigh, and the scowl drops off my face. "I know, I just don't know why you waited this long to tell me who you are. If you would've told me when we met in the parking lot on the first day of school, I would've had weeks to get this done, not days."

"I was hoping you'd remember me. It's crazy. I honestly thought your memory would come back once we spent some time together, and...you'd want to be like me. Be together—forever, just like we planned before," he whispers.

He's still holding on to the hope I'll love him. It's all over his face. "Were you planning on telling me once you figured out I didn't remember?" I try to read his expressions and when he doesn't look at me, it hits me. "You weren't going to tell me, were you?"

He shrugs. "I wasn't sure what I was going to do."

Heat creeps up my neck and my head feels like it's about to pop off. "You're fucking unbelievable!"

He reaches for me, but I swat his hand away. I leave him standing there as I flop down in my car seat and slam the door. That asshole had no plans of ever telling me he is a demon—my demon. He was just going to let my life line fade away and leave me with no other alternative but to become a demon and collect souls like him.

Revving my little four-cylinder and spinning the tires, I fling gravel all over the parking lot. In the rearview mirror, Rick fans the dust away as I tear out of the parking lot.

My eyes sting as I fight back the millions of tears threatening to spill out of them. I roll down the window, allowing the cool fall air to whirl around my face.

I make it home and run upstairs without saying a word to Mom. I can't deal with that scene right now.

Relief floods my body when I close my bedroom door. I let out a heavy sigh and slide down the door. My breaths feel labored and I grasp my chest. I can't go on much longer like this.

# Chapter Twenty Two

Last night I had to lie—well not exactly lie—about Rick and me breaking up. Mom's under the impression he dumped me. It was the only reason I could explain why I locked myself in my room and cried myself to sleep. She's better off left in the dark about most things, because truthfully, I don't think she can handle much more drama.

Dad didn't come home last night. He probably thinks I told Mom about our little conversation. I think she stayed up and waited up on him for a while. She doesn't know I heard her crying in her room well into the night.

I can sympathize with feeling betrayed and heartbroken.

My Converse shoes squeak on the hard tile floor as I walk to my Statistics class. Alicia would just die if she saw me mixing this skirt with my old sneakers and torn fishnets. I hate wearing the high-heeled shoes she picked out. They kill my feet and they aren't exactly conducive to soul collecting.

My neck burns with every slight little movement from lying in the fetal position all night. I massage the area with my fingers, but it's not really helping the pain.

"Did you eat anything?" Rick asks, startling me, as he walks beside me.

I roll my eyes. "When? You mean last night?"

"Yeah, then and breakfast."

Pain shoots down my shoulders as I shake my head.

He frowns. "You really should eat. Before and after. It helps with the..." Stealthily, his eyes dart around. "Muscle aches. After. You know."

Most eavesdropping people would assume he's talking about sex, not killing two big time sinners, and then stealing their souls.

I avoid the topic and continue to rub my stinging neck.

He readjusts his backpack and sets his charcoal gray eyes on me. "I can rub it for you, if you want?"

His hands stretch toward me, but I steer away. "No thanks. I think I got it under control."

"Come on, Nat. Let me help you. Please."

I groan, thinking of how nice some kneading on my aching muscles might feel. And maybe if Rick rubs it a little, I can get through the day.

Quickly, I glance around. The coast is clear. I nod and then toss my bag on the floor. I pull my hair back and expose my neck to him.

Rick lets out a little gasp, but quickly starts rubbing.

I throw a protective hand on my skin, knocking his fingers away. "Is there something on my neck?"

"No." His voice wavers a touch.

My eyes narrow. "You're lying."

I crouch down and dig in my bag until I find my compact. Standing slowly, I search out the view of my neck in the mirror.

My eyes bulge and I gasp. "What the..." I inch mirror closer for a better look at the faint black lines squiggled on my skin. "What the hell is that?"

My fingers scratch at my skin in a desperate attempt to erase the lines.

"Do you remember the tattoo on my chest?" My hand stills and I stare into Rick's face, looking for answers. My brain pulls up the image of a shirtless Rick the night I nearly had sex with him.

I'd like to forget that scary-ass, demonic tattoo—slithering snakes that formed a perfect circle and came to life—along with everything else. I learned about him that night. "Yeah?"

His lips draw into a tight line. "Well, you're kind of—"

My breath catches. "What? Getting one?"

He nods, his stormy eyes sad.

I shake my head. "No. No, no. No! Why? I've still got one day."

"Which is why you only have the outline. It'll fill in as time gets closer."

I stare at the lines in the mirror. "But if I succeed, it'll go away right?"

He grazes his bottom lip with his teeth. "It should."

"*Should*?" I growl and shove him away from me.

His brow crunches over his eyes. "I don't know. It's not like I've done this before. I only know what happens to a person changing into a demon. I've never actually helped a person back out of a deal. People usually die after I meet them, remember?"

My hair slides through my fingers and makes a black curtain over my neck, before squaring my shoulders.

Great. One more way Rick's completely ruined my life.

I turn away and leave him standing there alone. My eyes burn, but I refuse to let my emotions take over right now. I need to be strong. All I have to do is help Rick collect one more soul and this nightmare will be over. I can do this.

I head toward my next class.

"Wait up." Rick calls. I don't stop, but he still refuses to go away. "Look, I'm sorry. I didn't mean to be a dick," he apologizes as his arm rubs against me. When I don't respond, he sighs. "Natalie, please. Will you just talk to me?"

I roll my eyes. "What do you want me to say, Rick? That it's okay about the hideous thing on my neck, and it's totally not your fault?"

He touches my arm. "It is my fault. I get that. I'm trying to make things right between us. I need you to see that."

I shake my head. Now is not the time to piss him off. It's hard to be nice when all I feel is anger toward him, but I have to play nice until I get my soul back. I stop walking and show him a faint smile. "I know you're trying. I'm sorry I snapped at you. I'm sure it'll go away, right. What does it mean anyway?"

He smiles, but his eyes are still sad. "It's the devil's brand."

I bite the inside of my jaw. "Brand? As in what farmers do to cows?"

He nods.

"That's sick."

"It is." He shrugs and runs his hand through his hair. "But what can you do?"

We walk to my classroom door. "Nothing, I guess."

He turns to leave, but stops like he forgot something. "Natalie, meet me in the parking lot after you're done with classes today. We have work to do."

"You mean..." My eyes dart from side to side to see whose listening. "We can get the last one tonight?"

His eyes crinkle as he smiles at me. "So I'll take that as you'll be there?"

My whole body tingles with excitement and I fight the sudden urge to cartwheel down the hallway. "Hell yes."

His throaty laugh echoes down the hall as he takes a step back. The light from the fluorescent bulbs catch his eyes and makes them sparkle. "Then I'll see you later."

# Twenty Three

I rush into Art class and Mrs. Wood's narrows her eyes. She hasn't exactly been my biggest fan lately. You'd think she'd be over the whole paintbrush throwing thing by now.

A faint smile flirts across my lips as I take in our table. Stew's been a busy boy. He already has all of our supplies laid out, and he's working on his individual canvas. I'm actually surprised to see him considering Rick told him to stay away from me.

"Hey," I greet him casually, while my chair screeches across the floor.

He doesn't respond, really, just a quick nod, and back to business.

"Can you pass me the black?" Stew asks.

I locate the color he asked for. The black tube falls into his hand.

"Thanks." He says but doesn't look at me.

I watch him work for a few seconds, but he doesn't acknowledge me. "Are you alright?"

Stew shrugs. "Let's not talk about it."

I scratch my head, unable to concentrate on my art. "Are you mad at me?"

He blows a rush of air through his nostrils and scowls at his artwork. "I said I don't want to talk about it. For once in your life can you just let something drop?"

His words practically smack me in the face and I flinch. "What the hell is your problem, Stew?"

He shakes his head as his eyes search the ceiling. He's doing everything in his power not to look at me. "You didn't wait for me, yesterday. I'm starting to think you like keeping me in the dark. I nearly killed Trevor yesterday because of all this. Killed him, Nat. And you can't even wait for me like you promised to help me understand all of it. What if I killed someone else on accident while you were off alone with Rick?"

He looks me in the eye. Is he jealous? My teeth graze my bottom lip. Stew doesn't need to know that Rick thinks we have some sort of history together. I need them to work together, not fight. We have to fix not only myself but Stew as well.

When I don't answer right away, Stew mumbles, "I should've listened to Dad and stayed away from you."

My eyes narrow. "What's that supposed to mean?"

"It means"—Stew gathers up his things from the table—"I want you to stay away from me. Dad told me you're the reason this is happening to me. He says you're pure evil. I didn't want to believe him, but maybe he's right. Maybe *you're* causing this to happen to me."

A tear slips down my cheek. "Fine." I scoop my bag from the floor and throw it over my shoulder. "Don't worry. I'll probably be dead soon anyhow. Problem solved."

I head into the hallway. Dr. Woods looks up from her desk, but doesn't bother stopping me.

I duck into the ladies restroom, needing some space. My arms help me turn and pivot up on the ledge we collectively call The Smoker's Nook then sit down. The smell of stale cigarettes lingers around me. The rhythmic drip, drip, drip, coming from the faucet keeps me company.

I lean against the cold, green block wall and goose pimples cover my arms. I shiver. I don't remember it ever being so cold in here.

The temperature suddenly feels colder, and my breath puffs out like white fog. With wide eyes I look around. Nothing's in here. It's just me and my Frosty the Snow Man breath.

I tighten my black sweater around me. The faucet stops dripping and it catches my attention. I whip my head to stare at the sink and panic shoots through me because the water is still steadily dripping. There's no sound. Only silence.

The lump I clear in my throat doesn't make an audible sound, either.

My eyelids are open so wide that I feel like they might fold back into my skull. I frantically search the tiny room for danger. My breath comes out in ragged spurts, but I can't hear a thing.

The deafness I fear is confirmed when I jump off the ledge and no sound comes from my shoes hitting the floor. Hard. Shoving my index fingers in each ear canal and wiggling them, isn't helping.

What the hell?

Slowly, I pull my fingers out of my ears and they pop like breaking the seal on a suction cup, but it's still silent.

There's a sticky, stringy substance on my fingertips. I grimace and then wrinkle my nose as walk to the facet and stretch my hands toward the knob. They shake as I stare wide-eyed at what's covering my fingers—nasty-yellow fluid oozing from the still bodies of a little brown roach.

Quickly, I spin the knob and thrust my hands under the cascading water. The bug swirls down the drain as I scrub my fingers. Water still drips from my hands as I turn my head slightly to the side. I push my hair away from my ear.

A silent scream erupts from my throat as I frantically bat at the constant stream of roaches crawling out of my ear and start covering the side of my face.

I ram my head under the water and try to flush the bugs out. I squeeze my eyes shut as the water practically drowns me. Water blasts up my nostrils causing me to go into a coughing fit as I shift positions and start on the other ear.

"What the hell are you doing?" Taylor Gee barks.

Startled, I snap my head up.

I can actually hear her.

I thrust my body toward the mirror and stare in shock at my completely normal looking ears. Frantically I turn my head from side to side inspecting each ear thoroughly.

No bugs?

A sigh escapes my lips as I close my eyes in relief.

I reach for a paper towel and risk a glance at Taylor. She's staring at me with her arms crossed, like I'm a total crazy person.

This time, she has every right to look at me this way. What sane person sticks their head in the sink at school?

I try to cover myself with a fake little laugh. "Haven't you ever had such a bad hair day, you want to wash it and start all over?"

"You're such a freak." Her stance relaxes a little as she drops her arms. She walks to the paper towel dispenser, and then hands me one. "Of course, I've had days like that. But I'd never put my head in there." She gestures toward the white sink bowl. "I mean, you don't even have shampoo, do you?"

I shake my head. Cold water drips from my hair onto my shoulders, making me shiver.

She sighs as she runs her fingers through her hair, and stares at herself in the mirror. "God knows, I have lots of days I'd like to do over."

My hands stop blotting my hair, and I stare at her. "Your life is perfect."

She bites her bottom lip while she still gazes at herself. "Forget it. You're right. What room do I have to complain?"

She spins around and strides toward the door, and suddenly I feel like an ass. Maybe she has her own demons to contend with—not the literal ones like me of course—and I shouldn't be so judgmental. She's been trying to help me.

"Taylor, wait." She pauses with her back still toward me. "I'm sorry. I didn't mean—"

"It's okay," she snaps. "It's fine," she says before she turns to face me. "I just came to let you know that I think I found the answer to your demon problem."

Hope fills my chest. "You did?"

She nods. "In the book Grandma gave me, it says you have to sacrifice the demon who owns it."

Great. That's pretty much impossible. I've tried countless times to kill Rick without success. "Does it say how to do it?"

Taylor pulls a piece of folded notebook paper from her back pocket. "I wrote it down for you because I really didn't understand it. Hopefully, this helps you."

I take the note from her. "Taylor..." I open the note. "Thank you."

She smiles. "Good luck."

Once I'm alone, I carefully unfold the note.

> *To obtain a soul from a demon. The owner of the soul must sacrifice the demon that marked the soul. Meer mortal tools will not work on demonic souls. The sword of Michael the Archangel is the only weapon known to mankind that is fully capable of killing a demon. The exact whereabouts of the sword is unknown. Legend says the sword fell from Michael's hand during the war in haven and landed somewhere on earth.*

*Sorry, Natalie. This was all I could find.*
*Taylor*

My heart sinks. Looks like there's only one option since finding some lost, angelic sword doesn't even sound remotely possible.

I sigh and rub my face. Guess I might as well face the facts. There's no way out of this deal other than getting one more soul to take my place.

Rick's sitting at his usual table located in the back of the library, with his nose stuffed in a book—one he finds comical about demon's no doubt—when I walk in. With light footed-steps, I march over to him and slide into the seat next to him.

He raises his eyebrows. "Well this is a surprise."

"Yeah. This can't wait," I say while his eyes flick to my wet hair.

"What happened?"

I debate on telling him about the whole bathroom scene, but decide against it. No way do I need him to know that Taylor and I have been plotting to kill him. "Don't ask."

He laughs. "Well, I hope you didn't run into anymore levitating guys who freak you out."

I roll my eyes. "This isn't a joke, Rick."

His smile leaves his face. "I didn't plan on telling you that way, you know. It's just that, I was really into what we were *doing*, and I let my powers get out of check."

My face heats, and for the first time in a long time, tingles fill my stomach. Thinking about Rick that night, the way I was ready to give into him, floods my mind. "It would've been nice for you to tell me, instead of freaking me out with it."

The corners of his mouth turn upward, in a half smile. "Like you would've believed I was your demon."

This time I smile, because I know he's right. "I would've probably just accused Stew of telling you about it or something."

He runs his hand through his hair and pushes it away from his face. "Stew pisses me off. Why would you even like an asshole like that? I would kill to be with you."

I recall the story he told me in his car the other day. "You kind of did, didn't you?"

He chuckles and shrugs. "You're right. I guess that's how we're in this mess to begin with, huh?"

"So, you really did kill people? I mean, when you were human."

"Yeah, I can't say that was my best moment, but when I got to your family's farm and found you dead, I kind of went berserk."

"I really wish you'd stop saying '*you*'. It creeps me out."

"But it was *you*."

I shake my head. "No, Rick. It wasn't."

We sit in silence as he picks at the corner of his book, and my curiosity stirs about the girl he killed for to become what he is.

"So how'd your girlfriend die? She was murdered, right? And then you went after the men who did it and killed them."

He nods and his charcoal eyes appear full of sadness. "Yes. It wasn't my finest hour. I shot them both in the back, and in those days you had to give the man a fighting chance, not shoot him like a coward. The Sherriff saw the whole thing go down. The town's folk strung up a noose, demanding justice. But before they had the chance to hang me, Lilim came and made a deal."

"Why did you take the deal?" I whisper.

He pulls his lips in tight causing his jaw muscle to flex. "To see you again. Lilim told me if I take the deal, there was a possibility I might find you again someday."

"What's the deal between you a Dr. Fletcher?"

"What do you mean?"

I chew the inside of my jaw. "Well, I know why you want me to become a demon. What I don't get is why Lilim wanted to transition you into one? She wasn't some old girlfriend too, was she?"

Rick shakes his head. "No Lilim's interest in me was purely...physical."

My head pushes back. "Ew." Flashes of Dr. Lilim Fletcher and Rick tangled up in a kiss causes my stomach to lurch.

He laughs. "It never got that far. Trust me. You're the only woman for me. Lilim can't hold a candle next to you."

A lump builds in my throat, and I swallow it down. "Rick...I'm not—"

Rick cuts me off. "I know you don't believe me now, but it's true. You're just the same. It's you. I knew it when I laid eyes on you sixteen years ago."

A warm tear glides down my cheek as I think about how much he's been through just to try and find his true love again. True love like that only exists in movies and fairy tales. I can't imagine loving someone so much you'd be willing to do Satan's work, but I see the love in his eyes. Love he thinks belongs to me.

Rick rubs his eyes. "Look at me getting all mushy on you. New topic. One that doesn't bring tears to that pretty face of yours."

I dry my face with the sleeve of my sweater and clear my throat. "Oh yeah. I almost forgot what I came in here for."

He leans into me, and puts his elbow on the table while he waits on me to spill it.

"Do you mind ditching your classes, because I want to get this deal done as soon as we can?"

He leans back in his seat and folds his arms. "How soon do you want to leave?"

I look down at my watch. "Is now too soon?"

He shakes his head. "Let's go. I know the perfect one to collect."

# Chapter Twenty-Four

I lean on my elbows on the table at Drake's while we wait on our food. The aroma of greasy dinner food wafts around my face, making tiny cramps clench in my stomach as it growls. Rick insisted I grab lunch with him while we wait on our next soul collection.

"I think you did an amazing job the past couple of days," Rick says.

I shrug and pick at my black fingernails, not ready to hear about the great job I did murdering people. "I really didn't do anything."

"Are you kidding? You've shown no fear. And you're more than happy to punish scum bags. You'd make an excellent demon."

"Well, those guys all deserved it, but there's no way I want to do this forever."

My head begins to throb, and I remember I still have my hair pulled into a tight ponytail. I release the rubber band, shaking my hair free. I run my hands through it, instantly relieving some of the tension on my scalp.

Rick's eyes scan me while he wears an appreciative smile. "Your hair looks nice down."

My cheeks grow warm from his compliment and I fight back an embarrassing smile. "Thanks."

His gray eyes soften, and he licks his lips. An influx of heat of floods through me as his stare transfixes on my mouth.

The attraction vibe between us overwhelms me. I bite my lip and look away. Is it wrong to find your demon attractive?

I shake my head. Yes. It is very bad to think he's hot. He's a cold blooded monster and I think I still have some sort of feelings for Stew even though he's an ass.

What's wrong with me? Having a thing for two guys at the same time is a very, very bad thing.

I rub my forehead viciously, trying to rid the thoughts of his killer smile from my brain.

"You okay?" Ricks asks.

I need a subject change, quick. "So do you know where the next soul is?"

He clears his throat. "It's not a definite yet, but I think one will be popping up pretty soon."

My body tenses. "You mean, you already know who it is?"

Rick shakes his head. "Not exactly. I just sort of get this ominous vibe."

I draw my lips into a tight line. "I see."

"What?" He raises an eyebrow. "You think I'm lying?"

I tilt my head and eye him with suspicion as I recall him saying in the library he knew the perfect one. "Not lying, exactly. But not telling me the total truth, either."

"Believe me, if I knew who it was for sure, we'd already be on our way. Nothing's set in stone. We have to wait for the choices of the soul to put them in death's path. And in this part of the city, that sometimes can be a while, but I'm getting a vibe."

The skin between my eyebrows crinkle. "What you're like a psychic or something?"

His deep throaty laughs bounces around the restaurant. "No. I develop a connection with the soul I'm tracking. It's not an exact science or anything. I sort of have an internal compass, pointing me in the right direction of the soul."

"Is that how you find me?" I ask my eyes focused on his. "Through a *connection*?"

"Every time. We've been linked ever since I marked your soul."

I raise my eyebrows. "How many times have you used it on me?"

He smiles sheepishly. "Too many to count."

"So the time you saved me from Trevor—"

He nods. "Yes. I knew you were going to be there, and when I didn't see you, I used it to track you."

A flashback of Trevor's breath on my face makes me shiver. "Thank you for that. If you'd been a couple minutes longer..." I shake my head, ridding myself of the thoughts that threaten to flood my mind. "Thank you."

Rick reaches across the tables and touches my hand. "I meant what I said that night about Trevor. I would've killed him if you asked me to. Deal or not."

I smile. It would've been easy for him to kill Trevor. "No doubt. And I'm sure it would've looked like a suicide or an accident."

He grins. "I am pretty good at covering up my crime scene evidence."

I roll my eyes. "Whatever. I think you kind of enjoy it."

He shakes his head. "I didn't at first. I hated it and thought I made a mistake. My first assignment was difficult, and I lost the soul. But eventually I got used to it and started going after the really bad souls. But you..."

"Me?"

"Yeah." He squeezes my hand. "You're a natural. It's like you have a gene in place to show no fear to your prey."

My mind traces a path back to the two souls I've helped Rick to my place. Both times, it was like someone else talking through me, ready to punish both of those sadistic bastards. "Is that normal?"

He chuckles. "*Normal*? Who knows what that is in this situation? Demons are better than humans at allowing inner darkness to take over."

I swallow hard. "Inner darkness? Like my evil side?"

Rick nods. "But In your case I'd say it doesn't have anything to do with that. You've always been ready to put people in their place."

He says that like he's known me for ages and in his mind I know he thinks he has. He peers down at me with his stormy, gray eyes. Butterflies churn in my stomach, and even though I should hate him for what he's done to me, I can't help but be taken in by his handsome face.

I stretch my arms above my head so the thoughts of Rick will stop. I need to get away from Rick before he has the chance to convince me being demon is a good thing. "When can we get the next soul? I'm ready to get this thing wrapped up."

He frowns. "You want to be rid of me?"

Without thinking, I touch his arm in an attempt to comfort him. "It's not that." He wraps his fingers around my hand and I'm surprised by how nice the feel of his skin against mine is. "You're actually a good friend."

The smile on his face nearly touches his ears and then he gives my hand a little squeeze. "Friend? It's a start."

Ruining our bonding moment, the waitress sets our hamburger platters on the table. The food on my plate makes my mouth water as the smell teases my nose.

My stomach rumbles at the site of the food. I can't remember even feeling this hungry. Maybe there is something to this stealing souls business that drives a body into hunger overload. "Is it always like this?"

"What?" He asks as he squeezes ketchup onto his plate.

"The cravings."

Rick's eyes jerk up to meet my face and my heart gallops in my chest. "I've had one I can't shake since the first time I met you."

# Chapter Twenty-Five

I pull my hair back while in front of the mirror at Drake's. The skin on my neck has been burning all day. I gasp when the newly branded patch of skin reflects back to me. The snake tattoo outline is darker—the shapes of the snakes now totally distinguishable shapes.

My eyes widen as one of the tales of the snakes wiggle.

"Shit." The word whooshes from my mouth while I steady myself against the sink.

Lunch time is over and we need to stop screwing around. Time is ticking.

Rick sits in the corner booth and stares out the window completely relaxed. When I approach the table he peers up at me. His face morphs into a concerned expression when our eyes meet. "What's wrong?"

The fingers on my left hand clutch my throat. "It's starting to move. We need to hurry."

Rick nods and then stands. I'm glad he knows exactly what I'm talking about and doesn't make me say it out loud.

"Let's go." I follow him out of the restaurant and to his car.

The music already blasts throughout as I slide onto the cool leather seat across from Rick. The warm air blasting from the vents causes the spicy cologne he's wearing to swirl around me and invites me into him, but I refuse to let those kinds of thoughts distract me.

"Where are we going?"

"We...are going to a party," he says as he squeals his tires on the pavement while he pulls away.

I check the clock. "A *party*? *Now*? It's only four o'clock in the afternoon. Whose is it?"

Rick shrugs. "Some guy from school is having a get together."

Shoving my hair away from my face and tucking it behind my ear, I look at him. "Why are we wasting time at a party? Today is my last day."

He steals a glance at me. "Relax. We'll still get your soul. We're just going to kill a little time until one's ready to harvest."

Leaning back in my seat, I do what he asks and try to loosen up even though he's being ridiculous. The beat from the stereo pumps in the car's interior and vibrates my muscles. This is the last thing I want to do right now.

Rick on the other hand looks happy and completely ready to attend a party. He looks amazing in a black oxford and his long, brown hair neatly tucked behind his ears. I, on the other hand, look like a complete mess. My hair is still a little damp from the bathroom incident and most of my make-up gone.

"You don't look happy," Rick says. I don't answer him and continue to stare through the windshield. "You know being a demon isn't all bad."

"I'm not a demon yet," I remind him.

He pulls up in front of a house party in full swing. People pour from every possible opening and it's not even five o'clock yet. There are tons of people from Capital here, but some of the others I don't recognize.

"How did you find out about this party?

He runs his hand through his hair. "I don't know. Everyone was talking about it this week."

My brow furrows. "They were? Why didn't I hear about it? Not that I would've scored an invite or anything."

"I think you were a little too busy hating me to notice much else."

"You're probably right. I was pretty mad at you."

Rick grins. "*Were*? As in not anymore?"

I smile. "Don't push your luck, but yeah. I mean, you've put a lot of effort into helping me break our contract, so I don't totally hate you."

He nods and smiles at me. "Come on then, *friend*. Let's go try to have some fun."

I pop my door open and the club thumping bass from the party wafts inside the car. Rick strides around the car and closes the door behind me. We walk inside, shoulder to shoulder, our feet moving in step on the concrete.

His warm fingers take my hand. "Is this okay?"

I should recoil from his touch, but today he's been so nice to me, I don't mind his closeness. "Sure."

Once inside, the overpowering stench of cigarettes and spilled beer assaults my nose. Immediately heads whip in our direction. My defenses shoot up as the stares continue. I pull my hair down around my face, making an instant shield.

"Um, Rick? Why are people looking at us like that?" I whisper in his ear.

He faces me. "Probably because of what happened last time we went to a party."

My eyebrows furrow. "But that was forever ago. Why would that draw attention now?"

He grimaces. "Maybe because this is Trevor Humphrey's house?"

A lump instantaneously forms in my throat as my eyes grow wide. "*Why* would you bring us *here*?"

I turn to bolt from the house—no way do I need to deal with this right now—but Rick refuses to let go of my hand. "Because the soul is here."

The soul? This is bad. My stomach clenches. This means the soul is somewhere in this mass of my peers. Up until now, I've been pretty cool with stealing the souls of wicked strangers, but this next deal will present a problem. "I can't..."

Rick tugs my hand. "You have too."

He leads me over to the keg, fills a red plastic cup for me, and then hands it to me. Sipping my bitter beer, my eyes scan the crowd, wondering what terrible thing will happen here that's brought a death demon.

Rick takes a drink. "Come on. Let's go upstairs."

I take a step away from him. "What's upstairs?"

His eyes scan the ceiling. "Our assignment."

Knowing this is Trevor Humphrey's house makes my skin crawl with the sensation of a thousand bugs as we snake our way through the crowed staircase. People stare at us we walk past them, their eyes excited with the possibility of another fight in the air.

We make it to the top of the stairs and Rick thrusts his beer cup in my hands. "Are you ready for this?"

I didn't see anything crazy go down. He has to be kidding. "You mean right now?"

With a quick clap of his hands, he answers my question.

The party goes still and this place suddenly looks like a bad teen movie on pause. There's a girl to my left frozen in the process of spilling her beer all over the plush tan carpet below our feet, To my right there's a couple stuck in a permanent make-out pose.

Rick takes off in the direction of a bedroom door, but stops before entering and waits for me to catch up. He balls his hand into a fist and knocks two quick raps.

"Who the fuck is it?" I'd recognize that voice anywhere. It's Trevor Humphreys.

Shocked, I rub my face. "*He's* our next deal? I can't do this, Rick. There's no way I can't help kill someone I know."

"Yes, you can, Nat. You have too. Do you even *need* to see what his sins are?"

I shake my head. "I think I have a pretty good idea."

My mind flips back to all the encounters I've had with Trevor and my nerves bounce around under my skin.

"He's going to die tonight, Nat. He's drank enough liquor to poison an elephant, so either we make the deal or another demon will. Besides, do you really want to give up the opportunity? You can have your soul back after this."

Trevor Humphreys is by no means a friend. He is, however, Stew's friend, and he has a family that loves him. He needs to be punished for what he did to me, but it doesn't exactly warrant death, does it?

Rick throws open the door, revealing a pathetic Trevor laying on the floor in his own puke in the fetal position. The room permeates with the smell of vomit and urine. I plug my nose and breathe through my mouth. Trevor lifts his head and remnants of his supper drips from his chin. His bloodshot eyes appear glassy, and his head wobbles around while he tries to hold himself steady.

"What do you assholes want?" he snarls. "And why are you in my house? I didn't invite you. I hate you two."

"We've come to help you, Trevor." Rick's voice is calm, like he's talking to a frightened child.

"I don't need your help." Trevor falls down on the floor again. "Get out and leave me alone."

I begin to pace around in his bedroom because I can't figure out what to do with myself. I don't want to be here.

There are pictures of naked women all over Trevor's walls, and I guess that's a pretty typical thing for guys to have in their room, but some of the poses are so provocative they make me look away.

I know Trevor Humphreys is one—if not the—biggest asshole in the world, but I wonder if the whole incident with me was a one-time thing. Maybe he can be saved?

"Rick? Maybe we shouldn't take his soul. I mean, this is Trevor, and I know what he did to me was horrible, but maybe it won't happen again."

Rick shakes his head. "It will. You weren't the first."

My hand clutches my throat. "There were others?"

"Yes," Rick whispers. "One just a couple hours ago, but she wasn't as lucky as you."

I grit my teeth as I squeeze my hands tight at my sides, burrowing my nails in my skin. This needs to happen. I can't allow him to hurt anyone else. "Do it. Before he hurts someone else."

Trevor's glazed eyes shift between me and Rick. "Do what?"

Rick smiles at Trevor. "Help you, of course."

"Okay," Trevor slurs as he closes his eyes.

Rick kneels down in front of Trevor and holds out his hand. "Shake my hand, and tell me yes you want my help."

"Yes. Help me." Trevor's hand barely moves from his body, but it's enough motion to cue Rick to grasp it.

The shock of their agreement courses through my hands. I know what comes next, and for the first time, I dread it. Even though random thoughts of inflicting pain on Trevor have crossed my mind, I never dreamt I'd be the one to actually kill him.

Rick stands over Trevor glares down at him. "Trevor, this is for what you did to Natalie."

Before Trevor can say another word, Rick raises his hands and a strong wind blasts throughout the room, causing the only window in the bedroom to fling open. Rick's eyes narrow as he sets his sights back onto his victim. A steady breeze zips all around me and the curtains strain violently against the rod bolted into the wall. Every loose piece of paper close swirls in the air and it reminds me of all the times Rick would make an appearance in his child form.

My hair whips around my face as I glare down at Trevor. His eyes close and he remains oblivious to what's about to happen to him. With an outstretched hand, Rick levitates Trevor's limp body into an upright position and sends him sailing towards the open window.

Trevor's hands hang limply at his sides. His chin presses against his chest and the lashes of his closed eyes rest against his skin.

"Go on, Nat. Give him a push," Rick says while concentrating on holding him in the air.

I walk over to Trevor, and grab the back collar of his shirt in my fists, but get no reaction from him. He practically looks dead already.

My stomach churns, but I can't bring myself to push him out the window. I can't kill him. I don't have it in me. Sure my nightmare with Rick would be over, but I'd have to live with the knowledge that I killed Trevor Humphreys.

Trevor's face looks pale and distant. He no longer appears overpowering, but weak beneath my grasp. I shake him, begging him to fight back, that would make this a lot easier to not feel guilty about if he would at least attack me or something.

Suddenly, I feel like the monster.

Sucking in a breath, and pushing my hair out of my face, I know we can't take Trevor. We'll just have to find another soul. "Rick—"

"We have to do it, Nat." Rick doesn't give me a chance to say that I don't want to do this. "The deal's already been made."

Rick storms over and spins Trevor's body around to face me. He yanks my hand up and slaps it against Trevor's chest

I shake my head. "No. I can't"

Rick gives me a sad smile and then turns and shoves Trevor with my hand from the second story window.

No sound comes from Trevor. No screams, no shouts, no cursing. Nothing. Not a peep. He never even fought it. A couple seconds later a loud crack sounds from the ground below and my gut tightens.

I thrust my head outside to get a look of Trevor's fate. My mouth hangs open and my stomach lurches.

The empty pool below us is spotted with crimson from where his body landed head first. Trevor is unrecognizable. His face mangled beyond repair. Tears fill my eyes and I cringe.

"What have we done?" I whisper.

Rick puts his hand on my shoulder. "We had to, Nat. It's our job."

I shrug away from his touch. "It's not my job."

He walks over and takes my hand to examine my lifeline. "You're right. It's not your job anymore. I'll give you back your soul."

We enter the hallway and Rick pulls me back to the exact spot we were standing in at the top of the stairs.

"First things first." He raises his hands and claps them, bringing time back to its current state.

The girl beside me squeals as her drink lands on her shoe, and the couple on the other side continue to make out like crazy.

"Take my hand." I interlace our fingers, and he gives his hand a little squeeze starts up the energy flow between us.

Rick leads me down the stairs when we hear a shrill screams erupt through the house. They must've found Trevor's body. People scramble, pushing and shoving each other to get out of the door, and soon the house clears out like it's on fire.

I step out and see a crowd gathered around the empty pool. My body shakes violently and my legs wobble. I drop to my knees onto the concrete sidewalk.

I don't know if I'm cracking from all the shit I've been through or if this pain is actually real that's coursing through me.

With shaky fingers, I turn my hands over and as they throb with pain. My hands feel like I've stuck them straight into a campfire, and the heats spreading up my arms.

I gasp and stare at my palms. "My hands."

Rick scoops me into his arms and hugs me tight to his chest. "We need to get out of here."

The pain spreads down to the tips of my toes and then all the way up to my face. It's overwhelming, and the tears I've been fighting can no longer be hidden. They streak down my cheeks, creating tiny wet puddles on Rick's shirt as I sob into his chest.

"Rick?" I rasp.

He slides me into the passenger seat of his car. "Shhhhhhhh. I'll take you home. Just hang in there."

Once inside his car, Rick grabs my hand and bright light admits from his eyes. Heat sears my palm and I squeeze my eyes shut.

A scream rips up from my throat, just as Rick pulls his hand away and the pain stops. "It's done. You're you again."

Breathing hard, I stare down at my hand with wide eyes. My life line is so long now it wraps all the way around my hand. "It's over?"

Rick nods and touches my cheek. "You're free."

# Chapter Twenty-Six

Rick's hand steadies me with his hand on my lower back as he walks me to my front door. "I'm not leaving until I'm sure you're okay, you know."

Flattered that he cares for my now completely human wellbeing, I smile at him. "Thank you."

Light from the evening sun pours into the foyer as Rick and I step inside. "Mom?"

She doesn't answer and all of my following calls go without answer as well. I make my way to the kitchen and open the door to the garage. Mom's car is there, but still no sign of her. She should be here.

This is so unlike her and it sets panic off through me.

I shoulder past Rick and run upstairs to Mom and Dad's room. I knock hard on the door before shoving my way in.

Mom's on her massive sleigh bed crying with Dr. Fletcher standing over her grinning like an evil bitch.

I freeze in my tracks. "What the hell are you doing here?"

Tears flow down Mom's cheeks as she stares up at the demon before her and almost like she's in a daze she swings her gaze slowly to me. Her eyes are dark, like raccoon eyes and she looks hallow. Four empty prescription pill bottles haphazardly spread around the bed and my heart sinks instantly as the thought crosses my mind that she's attempted to end her pain.

"Mom?" I take a slow and steady step toward her. "What have you done?"

She sniffs and wipes her eyes with a tissue and then closes them. "Oh, Natalie, my beautiful girl. I'm so sorry."

"What are you doing here Lilim?" Rick's voice seethes with anger behind me.

Lilim steps away from Mom and casually takes a seat in and oversized chair to the right of the bed. "Nice to see you too, Rick. I've missed you."

Rick takes a step forward. "Leave Natalie and her mother alone. They have nothing to do with what happened between us."

Lilim laughs—a scathing one, full of malice. "Oh, no? I think she"—Dr. Fletcher points to me—"has everything to do with why you left me."

Rick shakes his head. "I don't love you, Lilian. I've told you that from the beginning."

Lilim stands and her bottom lip pokes out. "You never even gave us a chance."

Rick steps toward me. "There was never an us. You knew I was looking for Natalie from the first day we made the deal for my soul. Can't you just get that through your head and move on?"

Dr. Fletcher stands and then quickly sits down on the bed beside Mom. She pushes the hair back on my mom's forehead and I lunge at her. Rick grabs me by the shoulders.

"You stay away from my mother."

Lilim smirks and my skin crawls. "I'm afraid that's not possible my darling, Natalie. Your Mom called me earlier, depressed and suicidal over your father telling her today that their marriage is over. She thought since I did such a wonder job fixing you, I could help her through the worst day of her life."

I stare her down. "So, what? You encouraged her to take the pills?"

She grins wickedly. "I even brought them to her. Lethal doses, too. I told her sometimes it's for the best if people just end it all." Lilim looks down at mom. "I'm so glad she listened."

I jump over the bed, just as Dr. Fletcher claps her hands.

"You bitch," I scream as I grab a handful of her hair. "You are not taking my mother!"

Lilim knocks my hands away from her hair and then grabs me by the throat. The pressure from her grip makes my eyes widen and gasp for air. Rick attacks her with full force and bashes his fists into her arms in attempts to free me, but it's no use. She's stronger than he is. My eyes pound with pressure as my brain screams for air.

Rick backs away and conjures up a couple cement blocks in midair. He hurls them at Lilim's head. They crush against her skull and fragments pelt me in the face. Her hold on me loosens enough for me to break free from her grasp.

I fall hard on my knees to the floor, trying to regain my strength. Lilim turns and narrows her eyes at Rick before she creates a hammer to swings it in his face.

Blood pours from his nose, but doesn't let that bother him as he stays intent on attacking her.

All I can do is watch in awe. They both pull different weapons out of the air to use on each other, attempting to hurt one another the best they can—each weapon a little more deadly.

The use of pure demonic power around me makes my head spin. This is just like the time in the quad with Rick and Stew, but magnified times one hundred. I slump to the floor and I'm barely able to keep my eyes open.

Rick's face is red, like he's struggling to keep up with Lilim. He can't keep this up much longer. We need help, and there's only one person I know that could help level the playing field. I reach into my pocket for my phone and then dial Stew's number.

"Hello?"

"Stew..." I struggle to speak. "I need you. A demon is in my house. Going to kill my mom."

The phone slips from my grasp and I'm too weak to retrieve it to hear Stew's answer.

There's a loud grunt from Rick as Lilim shoves him against the wall. She whips a short handled knife from nothing and then plunges it into Rick's stomach.

"Rick!" I rasp.

Rick grabs the knife and his eyes grow wide as he stares into Lilim's face. She lets go of him and he slides down the wall. The knife still wedged in his stomach.

Lilim wipes her hand against her jeans and stands over Rick as his body goes limp. "You just need to be a good boy and stay out of this."

I squeeze my eyes tight as I watch Lilim stalk toward me. "Are you ready to make a new deal, Nat?"

My eyes widen. "A deal?"

She squats down and smiles. "I want your soul, Natalie. For whatever reason, you are the key to keeping Rick around, so as long as I own it I can track the both of you. So, what do you say? Your soul for your mom's. Again?"

I stare up at her, a deep electric burn—the familiar one that used to come every time Rick made a deal in front of me—covers my palms. My fists ball up at my sides. I dig my nails into my skin and take a deep breath. My family means everything to me. There's no way I'll let her have Mom. I'd give anything for her, including my eternity. "Okay."

Lilim smiles and holds out her hand. "I guess we can skip all the formalities since you know the drill, just shake my hand and we'll get this over with."

Rick's still out and Mom's chest is barely moving. There isn't really a choice here. I reach out to Lilim and she grabs my hand. Her eyes shine a brilliant white as she burns my skin to seal the deal.

"Stay away from her!" Stew shouts as he barrels through the door and tackles Lilim from behind.

I stare in horror as they roll around the floor, I glance over at Rick and he's starting to come to and attempting to pull the knife from his belly.

While Stew still has her occupied, I rush over just as Rick successfully removes the knife. He stretches his hand out and hands it to me.

"Stab her," Rick tells me. "He's no match for her. That will at least slow her down."

I swallow as I take the blood covered handle into my fingers. It's slick with Rick's blood and still warm.

I peer at the knife with trepidation.

"Do it," Rick rasps.

I nod and turn around. Lilim has Stew pinned, but she's not using her power on him like she did Rick. It's like she's merely trying to restrain him.

They both grunt as they struggle against one another, and she doesn't even hear me approach until it's too late for her.

I slam the knife into her back and feel her flesh tear against the blade. She cries out in pain and loosens her grip. She struggles to reach the knife in her back without success and opens her mouth and roars so loud that my ears ring with pain.

Stew wiggles free and rolls away from her, his breathing ragged. "Who the hell is she?"

She crouches down in front of us on all fours like she's ready to pounce on us. Rick pushes himself up from the floor and Lilim's eyes dart between Rick and Stew like she's debating on finishing what she started.

Rick stands beside me. "You can't take us both on. We won't let you have her. Leave while you still can."

I help Stewart to his feet, but never take my eyes off the menacing demon before me.

"You can't protect her forever. I will have her soul," Lilim growls before turning and throwing her body through the second story window.

Once it's safe, I run over to Mom's bed and lay my head on her chest. Thank God. She's still breathing. "Call 9-1-1!"

It's the longest ten minutes of my life waiting on that squad, but finally they arrive and start working on her. I ride in the squad and follow with her all the way to the Emergency Room until they kick me out of the room so that they can pump her stomach.

I turn to find Rick, leaning against the doorframe with his arms folded. "She's going to be okay, you know. There's no pull towards her now."

I shrug while tears threaten to expose my pain. "Yeah I know, I'm just glad she didn't make a deal with Lilim."

He takes my hand, turns it over, and runs his fingertips over the skin where my lifeline should be. It's completely gone once again. "I'm sorry you had to make another deal. I feel like I've failed you because I should've been there to protect you. I don't own your soul anymore. "

"My hands still burn. Will it hurt much more than this?"

Rick frowns. "A little."

A shiver ripples down my spine. "How much time do I have left?"

"Not long. Come on. We can't do this here."

Grabbing my hand, he pulls me toward the exit. "Wait. I can't leave Mom. What if she wakes up and needs me?"

He shakes his head. "There's no choice. If I don't transition you into a demon now, you'll die and I'll have to collect you. You only have so much time after you make a deal when you're over twenty-one."

My heart sinks as in all the chaos I've forgotten today is my twenty-first birthday. This is it—the last few minutes of life as I know it. Hand in hand I allow Rick to lead me from the hospital. Mom will be safe, because I don't feel her soul calling to me, so I know she'll be fine, but it's still hard to leave her alone.

We step outside into the cool, fall night air and that's the last thing I remember before I feel my body go limp and everything goes black.

The nothingness ends when I feel a little nudge on my shoulder. "Natalie?" Rick's calm and soothing voice rings in my ears. "You're safe. You're in my apartment."

An involuntary scream rips from my throat. Every cell in my body burns with what I can only guess is fiery brimstone. I wish like hell I can go back to sleep. There's nothing else to focus on but the pain of my whole body being on fire.

Both of Rick's hands hold each of my shoulders down firm against his mattress. "Listen to me, Natalie. I can make it go away, but you have to lie perfectly still and hold your breath."

Squeezing my eyes shut, I gasp as all of my limbs strain fighting against the pain. "I can't!"

He shakes my shoulders forcing me to stare into his eyes. "You have to or you'll die and go to Hell like the rest of them. I need to transition your soul. Please let me help you."

I wondered what happened to the souls once they made their deals. Killing the souls must've ensured a transition to Hell.

Tears flow from my eyes as I realize there is no other choice and hold as still as I possibly can. "Okay."

Rick rolls his right sleeve up and stretches his fingers out like he's going to palm a basketball. Before I can ask what I need to do, he lays his hand on my face, covering my eyes completely. All I can see is a brilliant white light glowing from behind my eyelids, and then I feel a pull—like the force of gravity—in front of my face. My sides shake, and pain rips through me as it feels like my entire body is being sucked out through my eyes. Against my will, my jaw thrusts open and a vortex of air forces down my throat.

I gag as my eyes roll back into my head and pressure fills my chest, nearly causing me to explode. And just when I think my body can't possibly take anything else being forced into it and I'm about to die, everything stops. It's so quiet you can hear a pin drop.

"Nat?" Rick whispers. "Are you okay?'

I open my eyes and slowly start to sit up. My bones move around inside my skin, like they're not exactly mine anymore, and I gaze up at Rick. "Do we have to do anything else?"

He shakes his head. "No. You're done."

"Already?"

He nods and takes my hand, holding my palm up next to his. Both are smooth and matching. There's no life line wrinkles to be seen. "You're branded. Now, you're officially a demon."

Remembering the snake tattoo that was developing on my skin, I rub the back of my neck and feel the snakes on my tattoo wiggle beneath my fingers.

"How will I know what to do?"

He grins. "That's what I'm for. I'll teach you everything you need to know."

My body shivers as he holds my hand. "I'm scared."

"Don't be. I'll never leave you." He touches his forehead to mine. "I do want to show you something now, though."

He reaches into his nightstand drawer and pulls out a photo. My eyes widen as I take in the site of us standing in a field of Forget-Me-Knots holding hands and smiling at one another. It's not a current picture. It's all faded and crinkled from the wear and tear of time. Something that came from the time period of the vision he showed me.

That's when it hits me. This is real. The connection I feel towards him isn't random or a demonic pull trying to unite us. I've loved Rick before, in another life, and he's never stopped loving me in over two hundred years.

"It's us," I whisper.

Rick grins. "I told you." He cradles my face in his hands and softly kisses my lips. "I will love you for eternity."

I kiss him back and allow him to pull me tight against his body. Being with him is right. He's fought to bring us back together. It's only right that I open myself up and completely try to let him in.

I knot my fingers into his hair just as he pulls away. "I love you, Natalie. We can take things slow until you love me back. I want our first time together to be perfect. We have forever to figure this out."

# Chapter Twenty-Seven

When Rick drops me off that night, he says to act normally and not to draw attention to myself, because I'd have to live life without people noticing any changes about me. Maybe it's a good thing people think I'm crazy. Crazy people tend to do weird things, like trying to adjust to their new demon body and powers.

Rick says we don't have to answer the call of all the dying people that we hear in our minds, but it does sit well with "The Boss" to be a good little solider—like I've ever been good at that. An eternity is a long time to do the same job.

I instantly wonder about Stew, and how he's doing after everything. Without thinking, I head around back. The round moon shines proudly, lighting up my back yard like a spotlight, and allowing me to see Stew lying out in his hammock across the fence—the place I first saw him at the beginning of summer.

When he sees me trudging up my back porch steps, he rises up and gives me a little wave.

I smile and I wave back. That must be enough to invite him over, because his feet swing out, and he starts toward me.

"Hey," Stew says.

I give him a fleeting smile. "Hi."

He runs his fingers through his hair as he looks away from me. "How's Rick?"

"He's okay. The wound healed up before the squad even made it there to pick up my mother, so now he's perfect."

He nods. "That's good. Demon powers are crazy, right?"

"Yeah, they're pretty screwed up." My body grows cold as I think about all the trouble demon shit has caused me over the past couple of days. I even killed someone I knew in order to save my own skin which ended up not mattering anyway, because in the end I still became a fucking demon. A single tear slips from my eye and I quickly bat it away.

Stew reaches out to touch my face, but it just feels wrong and foreign to have his touch now. The connection I used to feel towards him is gone. Maybe Rick was right, all we ever really had was his demon side seeking out my soul.

I step back. "I'm sorry. I'm with Rick now."

His brow creases and he draws his lips in tight. "But I love you, Nat."

Taking another step away from him, I wipe a tear away from my eyes. "Are you sure? Our connection doesn't feel as strong anymore."

He nods. "Just because the pull is gone doesn't mean I don't still have feelings for you."

I turn to dash in the house before I say or do something that will betray Rick.

"Nat, I'm leaving tomorrow." He says behind me and I freeze. "My dad, he finally broke down and told me the truth about what I am."

I whip around. "He knows you're part demon?"

Stew frowns, practically making his dimples disappear. "Yeah, he does."

"How would he know that?"

"Because my mother was a demon. Dad said Mom never died either. He told me that was a lie that he had to tell everyone because she had to leave. She didn't want to put me in danger."

I gasp. "She's alive?"

"Yes."

I tilt my head to the side. "What kind of danger?"

His gray eyes meet mine. "If I'm a around demonic energy, I become a monster myself. Mom left so I could have a normal human life"

That's how he never knew what he was. "So being around me and Rick..."

He nods. "Turns me evil, which is why now that I know what I am, I'm going to find my mother. I've been without her long enough. And I was hoping you'll come with me."

I frown. "I hope you find her, Stew, but I can't go with you."

Not wanting to wound him any deeper with a detailed explanation on how I may not fully be in love with him anymore, I turn around and head for the house.

I belong with Rick, now—the love of my past life. Somehow I can just feel that he's who I'm supposed to be with.

Rick says with time, I'll get the memories of my past life back. According to him, it'll be gradual, with certain things triggering a memory—like a person with amnesia. It'd be nice to know what kind of love we shared before, but from the look on my face in that picture, we were happy, and I would give anything to feel that free again.

My future as a demon isn't really clear. I mean, Rick said he would explain things in time and he'll always be by my side, but it looks like I'll have a lot of rules to learn about the soul collection game. Stealing souls for the devil was never part of my plan, but somehow I have to learn how to make this work.

This is going to be a hell of a year.

# Acknowledgements

With every book I write I meet more and more amazing people. Thank you, dear reader, for embracing this book and giving an underdog Indie author like me a chance to entertain you with the crazy stories that spill out of my brain. I appreciate every single one of you from the bottom of my heart.

Next comes some of the best writing pals I comes my writing partners. I couldn't have a better support system even if I wished for one with a magically granted wish. Emily Snow and Kellie Maine have been by my side through thick and thin and I am thankful each and every day that I have you two to lean on!

Katie Ashley has always assisted me in editing all my novels to this point, so I want to thank you for reading twenty thousand versions of this book and not complaining. You're edits are amazing.

Kristen Proby, you make me laugh on a daily basis. Thank you for brightening my days with your wicked sense of humor.

To romance blogging community. Thanks to you all Google can now find my books. ;) Thank you for always supporting me. I would name all of you, but that would take up most of the page, just know if you are reading this that I have much love for you and want to thank you for all the pimpage you do for me and my novels. They would seriously never be read if it weren't for you guys. Keep doing what you're doing. Us authors need you.

Christine Bezdenejnih Estevez thank you for EVERYTHING. Thank you for organizing the book tour for this novel. I know it takes a ton of time to do that and I can't tell you how much I appreciate all the work you've put in. Thank you for your keen eye and helping me catch all those pesky werid/inccorect words. You rock so much!

Holly Malgieri thank you for your words of encouragement when I'm down in the dumps. I couldn't ask for a better cheerleader!

My beautiful ladies in the Rock the Heart Discussion Group, you all rock so much it isn't even funny. Thank you for the laughs.

Jennifer Wolfel Thank you for helping me out with this novel. I know beta reading takes time, so thank you for helping me out and making this book better.

Nikki Sparks and Nichele Reese, what can I say but thank you for reading the rough draft of this book and cheering me on to publish it. Nikki, it's because of your love of the book that it's seeing the light of day. You got me excited about it again. Thank you from the bottom of my heart.

Last, but never least the two men in my life. Thank you for putting up with me. I love you both more than words can express.

# About the Author

*New York Times* and *USA Today* Best Selling author Michelle A. Valentine is a Central Ohio nurse turned author of erotic and New Adult romance of novels. Her love of hard-rock music, tattoos and sexy musicians inspires her sexy novels.

Find her:

Facebook

http://www.facebook.com/pages/Michelle-A-Valentine/477823962249268?ref=hl

Twitter

@M_A_Valentine

Blog:

http://michelleavalentine.blogspot.com/

Website:

www.michelleavalentine.com

2-16

DISCARD

CPSIA information can be obtained
at www.ICGtesting.com
Printed in the USA
LVOW01s1447080216
474191LV00023B/1502/P